BEGINNER'S LUCK
A PAUL GREY MURDER MYSTERY

Stacye –
Merry Christmas!
Cheryl Ritzel

TOLLING BELL BOOKS
ATLANTA, GA

Printed in the U.S.A.

This book is dedicated to my husband, Barry, and my daughter, Ashton, the two loves of my life.

PROLOGUE

Wilma Fleming's eyes flew open; she thought she had heard a noise, something like a tire blow-out. She lay still in the bed, not moving, not breathing, just listening. She lay there thinking perhaps she had imagined it or dreamed it. She lifted her head slightly to look at the clock. Without her glasses, she found the hands hard to read, but she thought it was about 2:00 A.M. She let her head fall back into the soft, down pillow and almost drifted back off to sleep, but she heard the noise again, a loud popping noise. She quickly sat upright, swinging her feet out of the bed. It was her moral, if not civic duty, to make sure everyone and everything was all right. There wouldn't be too much to check she thought as she donned her robe and slippers. She had only one neighbor; the rest of the houses in the area had gone commercial. Before she even reached the window, she heard tires squealing out of the driveway next door.

If she'd had Mr. Meeker's phone number, she would have called him to make sure he was all right, but she didn't have a number for him. She barely knew Mr. Meeker or anything about him, only that he was a bachelor. Still, determined to check on his well-being, she turned on the outside lights and carefully went out the kitchen door, which took her to a window of his antique gallery. A dim light was on inside.

Leaning across the shrubbery and rapping gently on the glass, she called out, "Oh, Mr. Meeker, I'm sorry to disturb you, but are you all right?"

No reply. She tapped louder and repeated her query. Still no response. She maneuvered herself into the shrubbery so she could look through the window, using her hands cupped around her eyes to cut out the glare.

Ralph Meeker lay sprawled on the floor a few feet from his office door. She could see his figure plainly. She wondered what had happened to him, but judging from the hole in his head, she knew he was dead.

CHAPTER 1

I don't remember the thirty-minute drive at all. My eyelids heavy, my thoughts sleepy, my mind switched to autopilot, and in what seemed like moments, without remembering how I got there, I was at home. The familiar sound of the pavement crunching under the tires, a welcoming sensation, I parked in the driveway. As I got out and stretched my six-foot-three frame, I looked toward our bedroom window. Feeling deep into my pant's pocket, I fiddled with the silver thimble inside. It was a gift for my wife, Lindsey; she was just about the only thing I'd done right in my life. I sighed deeply into the damp July night. I glanced back at the window, where everything looked normal. All the lights were out, yet, not knowing why, a wave of anxiety washed over me. I quickly unloaded my carry-on bags.

Hurrying up the sidewalk, I anticipated that wonderful feeling I get when I step inside my house after a trip. Door unlocked swiftly, I swung it open with my free hand and took in a deep breath. I released it in a burst as Lindsey rushed to me and grabbed my arm.

My heart leapt. "What are you doing up?"

I'd been traveling for years, and Lindsey never waited up for me when I was this late. I knew immediately, before I'd even finished posing the question, something was wrong. Was she hurt? Did someone die? Did she want a divorce?

"Don't they have phones at your job site?" she asked, pulling me down the darkened hallway to the living room. "Were there no phones at the airport? You didn't call me."

"What is it? What's wrong?" I asked, panic growing at the sight of tears on her face.

"It—it's Allan." Her body shook as she spoke.

I pulled away and held her arms down by her sides, searched her eyes. Puffy-faced with splotchy red cheeks, she had been crying a long time.

"Allan? What about him? Did he hurt you? Did you get in an argument?"

"No, no." She shook her head. "Dead, suicide."

"What?" I dropped my hold on her. I'd seen Allan the night before I left for my trip, alive and well. There had to be a mistake. I needed to sit down, close my eyes, stop thinking for a minute.

"It was in the paper today. I've been trying to reach you. I called your office. Didn't they page you?" Lindsey handed over the local news section.

"No," I answered dumbly. I swept away a pile of Kleenex tissues so I could sit down to look at the article, but the letters were not forming into words for me. Lindsey paced back and forth, rambling on as I struggled to read the paper.

"They say he killed someone, some antique dealer. They say he killed this man and then himself," she explained.

"They?"

"They—the police, the news—they say it." She pulled a fresh tissue to wring in her hands.

"When? How? I mean, good God, why?"

"Yesterday," she wailed. "They said he killed the guy two nights ago and then himself yesterday morning."

"But why? Why would Allan kill someone? He was a good person, liked by everyone. He didn't have any enemies, did he?"

"Well, no. Not that I know of." The tissue was tightly wadded now.

"You're like his daughter. You should know. Give me that," I removed the tissue from her clenched fist and holding her hands pulled her down to sit on the sofa.

"No, no enemies. I mean he is, was a Senator. Maybe political enemies," she shrugged.

"Who was the guy? Did you know him?"

"An antique shopkeeper. I didn't know him."

The eleven o'clock news was on its late-night repeat. Allan was their main story. "Senator Murder-Suicide." I became mesmerized by the upbeat newsanchor reporting the case.

"Allan Puckett, Atlanta's fortieth-district veteran Senator has been implicated in what is now classified by police as a murder-suicide. The Senator allegedly shot and killed art dealer, Ralph Johnson Meeker, early Tuesday morning before returning to his home and taking his own life. The police, tight-lipped about the case, have given no comment regarding motive or evidence. We go now to Rebecca Bartles at the police station downtown—"

"Ralph Meeker?!" I repeated in shock and amazement as the story continued.

"Yeah, why? Did you know him?" she asked, brows furrowed.

"I met Ralph Meeker only about a week ago on a late flight to Dallas."

CHAPTER 2

Ralph Meeker had been on the same late flight to Dallas/Ft. Worth from Atlanta as I was; I being on my way to the outlying city of Plano for several days of business work. Observing Mr. Meeker from across the aisle at 34,000 feet, I didn't like him from first sight. He was short and overweight and wore an expensive suit and lots of gold decorations that I would hardly call jewelry. His nose was red and puffy, aggravated by the altitude change, so he sniffled constantly as he spoke with the woman beside him about teakwood dressers. He knew altogether too much about teakwood dressers, and his victim was visibly distressed with her predicament. Finally, when there was a lull in the conversation, the woman decided to take a nap. He turned in search of another soul to speak with.

To avoid attracting his attention, I averted my eyes from him and back to the persons in my own aisle. The young girl next to me was playing solitaire, while the gentleman on the other side of her, presumably her father, read the stock exchange. He grumbled something unintelligible, obviously frustrated he stuffed the pages into a briefcase and was coaxed by the young girl into a game of cards.

My gaze was startled upwards as the person in front of me turned around, knees in the seat, and extended his right hand.

"I'm Ralph Meeker," he said.

"Paul Grey," I said, as I reached to shake his hand.

He gave it a quick jerk, a power shake. He had changed seats mid-flight in an attempt to find someone to converse with.

"You're the teakwood dresser fellow," I said somewhat sarcastically. "I couldn't help but overhear."

I hoped my tone would deter him, but he persisted.

"Arts and Antiquities, to be precise," he sniffled proudly. "I own an art gallery in Atlanta. I do a little bit of everything—furniture, stained glass, classic artworks, even pottery and African pieces. I can get practically anything anyone wants, for a price."

"Do you always use your sales pitch on strangers in airplanes?"

"Well, no." He paused to sniff again. "But I never know where I'll find business, so I try to mention it in conversation whenever possible."

He handed me a business card.

"I see. I'll certainly call you if I ever need any art or—," I glanced at the card, "or antiquities."

Sensing that our conversation was over, Mr. Meeker went on in search of more business contacts. I stuffed the unwanted card in the ashtray and thought nothing more of it.

However, my path collided with Ralph Meeker again on the return trip, a strange coincidence. He recognized me immediately, and like a leech sucking out my life blood he struck up more conversation, going into excruciating detail about all the pieces in his current collection. Most of the time I tuned him out, throwing in an occasional affirmation or nod to keep him pacified. It was the longest two hours of my life. I was extremely relieved to be able to leave him behind at baggage claim. I knew I had packed light for a reason.

The next night, Lindsey and Allan were hosting a dinner for her election campaign. Allan was Lindsey's mentor and her only parent since her real mother and father had died in a car wreck when she was sixteen. Lindsey, an only child, with no other living relatives, except an aunt in Minnesota, would have had to move, but Allan convinced the aunt to let her come live with his family. At that time Allan was working as a police officer and finishing his last term at law school. He and his wife, Margie, had three other children that would keep her company and help her adjust. Their families had been close anyway, so it wasn't a traumatic experience to move in. She stayed with them all through college, and they would have helped her pay for graduate school had she wanted to go. Instead, she was ready to marry me and had found her true calling in politics. By then Allan was a Senator, had given her a part-time job at the capital, and that was all it took. She was hooked. She worked as a lawyer's aide to pass the time until she could become an elected official. Now was the time.

The dinner was to start at 8:00 P.M. At seven, Lindsey was in a panic.

"Oh, Paul, what should I wear, the red suit with the skirt or the navy pantsuit?" she asked.

I knew I was in trouble then. It appeared that I would have had a fifty-fifty chance, but there was never a right answer to a question like that.

"The navy pantsuit," I said. I waited for the response, pretending to be engrossed in my cable television program. She held the navy up to her neck.

"Really? You don't think it makes me look fat?"

I looked up and down her beautiful, slender body.

"You? No, but if you think it does, wear the red," I said.

She held the red up in front of the mirror and wrinkled her nose. I could watch her face in the reflection from where I sat on our bed.

"The red? You don't think it clashes with my hair color?"

She had straight, chestnut, shoulder-length hair. It shone like polished cherry wood.

"I think it looks fine, but if you really want my opinion, I like you without anything on," I said. She caught my looking in the reflection.

She tilted her head. "Very interesting idea, but not appropriate for tonight's dinner."

She tried on both outfits and then decided on neither.

"I'll wear my black dress," she said emphatically.

"Black?" I questioned her choice. "It's not a funeral, you know."

"I know, but it's a powerful outfit. I feel confident in it."

"OK," I shrugged, knowing this was only the beginning of the ordeal. We still had shoes, handbags, and make-up to go through. Lindsey was a "clothing horse"—collecting clothes was her hobby, even though she claimed it was a necessity. During her campaign she'd been in the spotlight, appearing on the news and a morning talk show, and speaking to groups. Being young and female were a rarity for a Senatorial position and all the political hype made her self-conscious about what she wore out of the house. This was a convenient excuse, and although she would never admit it, I secretly knew she wanted to be rich enough to never have to wear the same thing twice. I could tell by the way she walked through the clothing department, hands wandering over the fabrics' textures as she went.

"Ooh, this is nice," she'd say.

"But you already have a royal blue blouse," I'd protest.

"I know, but this one—," she'd say and launch into some reason why the one on the rack had to go home with her—better color, more buttons, less buttons, smaller collar. I didn't mind really. I loved to spoil her.

On the other hand, I was restricted to one good suit with dress shoes, one pair of jeans, and one pair of sneakers. Even if we had the money, I probably wouldn't want more clothes, but we were on a tight budget. Her campaign for a Senate seat had all but sucked us dry. I teased her that before the election was over we would have to move out of the district to a less upscale neighborhood. This would disqualify her candidacy. She never thought that my joke was funny, probably because it rang close to true.

"They'll eat me alive." She was muttering something about not being able to take a leather purse because of animal activists or some such nonsense.

I reassured her. "Tonight the people have come to meet you by choice. They're your supporters."

She appeared around the corner from the bathroom.

"You're right." She smiled. "I should relax. No more worries."

"Good," I said.

I went back to watching my cable show, which was teaching me how to build a gazebo. Would I ever need this knowledge? Most likely not, but I watched, fascinated anyway. I was, of course, already dressed and ready because men are faster at that sort of thing.

Lindsey reappeared a few moments later. "Paul, which shade of lipstick should I wear?"

"Uhhhh," I said and fell backwards onto the bed. Lindsey stared at me in confusion. It was going to be a long night.

The dinner party started at eight o'clock precisely. Actually, dinner was a misnomer—hors d'oeuvres party was a more appropriate title. People could mingle and talk as they enjoyed the luscious food and elegant decorations of the large conference hall at the Radisson Hotel. About a hundred people attended, of which I was sure I knew only three—my wife, Allan, and his wife, Margie.

We all sat in folding chairs at the front of the room with a large podium in the middle. Everyone else milled around, talking. A few seats were spaced along the perimeter of the room, but they were mostly empty.

Allan approached the mike and introduced Lindsey to the guests. Then Lindsey made a short speech outlining her beliefs and goals for the community. Allan, who was retiring this year after twelve years in the Senate, hoped to turn the district over to Lindsey so she could continue his work.

During the mingling, I met lots of people I wouldn't remember. I talked superficially with everyone I met about sports and weather and family values. Some of the guests were big shots, so I could say I hobnobbed with Atlanta's best and brightest, but most were average folks that I couldn't for the life of me name a single one of them the next day.

At about eleven o'clock, things had wound down considerably. I was losing my voice and had lost Lindsey, too, in the mingling process. I stood by the bar and sipped my glass of wine, looking for her. I didn't see her, but I saw Allan. And Allan was arguing.

He was over by the exit doors, talking adamantly to a shorter man, who had his back to me. I could not hear them, but Allan's body language gave him away. He scowled as he spoke and shook his arms and waved them about, distressed. Curious, I walked closer.

Being six-foot-three has its advantages. I was a good head above the rest of the crowd, and I could keep my eye on them as I approached. Allan grabbed the shorter fellow and shook him. The short man broke away and in doing so turned partly toward me. For an instant I thought I recognized him, but then the feeling was gone. I circled around closer now.

Despite the visible frustration on Allan's face, he was speaking in hushed tones, and I could not overhear the conversation; however, I could see the other man's face now—no mistaking him. It was Ralph Meeker.

CHAPTER 3

I couldn't forget Ralph Meeker. I'd spent two hours face to face with the disgusting little man. The two men continued to argue in the corner. I was about to approach them when someone grabbed my arm. I spun around to face Lindsey. By the time she got through telling me the party would be over soon, both Allan and Ralph were gone. That was the last time I saw Allan alive.

After relaying my story to Lindsey, I lay with her in the bed, stroking her hair. I still couldn't believe Allan was dead, I had just seen him a little over forty-eight hours ago. I had seen the two men arguing, why hadn't I done something? I might have been able to prevent his death. Feeling tremendously guilty, I resolved to do what I could now to make up for inaction earlier. I tried to come up with any reasons why Allan would kill someone, much less himself. It didn't make sense. What could an art dealer and a Senator have had going on between them that could lead to murder? I could make no connections. I sighed deeply and Lindsey stirred.

"Rest," I said. "Try to sleep."

"OK," she murmured with closed eyes.

Alone with my thoughts, unable to take my own advice, I was incapable of sleep. Maybes ran rampant through my head. Maybe we didn't know Allan as well as we thought we did. Maybe he just cracked. Maybe he was taking bribes. Maybe he killed Meeker. They were fighting, and he was as capable as anyone else. Could it be true?

Allan was as much a father to me as he was to Lindsey. He had always been loving and honest with us, but putting that aside, even fathers can do dastardly things. I tried to look at the situation more objectively. Allan had never told a lie, which is quite an accomplishment for a politician. The public and even the news media respected him. So many things about the man were decent and wholesome; he donated to charity, he was an intellectual, and he rarely let his voice rise or his temper control him. A man like that could not be guilty of murder. So if Allan wasn't guilty of Ralph

Meeker's murder, why would he kill himself?

I concluded he must have been murdered as well—foul play, a third party, someone still at large.

The first step would be to talk with Detective Jeffries, the officer in charge of the case. According to Lindsey, the police considered it almost an open-and-closed case, a murder/suicide. I hoped they could tell me what evidence they had to support their position. I felt confident they would talk to me. Lindsey knew several of the police officers on the force from her work as a lawyer's aide. She worked for a well-known, local attorney named Robert Mayson. Colleagues in the industry had tried to nickname him "Perry," but it never stuck. Everyone just called him Mayson.

"I have to be at the station at eight this morning, anyway," Lindsey said and rubbed her red, puffy eyes. She had slept, but restlessly, sometimes crying out in her sleep. "I'm meeting Mayson for some preliminary work on a drug case. While I'm there, I'll see if I can arrange a meeting with the detective."

"You can't work today. Look at you," I insisted.

"I have to go. I didn't work yesterday."

"You can take another day off. We have the viewing this afternoon. Mayson will understand."

"No," she dabbed her eyes gently to avoid smudging her make-up. "I need to go. I can't hide away."

"Then I'll come with you. I don't have any installations today, and I've already accumulated 100 of my 160 hours for the month." I hunted around in the pockets of last night's pants for my wallet, keys, and comb.

"That's fine. The sooner we talk to the police, the better. This whole situation is ridiculous. Someone—" Lindsey's eyes glistened.

I brushed a runaway tear from her cheek. I knew Lindsey was strong, but I would have to help her. I would have to be even stronger. I couldn't let my emotions control me, not now. I squeezed her hand and passed the thimble I'd bought into her palm. "I love you," I said, a simple reassurance.

She looked down at it and let it roll in her palm. A smile broke through. "I love you, too."

Mayson was already at the station when we arrived a few minutes after nine. He was seated in the meeting room, along with Chief Blumberg. Between the two men was a long, worn, rectangular, wooden table. The stain was patchy, dark in some areas and whitened in others. One end had been picked at by nervous fingers and etched and scratched by guilty nails. The walls were cheap wood paneling and glass. In the center of the table was a pitcher of water and four glasses. Chief Blumberg, a big, impressive man, puffed gently on a cigar. He had dark, tanned skin and was wearing a dark suit. The halo of smoke and his grizzly old face made him look more like Mafia than police. Above his head on the bulletin board "Most Wanted" mug shots from all over the country and a "No Smoking" sign were posted. Mayson stood up as he saw us approaching.

"Glad to see you made it, Lindsey," he reached out and gave her a sympathetic pat. "You don't look like you got much rest."

"No." Lindsey grimaced.

"Good to see you, too, Paul," he added and shook my hand heartily. "This is the Chief of Police, Chief Blumberg."

"Nice to meet you," I responded.

"Chief." Lindsey greeted him with a nod.

The Chief didn't answer. No emotion stirred within him. He just nodded acknowledgment of our presence. He snuffed out his cigar on the table.

"I was wondering, since we're all here," she started and paused, glancing at me for mental support. "Um, since we're all here——"

"Spit it out, Mrs. Grey," the Chief urged.

"Is there any way, I mean, would you have time to talk with us about Allan Puckett? About his case?"

I think the Chief was going to deny the request, but he softened. "I guess. Let me see if Jeffries is still here. His shift ended at seven, but he usually hangs around. It's his case."

"Thank you," she replied and smiled.

"Yes, thanks," I enjoined.

He looked at me distastefully. "I'll be right back." He struggled out of the chair.

"Have you got the file on the Fuentes woman?" Mayson asked. "I'm meeting with her next."

"Right here," said Lindsey, handing over the file.

"Have you found out who our judge will be for this case?" He flipped through the papers.

"It's all in there."

"Good work. I've got to go." He shut the file. "Will I be seeing you in court later?"

"Yes." Lindsey nodded.

"Take it easy, Lin." He rested his hand on her shoulder for a moment. "I will."

With Mayson gone, we both sat down in chairs at the conference table to wait for Chief Blumberg.

"I don't think the Chief likes me," I whispered. Trying to keep the atmosphere light, I spun the chair around in a circle.

"He doesn't like anyone," Lindsey reassured me. "He's old and crotchety. You have to get used to him."

"No thanks," I replied.

Chief Blumberg rounded the corner, accompanied by a stout, freckle-skinned, dark-haired officer. The Chief pointed us out. The officer entered the room.

"Hello, I'm Detective Jeffries." He shook both our hands as we stood to meet him. "Chief says you wanted to talk about the Puckett murder-suicide."

"Yes," we replied in unison.

"What would you like to know?"

"We understand that the case isn't being investigated any further, has it been closed?" I asked. "We just can't see how. There are so many questions that are still unanswered."

"Like what?"

"Like what kind of evidence you based your conclusions on, how you figured out what happened, why you ruled Allan's death a suicide, all the details."

"Well, " He paused. "Where should I start?"

Neither Lindsey nor I responded. We waited for him pensively.

"OK, evidence. It all comes down to the weapon. The gun used to murder Ralph Meeker was the same gun Senator Puckett used to take his own life. It's that simple."

"Couldn't more than one person own the same type of gun?" I inquired.

"Yes, but this gun was fairly unique, a Colt Army revolver. It came from a set of guns at Ralph Meeker's shop, but we found it in Puckett's hand at his house. We concluded he shot Mr. Meeker with it then took it home. Originally he probably didn't plan on killing himself; perhaps guilt made him do it. The tests we ran prove without a doubt that it was the same gun."

"Can you explain? What type of test?" I asked.

"A ballistics test. When a bullet leaves a gun, the barrel marks the soft shell. Each gun barrel leaves different markings, just like a fingerprint. No two fingerprints are alike and no two gun markings are alike. We checked the bullets of both crime scenes and they match."

"Did you check for fingerprints? And what about a powder or metals test? What about blood?" Lindsey asked. This was her territory.

"The fingerprints on the gun were smudged. The other gun tests were inconclusive. No blood at the Senator's. He could have ditched the shoes."

"Re-run the tests," Lindsey demanded.

"No."

"You can't be sure Allan shot himself without those tests," Lindsey said.

"That isn't enough evidence for us." I shook my head. "Someone could have shot both of them and just made it look like Allan committed suicide."

"Not very practical, but possible. This case isn't closed—yet. We have to look at all angles in a case like this. That's why we treat all mysterious deaths as murders; however, we have other evidence, not as important as the gun, but still it supports our conclusion of suicide."

"Like what?" I asked.

"At Mr. Meeker's shop we found fibers from the Senator's clothing. We think there may have been a struggle. Also, an old lady, Mr. Meeker's neighbor, claims to have seen a car like Puckett's at the shop many times in the past few weeks. She says she saw his car leaving after a gunshot woke her up."

"But—" I started.

"They were fighting at the party. Doesn't that seem to fit the scenario?" the detective continued.

"Well, they weren't really fighting," I explained. "They were just arguing. I saw them."

"What were they arguing about?"

"I don't know that, but I do know Allan didn't kill anyone. He was an ex-police officer and served the government for years, for God's sake."

"How do you know he didn't kill anyone? In a fit of anger, people, even police officers and Senators, will do things you would least expect. He killed Ralph Meeker, and then in his deep regret the next morning, he took his own life. All of the evidence suggests and supports this."

"He didn't do it," I claimed. "There was no motive."

"They were fighting. There was a disagreement of some type. We don't know what it was about, but we will. Tension existed. That signifies a motive."

"Allan wouldn't kill himself," Lindsey said.

"Even out of extreme guilt or self pity? Even out of fear of life in prison?" the detective asked.

"I think the whole thing is a set-up," I said.

"This could all be circumstantial." Lindsey went into cross-examination. "The neighbor that identified the car may be mistaken. It would have been dark. You said she was old. And a fiber transfer can occur at almost any time. You should know that."

"Why would someone go to all that trouble? It seems improbable that someone would go to all the time and effort to frame someone and then kill them in an apparent suicide," the detective continued. "That's what you are suggesting isn't it?"

"Yes," I explained. "It looks to me like you have a highly intelligent murderer on your hands, Detective. Someone who killed Ralph Meeker and then Allan, to make it look like a murder-suicide. It's a better plan than just framing someone, because with the framed suspect dead there are no witnesses. It makes a perfect crime."

The detective shook his head. "There's no such thing as a perfect crime. And which is more logical—a situation which you are describing where a third party kills both men in a huge conspiracy cover-up, or Senator Puckett kills Ralph Meeker in the heat of an argument, then takes his own life in regret rather than face years in prison? If you think about this rationally, you'll see we're right. Trust us, we'll take care of it," he continued. "Here is my card and my home phone number. My partner on this case is Detective London Shope. She can help you if I'm not available. Call either one of us if you need anything."

"Thank you." I took his card.

"Are you going to run those tests again?" Lindsey asked. "Because I can go before a judge and have them ordered."

"No, they're a waste of time and money in this case; besides, the body has already been taken to the mortuary for burial and a court order will be too late." He shook his head and continued, "I understand how you both feel—"

"You have no idea how we feel," Lindsey interrupted, her voice quavering. "You have no idea."

With that she jumped out of her seat and burst out of the room. I followed in hot pursuit, leaving the detective behind speechless. I caught up with her on the front stairs. I gently reached for her arm.

"Wait for me," I said.

When she got to the sidewalk, she paused. She paced back and forth twice, then stood in front of me and looked into my eyes.

"Paul, what are we going to do?" she asked. "How can they believe that about Allan? How can they say those things? I can't tell Margie all that stuff. It would crush her."

"So don't tell her." I shrugged.

"Don't tell her?"

"Don't tell her. We'll figure it out. We know the police are wrong. As improbable as it might be, they're wrong."

"What are you saying?" She tossed her head to get the hair out of her face.

"I'm saying I'll investigate it myself. I'll find out who killed Allan."

"You have no experience investigating. You can't." Lindsey folded her arms.

"I can. You have the law and research background and lots of connections. With your help I can do it."

Lindsey looked at me skeptically. "What do we say to Margie until then?"

"Tell her the police are still looking into it. That's kind of true." I headed toward the car.

"OK, so what's our first move?" she asked, following.

"How hard would it be to get a list of the guests from your party on Monday?"

"Not hard, why?"

"Most people that are murdered are killed by someone they know, right?"

"Right," Lindsey agreed. "But maybe not in this case."

"I'd like to look at the guest list. They're all people who knew Allan. It's as good a place as any to start looking for suspects."

"OK," Lindsey said, "Jo should have it at our campaign headquarters."

By now we were to the car. I opened the door for her and she climbed in. I walked around to the driver's side and slid behind the wheel.

"We also need to ask Margie when she and Allan got home Monday night. He might even have had an alibi for the time Meeker's murder occurred," I suggested.

"What are you, Detective Columbo now?" She winked at me.

"No, but let's go get that guest list."

In less than a half-hour we were at Lindsey's campaign headquarters, a cheap unit at a local strip of stores connected to a grocery. It was a hole in the wall as far as I was concerned, but we could afford the lease. Her name was emblazoned across the front of it, for hundreds of shoppers to see every day. Someone was always there in case an unwary citizen should approach and request information. In all the times I had been there, I had never seen any passerby approach. If they had, they'd probably have been pounced upon by bored and overzealous volunteers. This was also the location from which all other aspects of the campaign were planned, implemented, and supervised. All yard signs, bumper stickers, and magnets originated there. All calls to and from voters were placed there.

A door chime announced our arrival. Two black metal desks stood guard, one on each side of the room, each equipped with a phone. Two uncomfortable-looking but matching armchairs from my great-aunt Susan that we had purposely never found a spot for in our home were strategically placed in front of each desk.

Behind one desk was a collapsible banquet table stacked with literature and brochures, statistical tables, graphs, and phone lists, reminiscent of our home office, which was buried under a similar slush pile. Underneath were boxes of magnets and pins and bumper stickers. Behind the other desk was a fax machine and two folding chairs. In the rear center was the door to Lindsey's office, which contained her desk, one armchair, and a copier. In the corner, yard signs were stacked against the wall.

Jodi Barrett, the campaign organizer, appeared from Lindsey's office with a stack of copies in her arms. She placed them on her desk. She was wearing a cheery expression, almost a laugh, unwarranted, considering the past two days' events. Her long blond hair tumbled over her shoulders as she walked toward us, arms open for a hug.

"Hi, Paul." Her words oozed. "Long time no see."

I gave her a hug half-heartedly. With my height and her slim, petite figure, I still engulfed her. She took a step back and smiled. Her smile made me uncomfortable. She was definitely not what I pictured as a political science type, then again neither was Lindsey.

"Lin, I'm sooo sorry to hear about Allan," she consoled. "We all loved him."

"I know. I don't want to talk about that right now. What's going on, anything?" Lindsey asked, taking a stiff posture.

Jo went back to her desk. "Here are your calls. Mrs. Hunting wants her sign down. She says all the neighborhood dogs are using it as a territorial marker and it's ruining her grass. You should talk to her."

"OK, I will."

"Also, the opposition called to challenge you to a debate."

"Televised?" Lindsey's back straightened with a hint of excitement.

"No. At a town hall meeting."

"Oh, tell them I'll think about it," she mumbled and slumped, obviously disappointed. "Anything else?"

"No, what did you come in for?"

"Do you still have the guest list from Monday's party?"

"Yes. It's on your desk."

"Thanks."

Lindsey and I went into her office and shut the door. The office was all of eight feet wide and twelve feet long with glass windows facing the front and her desk on the left. We both took a seat. Jo looked after us with curiosity.

Lindsey sifted through the papers on her desk. "Here it is." She handed the list to me. "I'm going to return some calls, OK?"

I nodded. I sat down in the armchair and read down the list. To me it read like the Fortune 500 and was almost as long as the telephone book. I recognized a few of the names, and I knew I had met some of them the other night, but I couldn't picture any faces to go with the names. I wasn't exactly sure about what I was doing. I had the dinner party list. Since both men had been killed by the same gun, I would need to compare names of persons they knew in common. Now I needed a list of Ralph Meeker's friends or acquaintances to compare to the dinner list. Any matches would be good leads. And since Ralph wasn't telling, I'd have to come up with a plan.

Lindsey appeared to be in between calls. She was staring into space, a faraway look to her eyes.

"Hey, Lin," I said.

Her attention focused.

"Is there any way I could get into Ralph Meeker's shop?" I asked.

"What on earth for?" She looked at me aghast. "Why would you want to go there?"

"To look for a client list, or address book, or something, a clue maybe."

"You think you can find something the police haven't?" she asked, almost laughing at my feeble attempts at sleuthing.

"Maybe," I said. "They think the case is closed, so why would they look for any evidence that says otherwise?"

She shrugged. "I guess you can get in. The scene should be released since the evidence collection is over, but you'll be on your own. I've got business at the courthouse. And don't forget we both have the viewing at three."

"I'll meet you at the courthouse at two. Can I have the car?"

"Yeah, I'll take a cab."

She seemed hesitant about letting me go. Maybe because she didn't like the idea of me poking around some dead guy's house. Maybe because she didn't want me to leave her alone.

"Are you sure?" I needed a smile before I would go.

"Yeah," she grinned. "Go on, Sherlock! Do your thing."

"Great, thanks!"

"I'll call Mayson's secretary and have her notify the police station. She can arrange to have someone with a key meet you at Meeker's shop. I'm sure we can come up with some little white lie to get you in."

"Thanks." I gave her a kiss.

She smiled as I left, like a mother of a wayward child.

"See you later, Paul," Jo said.

The door chimed as I walked out.

CHAPTER 4

I drove to Ralph Meeker's shop. Traffic congestion on the roadways slowed my trip. Lunch hour was approaching and travelers zipped in and out of intersections and local eateries. Long waits at traffic lights were common in that busy area almost any time of day.

The shop was a freestanding building that at one time, before city expansion, had been a small ranch home. Although multiple facelifts had been applied, the place was run down now as was witnessed by several colors of peeling paint around the windows. A beautiful oak and stained glass door complete with an ornate doorbell at the entrance belied the rest of the shabby exterior. A small brass plate above the doorbell announced "Atlanta Arts and Antiquities" in elegant script. No one was waiting at the shop as I had anticipated.

I tried the door. It was unlocked. I debated about waiting for someone to arrive. Perhaps someone had already come by and unlocked it for me. I decided to go ahead in.

"Hello?" I called. No one answered.

Inside was bigger than I had expected. Most of the interior walls had been removed to create one large room—the showroom. To the rear were two doors—one open and one shut. The door that was open led to a small office. I assumed the shut room to be the bathroom. I stood in the front doorway for a few minutes. I wasn't sure I should go in. Maybe I should put on gloves, I thought.

"Can I help you?" boomed a voice.

"Ahhh," escaped my lips; my heart leapt. I turned to see a police officer in uniform. "I— I'm with Mayson, the attorney. I was going to check things out," I stumbled.

"OK," said the officer, who had arrived stealthily under the cover noise of passerby traffic. "Just don't disturb anything, and let me know when you're done. I'll be in my car." He turned to go back down the walk to the driveway.

"Um, could you help me for a minute?" I asked.

"Yeah," he said.

"Possibly you would know, are the police through collecting evidence?" I inquired, although I knew the answer.

The officer looked at me blankly and remained silent.

"I mean, have they removed the body?"

"Yeah, the scene is released."

"Did they dust for prints?"

"Yeah, the scene is released."

"Can you be more specific, tell me anything else?" I had no idea what a 'released' scene meant and I didn't want any gruesome surprises, so I prodded this man of few words. I could see doubt in his facial expression that I was with the attorney's office and had experience in these matters.

"The usual," he said, pausing for a great length of time and looking me steady in the eyes. "First they photographed and diagramed and measured everything. Then they completed an alternate light scan for blood and fingerprints. They vacuumed for fibers. They took any weapons to ballistics and the body to autopsy."

"The usual. Thanks, that was very helpful," I said. "So the scene has been released? I'm free to walk around in here?"

"Yes, but don't touch anything," he repeated his warning. "And watch your step. There hasn't been a clean-up yet."

"OK."

Left to myself, I stepped cautiously inside. I felt like I was on an amusement ride. At any moment a skeleton would pop out or drop from above. My adrenaline was pumping, but for no apparent reason. The store was very ordinary.

The cluttered showroom smelled of mildew and old things. The scent filled the room even though all the windows were open. Dusty sunlight filtered through. It was hot, no breeze. On the walls hung Oriental rugs and mirrors in gilded frames. I walked around the room clockwise. It was an odd assortment that reminded me of a flea market or oversized garage sale. In every direction were pieces of furniture and cases of trinkets. I recognized one of the items Meeker had proudly told me about. Meeker was an eclectic collector.

On the other side of the room were rows of shelves and picture racks. The shelves contained things like silver tea sets and china. Picture racks were filled with canvases and frames to the point of overflowing. Simultaneously, several small clocks and a large grandfather rang out the hour. I wondered how long the grandfather clock would run without Meeker there to wind it.

Directly to the left of the office door, in the corner, was a gun display case. I stepped to the gun case to take a closer look at the weapons inside.

A smaller box inside the case had an empty slot where one of two weapons was missing. I knew from the police detective that this must be where the murder weapon had come from. Three weapons remained on display inside—two rifles and a revolver. On the window sill to the left of the case was a strategically placed box of disposable latex gloves, presumably put there by the late Mr. Meeker to protect his treasures. I put one on each hand. In the ninety-degree heat, the latex made my hands sweat, but then I could really investigate. I carefully removed the smaller box that still held one revolver. The killer must have been familiar with the shop in order to know the gun was there, complete with ammunition. The gun case was oak with a velvet lining with niches for two revolvers and for the bullets. I removed the remaining revolver and examined it. It was, according to the tag, a double-cased set of Colt Postwar Single Action Army Revolvers in a .357 Magnum caliber. It felt like a brick in my hand. The cylinder where the bullets were housed was engraved, and the grip was ivory. I checked the cylinder for bullets. The firearm was fully loaded. I closed it carefully and laid it back in the case. I replaced the entire box in the cabinet. Then I visually examined the two rifles—a Winchester Model 70 and a Weatherby Mark V, also a Magnum. I guessed these were not inexpensive, pawn shop type items and concluded Meeker's murder had not been a result of theft, or these items would be missing. I left the display case open like I had found it. I left the gloves on; I wanted to examine everything else.

The door on the right turned out to lead to a bedroom with a bathroom and a kitchen area with a storage closet. As I snooped around I was careful to replace everything exactly like it had been. A glance over my shoulder assured me I was alone. I checked the kitchen. Ramen noodles appeared to have been that man's staple diet. In the bedroom I looked under the mattress and through the clothes in the closet. Checking all the pockets, I found a gas receipt, some spare change, and a roll of film. I confiscated the film and the receipt, but replaced the coins. I tapped the walls, looking for a compartment or something mysterious, but I found nothing.

In the bathroom I found a pet food dish and litter box. I called out for the cat, but no animal responded. I thought the cat might be outside, so I went to the front door and called for it.

"Heeeere kitty, kitty, kitty," I called and bent down to look under and around the hedges.

The police officer looked up from his magazine to stare at me. The expression on his face, one eyebrow raised in question, was a mixture of amusement and doubt. I returned to the house, embarrassed.

I finished my check of the bathroom with a glance inside the medicine cabinet. A few over-the-counter drugs and a prescription allergy medication were not the big clues I was after. That left only the office to be explored.

I approached the office slowly, not knowing what to expect inside. A bad odor, unlike anything I had ever smelled before, lingered in the room, but it wasn't overpowering. After a few minutes I couldn't smell it at all anymore. The breeze had picked up and that helped. A storm was probably moving in.

I thought that the sight of blood might make me sick, but instead it was like walking through a movie set. I didn't know Meeker and that helped. Uncannily desensitized, my attention focused immediately on the blood—set, dried, and cracked like black ice. It wasn't red and oozy. The blood was pooled in the middle of the room with a mist of droplets around it, mostly to the front of the room. A few droplets smudged by feet, no prints. A tape tracing marked the location of the body, and a section of the wall was missing. I assumed it had been cut out because that was where the bullet had been deposited. Judging from the location of the body and the blood stains, it looked as if Meeker had been shot in his midsection, possibly the heart. *Why hadn't the killer shot him more than once to be sure to finish him off?* I would need to interview the coroner or get an autopsy report.

I looked around. Cavernous and dark, the room was about fifteen feet square with one barred window. Out the window, I could see the neighbor's house. Facing the door was a metal desk and a filing cabinet. The chair behind the desk was pushed back, and there were files open on the desk. The desk blotter was stained with coffee, but there was no mug. A pair of glasses lay folded up and placed to the right side. I sat down at the desk. *Was Ralph Meeker near- or farsighted?* I held the glasses up to my eyes. I couldn't tell. If he was farsighted, he should have had the glasses on when the killer approached. The open files, the blood stain—they told the story. Ralph must have been working at the desk when he heard something or someone approach. He got up, pushing the chair back, and came around to the front of the desk. The killer probably remained near the doorway. Ralph got to the middle of the room and then the killer, having the gun from the display case, shot Ralph in the stomach. Ralph then slumped and fell forward. The whole incident probably took only ten to fifteen seconds to complete. I pocketed the pair of glasses, too. I was probably going to be in a lot of trouble for this.

I examined the papers on Ralph's desk. The folder on the desk was full of shipping receipts. Nothing out of the ordinary. Remembering the Hardy Boys and other childhood crime solvers, I looked under the desk and the desk drawer—nothing. Where would he keep an address book?

Most likely he kept it in the two-drawer filing cabinet behind the desk. I pulled the top drawer open. It was stuffed full of papers. I flipped through the files. Two things were obvious. Meeker was not one for neatness or organization, and he desperately needed another filing cabinet. I could barely squeeze a finger between the files to keep my place. The files were mostly receipts and sales tickets. A file folder labeled "BANK" was empty.

Perhaps someone took the contents already. On the inside of the folder was a scrawled number—12054901100. I wrote it down and tucked it in my pocket. It was probably his account number. I replaced the folder.

The second drawer was full of office supplies like tape and staples, paper and pens, and a Rolodex. I immediately pulled out the Rolodex. I felt like a super-sleuth. I took the list Lindsey had given me out of my pocket and began comparing names. Thirteen names, including Allan, were common to both lists. Feeling elated and accomplished, I put the Rolodex back. Then I examined the underside and backsides of the file drawers. Sticking an arm into the back recess of a file cabinet is not an easy thing to do. I had to remove several handfuls of files in order to make the fit. Something was there, clinking around as I tried to grasp and remove it. To my disgust, it was only a paper clip. I felt around again to be sure, along the bottom, the sides, and up the back wall. Nothing more.

I moved to the middle of the room and scanned slowly in a three-sixty. Having never been there before, to my eye it looked as if nothing had been disturbed. I got down on my hands and knees and put my eye level with the plane of the floor. This new angle yielded nothing but dust bunnies that had escaped the police vacuums.

I had one last place to look, behind the rug that hung on the wall. I crossed my fingers for a safe or something, but all I found was more dust, which released into the air as the rug fell back into place. But wait, there on the floor, stuck into the tassels was a small white card. It was a rectangular piece of laminated plastic. I picked it up and flipped it over. My stomach turned into knots and I felt nauseated. It was a name badge from Lindsey's dinner party—Allan's name badge.

This can't be good. Do I put it back? Was this a test? The officer had said not to touch anything. Maybe it had been planted. I stole a furtive glance over my shoulder as I slipped it into my pocket. If I left it or told the police, it would only be added to evidence against Allan. I removed the gloves. Then I left the store. The officer was sitting in his squad car with the windows down, no air.

"I'm done," I called out to the officer from the walkway. "I'm going to talk with the neighbor now."

The officer nodded and started his car. I turned to the neighbor's house, cut through the grass, and knocked on the front door. In a few moments it was answered by a hunchbacked, gray-haired woman.

"I'm Paul Grey," I introduced myself. "I'm investigating the murder of Ralph Meeker. Do you have a minute?"

She stuck her head out and looked around. Seeing the officer's car next door sitting in the drive, waiting for a break in traffic, she allowed me inside.

"The report says you saw a car leaving Mr. Meeker's house the night he was killed," I said. "What time was that?"

"I'm not exactly sure." She twisted her hair. "I think it was around two in the morning. I didn't have my glasses, so I couldn't read the clock."

"Where are your glasses now?" I asked, thinking about the pair in my pocket.

"They're in the kitchen. Come," she said and motioned for me to follow her. "Would you like some sweet tea?"

I nodded and she poured a large serving of the refreshing liquid.

"Tastes so good on a hot day." She smiled, delighted that I was enjoying the beverage.

"Yes, thanks." I sat down at the table with her and noticed her glasses lying next to a book she was reading—*Wanderlust* by Danielle Steele.

"Books like that make me feel young again." She blushed as she quickly put it away.

"You're farsighted?" I commented and pulled out the pair of glasses I had found. "Will you try these on and see how they work for you?"

She took the pair and put them on. "Nope, no good."

"Did Mr. Meeker wear glasses?" I asked.

"I don't know for sure. I don't think I ever saw him wearing any." She passed the pair back to me.

"What were you doing up at 2:00 A.M.?" I asked.

"I heard a noise. It woke me up," she replied.

"Tell me exactly what happened, as you remember it," I instructed.

"Well, I was sleeping when I heard a loud noise, which I now know was a gun-shot, and it woke me up. I thought it might have been a blown tire or that I had imagined it, so I lay there awhile, waiting. I should have gotten up right away, but I didn't think there was anything seriously wrong. Then later I heard the same noise again and then tires squealing, so I went outside to check on Mr. Meeker."

"Is that when you were at the window and saw the car leaving?"

"I only heard a car leaving," she said. "I didn't see it."

"The police reported you saw a light-colored car leaving Mr. Meeker's house," I insisted.

"No, no. I saw a car, like the one they showed me, many times in Mr. Meeker's driveway, and that night I heard a car leave, but I don't know it was *that* car. It sounded a lot like that light-colored car but it's hard to say."

"How much time went by after the first noise before you went to investigate?"

"I'm not sure. I think I may have drifted back off to sleep. Like I was saying, I really didn't think there was anything serious going on, or I would have done something right away."

"How much time do you think went by?" I asked.

"Maybe fifteen minutes?" She shrugged.

"Did you ever see Senator Allan Puckett at Mr. Meeker's house?" I looked straight into her pale eyes.

She shook her head. "Never. I didn't pay much mind to the comings and goings over there. He has a shop, so lots of strangers are in and out."

"Thank you. You've been a great help." I shook her hand.

Once back across the yard and into my car I pulled out the nametag. Despite this nagging piece of evidence, I was pleased with the ease in which I had gathered the information I wanted. I was impressed with myself. I had always thought private eye work was harder. Already I had discounted one piece of evidence against Allan—the witness. And as for the nametag, I folded it back and forth to weaken the plastic so I could tear it in half again and again. I shoved all the parts in the ashtray and used the cigarette lighter to melt them beyond recognition. *Only just begun and already I'm destroying evidence—what a wonderful start!*

Hoping I had made the right choice, I drove over to the courthouse to meet up with Lindsey. Feeling proud, I puffed out my chest and strutted my stuff as I entered the courthouse in search of her. Even the guard who made me empty all my pockets and walk through the firearms detector twice couldn't squelch this feeling.

Lindsey and Mayson were in Courtroom No. 2, still waiting on their case to be called. I took the opportunity to check in at my office. One of the benefits of my job was not having an office or set work hours. I worked until I accumulated 160 hours in a month. There was no overtime. If I earned all my hours in the first two weeks, then I could have the last two weeks off. Usually it didn't work out that way, but it had sounded good when the company had presented the idea to me at the interview. I called my voice mail, which confirmed I had no new messages.

I unfolded the list of names I had made at Ralph Meeker's. That list being my main lead, one way or another I would have to narrow it down. The most straightforward approach would be to start by checking alibis, but running around town throwing accusations at Lindsey's supporters wouldn't be productive for her campaign. I would have to be careful. Just because they were at her party and happened to know both Allan and Puckett and Ralph Meeker did not constitute proof of guilt.

I also had the number from Ralph's file. I decided to check some local banks to see if the number was to an account at one of them. I stood at the pay phone booth and flipped through the yellow pages, looking up names and branches of banks in the area. I wrote down their numbers. Lindsey was going to be a while, so I began calling them one by one. When I called the first bank, I wasn't sure what I was going to say or do. The teller answered and the words just started coming out automatically. I wasn't accustomed to lying, but somewhere deep inside I had the instinct.

"American National Bank. This is Teresa. Can I help you?" she said.

"Yes, Teresa. I have a question. I have a check from someone who

banks there. Can you tell me if the funds are available before I deposit it?"
I asked.

"Certainly," she said. "Read me the account number."

I read the number to her.

"Just a moment," she paused, "Give me the name on the account,
please."

"Ralph Meeker."

"Sir, I'm sorry, but that is not a valid account number. Are you sure it's
a real check?"

"Oh, my," I feigned dismay. "I don't know. I'm sorry."

"No problem," she said.

I hung up and called all the banks in the area and questioned them in
the same manner. Not one of them had that account number for a Ralph
Meeker which could mean many things—the number was wrong, or
outdated, or to an out-of-state bank, or even that Meeker was using a false
name. In all cases the number seemed to be a dead end.

I walked back to courtroom number two, went in, and took a seat in the
third row next to Lindsey.

"Are you busy right now?" I whispered.

"No. This isn't one of our cases."

"Any idea what this could be?" I handed her the piece of paper with
the number on it.

She looked at me questioningly, but I just shrugged. She studied it for
a few seconds and then shook her head. "No idea," she announced and
handed it back.

Several long minutes later, her case was called. Lindsey and Mayson
went to the front of the courtroom. The judge looked over the evidence file
before him and in less than five minutes decided formal charges were to be
made against their client. After the decision was passed, Mayson and
Lindsey had some minor discussion. Lindsey came toward me. I stood up
and joined her.

"Did you find that number at Ralph Meeker's shop?" she asked as we
left.

"Yes. I was hoping it was a bank account number. Then, somehow, I
could look at his financial records and get some idea of what was going on
in his life."

"I wouldn't think it would be that simple," she said sympathetically.
"That number could be anything. It could be the combination to his luggage
for goodness sakes!"

I contemplated the needle in the haystack theory.

"Maybe we should turn it over to the police?" Lindsey suggested.

"Are you crazy?" I blurted. "I probably shouldn't even have that
number and that's not all I have."

"You're right. No point in getting ourselves in trouble. What else did you find?"

"I— I found a roll of film that we can drop off for developing."

"Stealing a dead guy's film?" she asked, seeming not to notice my hesitation.

"Yeah." I rolled my eyes sheepishly. She didn't need to know about the nametag.

Lindsey shook her head in disbelief. "Great, just great. I'm married to Magnum PI."

"I know!" I grinned at the challenge. "Isn't it great?"

CHAPTER 5

We dropped the roll of film off at a one-hour developing service on our way to Parson's Funeral Home. We were late and feeling guilty. We arrived at the end of the scheduled viewing hours. The only persons present were Margie and her two sons, with their families. Their little ones were hungry, so they were on their way out as we entered. Margie looked relieved to see us. She probably didn't relish the idea of having to sit in there alone. She looked old and frail, wrapped up in the embrace of a love seat. We leaned over and hugged her in turn.

"So far, so good." She had anticipated our first question. "I think I'm still in shock."

"Me, too," I replied.

"It's so hard to believe. I feel so unprepared." Lindsey's eyes flitted across the casket.

"I know. When I left for work that— that morning. He was fine. We— we had breakfast together. He kissed me good—." Her gray eyes flooded. I can't believe he's gone."

"At least you left on good terms, with no regrets."

Margie nodded in agreement, dabbing her eyes.

"We were good Christians," she said. "I know he's gone to a better place, but I can't help but wonder how anyplace can be better than here with me. Is that wrong of me? Is that selfish?"

Lindsey shook her head and her eyes began to well up with tears, as did Margie's. I removed myself to a safer place, somewhere away from them so I wouldn't cry, too. I walked up to the casket to pay my last regards. It was a closed casket. It smelled of pine and roses. I bowed my head silently, reverently. *Allan, I'll find out who it was.* I placed my hand on the casket. Then I took a few minutes to look at all the tags on the bouquets. "With Sympathy" and "Our Deepest Regrets" they all said.

"Paul," Lindsey said, her hand on my shoulder. I turned to her. "Margie wants to ask you something."

Like leading a horse to water, she took my hand and guided me to the sofa where Margie sat, rubbing her eyes with a fistful of tissues.

"I was hoping you could go by the house and pick up some things for me," Margie explained with renewed composure. "I've been staying at the hotel with the kids, but I don't have any of my things. And I can't go back to the house."

"Ummm, " I paused, unsure of my bravery.

"I'd ask one of my boys, but they don't know the house like you do. If you can't, I understand." She bit her lip—again fighting tears. "The kids can help me buy some new things to tide me over."

"No, no. I'll go," I insisted.

"Thank goodness. I really need our papers from the safe." I could see her relax.

"Papers?"

"Yes, our wills and bank account papers. Without the account numbers, I don't have access to any of our money, and I don't think any insurance checks are going to come through, you know, suicide and all."

"No insurance? You have no money?"

"We, I mean, I have money. I just need to get into the accounts."

"I'll go. I'll try."

"Oh, thank you." She patted my hand and closed her eyes.

Silence fell. There wasn't anything I could say. Every time I thought of something to talk about, I bit my tongue and held back. *What if I said something upsetting?* It appeared Margie and Lindsey couldn't think of anything either. I needed to pick Margie for information and if I didn't ask her then, I might not have ever gotten the courage. Finally, I decided to take the plunge.

"Margie," I began. She tuned in on me. "I'd really like to know where Allan was after the party the night of Meeker's murder."

"I don't know."

"You don't know? You weren't together?" I inquired.

"Wouldn't that have been nice? That would blow the police's theory."

"You know what the police think?" Lindsey asked with some surprise.

"Of course, honey. I may be old and grieving, but I still read the report. I want to know."

"So you weren't together?" I repeated.

"No, we both had been working and had gone to the party in our own cars. So we drove home separately, too."

"Didn't you both get home around the same time?"

"No. He came in much later. It was after 3:00 A.M."

"Three? Isn't that a little unusual?" Lindsey asked.

"No." Seeing a need to explain she continued, "He likes, I mean liked to go to bars."

"Bars?! But Allan didn't drink," Lindsey said.

"No, he didn't. If he had anything weighing on him he'd go so he could listen to all the problems other people talked about. It made him feel better every time. He'd come home and tell me how good we had it."

"I never knew that." Lindsey's eyes welled up.

"What bar was he at that night?" I asked. "What was weighing on him?"

"I don't know either answer. He liked O'Malley's. He went there often." Her voice was hollow and distant.

"Did you tell this to the police?"

"Yes, but I don't know for certain that he was there."

"We could call the bar and ask the bartender if he knew Allan, or if he remembers Allan being there that night," Lindsey suggested.

"Exactly what I had planned," I said.

"Why would you do that?" Margie asked. "Won't the police do that?"

Lindsey and I exchanged knowing glances before she responded, "I'm sure they will, but there's no harm in us following up, too."

"If Allan was there, then he couldn't have killed Ralph. And if he didn't kill Ralph, then he wouldn't have the gun or the reason to kill himself. If it wasn't suicide, you ought to at least be able to collect your insurance," I concluded.

"He couldn't have killed himself, but I don't know which is worse—believing he killed himself or knowing someone took his life from him."

"Try not to think about either," Lindsey encouraged and then addressed me. "In the meantime, I'm going to take Margie to the hotel while you go by the house for her things. You can meet us there."

"Now?" I panicked a little.

"Yes, somewhere in here is a list of what I need." Margie rooted through her purse and handed me a slip of paper and the door key.

We parted ways. I took the car to Margie's house.

In the dead heat of afternoon, my dampened shirt clung to my back as I got out of the car. I was nervous and hot. I surveyed Allan's house as I made my approach—nothing unusual. I held the key to the house tightly in my hand. It dug into my skin, leaving its print in my clammy palm.

Just get in and get out. Pick up the things for Margie and get out. The door opened easily and swung wide into the foyer. Ralph Meeker's place had been easy. He was a stranger. His death did not affect me. I had felt removed. His death scene was no more emotional than what I saw every night on the news or cable movies. Allan's on the other hand was frightening. I stood frozen to the front steps. I felt I could not go in.

The air-conditioned coolness from the rooms inside began to mingle with the unbearable heat of the outdoors. The wisps of air wrapped around me like cold hands of death and enticed me in. The house felt empty, like it had been deserted for years. The hall seemed hollow. Pictures of the couple and their offspring peered at me from the walls. I shuddered as the inside air penetrated my sweat-dampened shirt for a super-cool.

Faintly, I could smell breakfast—breakfast for Allan and Margie. I went through the living room to the kitchen. The greasy bacon pan was still on the stove. The dishes were piled in the sink. Perfectly normal. However, I didn't need anything from the kitchen. I was just wasting time, delaying the trip to the back of the house.

The far end of the house did not smell like bacon but was reminiscent of rotten fruit—sickly sweet. It made my stomach turn. It was a good thing I hadn't eaten at all that day. I needed to get clothes from the bedroom and papers from the office. I got the suitcase from the hall closet, right where Margie had said it would be.

The doorway to their room was shut and sealed with crime scene tape. I snapped the plastic tape and opened the door. I hastily collected some clothes and underwear for Margie, constantly aware of what lurked beyond the bathroom doorway. A mirror above the dresser where I rummaged granted me a reflection of a bathroom wall. I shut the drawer I was searching. Curiosity prevailing, I approached the bathroom.

The room was a flood of light blue tiles. Light spewed from a window. The tub was spattered with dried blood and tissue. I gagged and lunged for the toilet. Dry heaves wracked my body as I cradled the seat, but there was nothing to bring up. Meeker's scene had been cleaner, easier to handle.

When the wave of nausea passed, I was able to open my eyes and get up. I noticed on top of the tissues in the trash can was a man's disposable razor blade. Strange. I examined the razor on the sink. It had a new blade in it. Some oil was still left on the steel blades, but it had been used. Hair stuck to the sides of the sink raised my suspicions. Had Allan shaved that morning before his death? Why would someone shave if he was going to commit suicide? Furthermore, why climb into the tub to shoot yourself? Wouldn't it be just as easy to sit on the toilet or do it standing up?

I examined the grizzly scene as objectively as I could. Evidently Allan had laid down in the tub, his feet under the spigot, and shot himself in the head. Blood and tissue had exited the back of his skull, and the bullet had apparently lodged in the tiles behind his head. A section of the wall there was missing, having been cut out by the police. Most of the blood had oozed its way down the drain, but in the basin of the tub I could discern where blood had pooled under his legs and torso and remained after the body had been carried off. A gag reflex closed my throat several times in rapid succession. I turned for the toilet again until the sickness passed.

A further examination of the dried blood revealed bits of clothing and fibers that had stuck to the bottom when they pulled the body out. *Why would he shower and get dressed?* There were too many questions that needed answers. I needed an autopsy report on both Allan and Ralph to help answer those questions.

I wrapped up my investigation of the bathroom since it was getting late. I collected the rest of the clothes and papers for Margie, locked up the house, and met them at the hotel. Margie was grateful.

Lindsey and I left together saying hardly a word. I knew we needed to eat, but I wasn't even hungry, especially after what I had seen.

"I don't want to cook," Lindsey complained, reading my mind.

"Neither one of us has eaten all day. We need to do something. Let's get something out."

"How about that new Italian place—Gianni's?" she suggested, smiling.

The thought of Italian twisted my stomach into knots, but this was the biggest smile I'd gotten from Lindsey in the past twenty-four hours.

"OK," I replied, but not before checking my watch. I couldn't investigate anything more that day anyway and the film developer was on the wrong side of town.

Most of the food was wasted on our plates. The chicken alfredo I'd ordered would have been excellent under different circumstances and the atmosphere romantic, but Lindsey was still so distant, and I kept thinking about my mystery. That night as I lay in bed and drifted into sleep, the pieces of the puzzle ran through my head over and over. The number, the roll of film, the razor blade, the list of names, autopsy reports.

Somehow I awoke refreshed. Still in my underwear, I went into the bathroom and pulled out my razor and toothbrush. I hadn't shaved in two days. As I held the thin blades to my neck and applied pressure, visions of Allan's bloody bathroom came to me—the tub, the tiles, like still photographs—blood, blood, blood. Like a bad horror movie or nightmare I could see Allan in my vision, his head snapping back with the squeeze of the trigger.

"Are you OK?" Lindsey asked as she entered the bathroom for her brush.

"Ow! Damn! I cut myself." Startled, I realized I was bleeding where I held the razor to my neck.

"Are you OK, space cadet?" she repeated, handing me a wad of toilet tissue. "What were you thinking about?"

"I— I don't know," I replied before her question had time to sink in. "I was thinking about Allan. I found a new blade in his razor and hairs in the sink. Why shave at all if you're going to do yourself in? And why a gun? Why not take pills or something? I mean, how does someone decide how they are going to die?"

"Most of us don't get to decide," she said. "But if someone is set on killing himself, I'd think he or she would try the quickest, most assured way, like a gun. Someone not as serious might try stuff like pills, so they can be found and rescued."

"So, Allan, to be sure he did it right, used a gun?"

"Probably, if he killed himself. But he didn't kill himself. I thought you were of the belief he was murdered as well." She put her hands on her hips.

"I'm just pointing out the details the police missed."

"Well, go on. Surely you have more observations than just the razor."

"Um—"

"Go ahead. I can handle it," she assured.

"Um, well, he was in the tub like this," I climbed in to demonstrate. "And he was shot in the head. I don't know exactly where."

"And?"

"Nothing else. Well, something's not right. It doesn't sit well with me. I want to see the autopsy reports." I leaned back and closed my eyes, thinking.

"Are you going to shower now?" Lindsey hovered over me. I sensed her there.

"Mm-hmm." I nodded, my eyes still closed, thinking.

"Good," she yelled as she turned on the cold shower water full stream.

She giggled and ran as I scrambled to get out of the tub. I couldn't get out fast enough.

"Some detective you are," she teased from the safety of the bedroom. "I can't believe you didn't see that coming!"

CHAPTER 6

Using some insanely hot water, I showered and then dressed. I unpacked my travel bag. It had sat untouched, and the contents were odorous and wrinkled. I folded my dress shirts and suit to take to the cleaners. This behavior drove Lindsey crazy. She would scold me saying, "They are dirty anyway; who cares if they are wrinkled and bunched up or not?" But it was a ritual. I always folded them. She always rolled her eyes when she saw the pile.

I dropped the dry cleaning off on my way into work. Friday morning was my usual day to go to the gym and work out, assuming I had no out-of-town trips. The employees' gym was located on the basement level of my office building. Modest in size, the mirrored walls gave a false impression of additional space and more equipment than there really was. It was extremely cold in the gym, and it stunk of sweat. I always began my workout with a few arm and leg stretches because I had reached the delicate age where omitting this would result in cramps and aches. Then I rode the bike for fifteen minutes using a program of medium difficulty, which gave the illusion of a hilly, rolling countryside.

A younger female employee entered the gym, glanced over at me self-consciously, and then began her workout. I finished on the bike and went to a weight machine, and then I headed for the showers.

I had brought my business clothes—a pair of khakis and a company-embroidered polo shirt. I re-showered then dressed in those. I reported to my office, or rather my partitioned cubicle, by promptly 9:00 A.M. I had an installation at eleven across town, so I had time to make a few business calls before I had to leave. I returned my messages and scheduled two installations for August. With those tasks out of the way, I headed out for my appointment.

The installation was for an insurance company located in the eastern suburbs of Atlanta. Phoenix Insurance had expanded into a new section of office space and needed all of their cables installed inside the walls before the final build-out and delivery of the workstations. I met with Joshua Higgins, the office manager, for a few minutes. He showed me where the equipment and wires had been delivered and were being stored, then quickly left me to do my work. A secretary was down the hall in case I should need something or someone.

I worked steadily for two hours before my rumbling stomach decided it was time to break for lunch. I went by the secretary's desk to tell her I was leaving and would return shortly. She was busy jotting down a message for Mr. Higgins.

"He'll hafta call you back, ma'am. He's in a very important meeting for the next thirty minutes or so," she said.

I glanced through the glass windows to Mr. Higgins' office. He was hunched over his desk sucking down a cheeseburger, fries, and a Coke, alone. I always knew that's what happened when someone was in a "meeting," but this was the first I'd seen it.

"OK. I'll tell him," the secretary continued. "Melinda Patterson, 205, OK. 535, OK. 1215." She paused. "Yessss, he'll call you back today. Goodbye."

The secretary looked up at me and smiled expectantly. When I didn't say anything, she started talking.

"Poor woman," she said. "Her house flooded, and she didn't have flood insurance—only hazard insurance."

But I wasn't listening to her as she droned on about coverages. I was looking at the upside-down phone number—205-535-1215. My mystery number began with 205.

"I'm going to lunch," I said to cut her off. "I'll be back."

She nodded and stopped ranting. "OK."

I wasn't even to the car before I had out the piece of paper with the number on it from out of my wallet. It could be a phone number. Easy enough to try. Leaning on the hood of the car, I wrote the number completely, including the dashes. As soon as I finished the installment job I could go to Lindsey's office and test my theory.

I didn't even go to lunch. I crossed the parking lot and went right back inside, past the secretary and into my work area. The secretary looked up at me, completely confused. I finished my work in another two and a half hours and then went to Lindsey's campaign office. On the way I picked up some fries. I was so excited that I hastily inhaled them.

I barged through the door of the office, sending the chimes into overdrive. Jo jumped up, startled, from her desk. She had one ear on the phone. Relieved to see it was me, she held up a "one minute" finger.

"I'm just going to the back," I interrupted her discussion of welfare issues with a possible voter.

"Excuse me," she said covering the mouthpiece. "Lindsey isn't here."

"I know," I said.

"What can I do for you Paul?" She smiled as she asked.

"I need to use the phone." I moved around her.

"I'd suggest you get a cell phone, but then I wouldn't have the pleasure of seeing you."

Not wishing to fall into a quasi-sexual conversation with her, which is where her talk tends to go, I politely indicated her waiting party and disappeared into the safety of Lindsey's office.

I shut the door. In my younger days I'd have jumped over the desk to speed things up. I was breathless as I dialed the number. It rang and rang and rang. Finally it was answered. I kept my fingers crossed.

"First Savings and Loan. This is Amanda. May I help you?"

This was it. I just knew it had to be it.

I didn't know what to say, so I hung up. I picked up the phone book from the floor by the desk and flipped to the information pages in the front. There it was—AREA CODES. I scanned the list for 205. Alabama. My first real clue.

I immediately called Lindsey at her office.

"Mayson, Clark, and Clark Attorneys—"

"Hey, it's me," I interrupted. "Guess what?"

"I have no idea." Lindsey was dumbfounded.

"I think I found it," I said.

"Found what?" she asked, still thrown.

"The bank. Meeker's bank. That number was a phone number," I said.

"Oh," she said.

"Try to show a little more enthusiasm," I prodded.

"Wow," she attempted. She was even worse at pretending enthusiasm when there was none there.

"That's much better."

"I'm sorry. It's just not been a good day."

"What's wrong with today?" I asked, presuming she had been thinking about Allan. "You seemed in good spirits this morning when you almost drowned me."

"Well, that part was OK." Her voice lightened a little.

"So what's the bad part?" I asked.

"There was a dip in our opinion poll today. It places me behind Samuel Kingman. I guess it's because of Allan's connections with Ralph Meeker's death."

"Should that affect you? You know I don't get all that political stuff." Despite my non-understanding of things political, I knew what was coming. I felt my heart drop. Our life savings, our futures were all invested in her campaign.

"I knew there would be a backlash—"

"In English, please," I insisted.

"People think I'm not a good person because I associated with Allan and Allan might have killed another man. People are less likely to vote for me."

"Well, maybe when we prove it wasn't Allan, the polls will go the other way."

"Maybe."

"We could get help from the press," I suggested.

"We'll see," she said. "Let's just wait and see. The money is already spent. We'll just have to wait and see."

"I think I should call or visit the bank," I concluded.

"What bank?" Lindsey was confused by my train of thought.

"To prove Allan's innocence, I must follow all leads. I need to go to Ralph's bank and see if I can get access to any of his records."

"Assuming you found the right place and that there is something worth getting," she countered.

"I'll bet my life there is. We could go and say we were his next of kin or something."

"Aren't you going a little far? You can't do that." Lindsey's tone was on the verge of an argument. "Besides, you don't even know the account number, if there even was one. He might not have even had an account there. Maybe he had a loan there, or a safe deposit box."

Why does she always have to be the devil's advocate? Everything always became a debate with her when her emotions weren't right.

"I just need a plan," I said, trying to smooth her ruffled feathers.

"A plan, huh?" she said. "Fine, but you're on your own for that. I've got work."

"I've got work, too," I said, my pride slightly injured. "Just not right now."

"I didn't mean it like that," she explained, her voice softening again. "I have enough to worry about. I don't want to have to worry about you."

"Don't worry about me. I'm a big boy," I explained.

"Paul, Allan is dead. We can't change that."

"I'm not trying to change that. I'm trying to find out who killed him."

"All I want to do right now is win this election. I don't care who killed him."

"What? What are you saying? Of course you care."

"All I have left of Allan is his district. If I lose that, I've lost everything."

"You haven't lost me," I reminded.

"I know. I meant everything between him and me. Everything he built for himself and for me."

"I want to help you win. Trust me. Solving this case will help you win.

Do you want to know who killed Allan?"

"Yes."

"Well then, help me help you. Don't shut me out. Don't put down my efforts."

"Paul, I can't be enthusiastic about all this. You can't expect me to be happy, not yet. She sighed heavily into the phone.

"I'm going home now. Why don't you go home now, too?" I suggested.

"I will. I have to finish up. Will you pick up something to eat?"

"Sure. I love you," I said as we hung up.

As I was leaving, I passed by Jo, who was engrossed in a steamy romance novel. *Didn't she have some campaigning, or something worthwhile to do?*

"I'm going," I said.

She looked up. "OK."

I took a step toward the door, but then turned back to her. Her gaze was still upon my lower extremities. Her gaze lifted to meet mine.

"How is the campaign going?" I asked her.

"No way to really know." She shrugged.

"I heard about the poll. Do you think Lindsey still has a chance to win?" I asked.

"I don't know." Jo's look was grim. "If you want to make a judgement for yourself—" She reached into her desk drawer. "When I opened the mail, I pulled these letters out of Lindsey's pile. I didn't think she needed to see these. And here are today's newspaper poll results." She turned and picked up some papers then handed the whole pile to me.

"Thanks," I said. I took a few minutes in the car to look at the papers Jo had given me. The letters were not your everyday fan mail. One even included a death threat on which Jo had written the date and name of the police officer she had reported it to. The opinion poll was just as Lindsey had explained. I stuffed them all under the seat of the car and went into the grocery store. I spent fifteen minutes trying to decide which heat-and-serve casserole to buy. There were so many varieties, and I wasn't in a decision-making mood. I finally selected one with broccoli, rice, and cheese. Then I swung by and picked up the film.

I tore open the package. My heart pounding out of my chest, I lifted the flap and removed the prints.

CHAPTER 7

I flipped through the photos, one by one. Most were pictures of some kind of vacation. Some were pictures of paintings, undoubtedly from a museum somewhere. The last print was the most interesting. It was the cat, a brown, fat tabby that proved animals resemble their owners. It was Ralph's cat. I recognized the background as a section of Ralph's shop. Like so many people, myself included, Ralph had used the end of the roll of film on his beloved pet. *But where was that cat now?* My suspicion was that someone had removed the cat, probably the police, and taken it to a shelter. I'd have to check on it. I stuffed all the photos back into the envelope and went home to take care of my wife.

When I arrived, I quickly cleaned up and heated dinner so Lindsey wouldn't have to. Then I waited. When she arrived home there was little discussion. We both knew it was not a night for words. Usually Lindsey would let me make the advances and be in control. But in a situation like that day, when she felt she'd lost control, she wanted to exert a little power. She pushed me up against the wall of the foyer where I greeted her, pressed against me, and began roughly pulling off my shirt and tie. I took the cue.

We never made it to the bedroom and our casserole got crusty, but neither one of us cared. When we were through, all I could say was a breathless, "Thank you."

She smiled and said, "You're welcome."

"Aren't you going to thank me?" I joked.

"Yes." She leaned over and kissed me. Her body brushed me as she picked up her bra and shirt from where they had been hastily discarded. "Thanks," she said and blew me a kiss as she left the room.

Some people would say that married life is boring. I would say it's what you make of it. For me marriage was reliable, like a pair of favorite jeans. No matter how many times you wore them, you still loved them and they were the perfect fit. There may have been some things you didn't like about those jeans, for example, the pocket was worn through, but they were still your favorite pair, and without them things just wouldn't be the same. It seemed to me, marriage, or at least a good one, should be the same way. It's comfortable. You always know whom you'll fall asleep next to and, more importantly, who'll be there when you wake up. And you don't have to worry about catching some godforsaken disease.

As for Lindsey and how she felt, her purpose had been as much desire as it was stress release. She had regained some control over the world and her surroundings and that made everything all right.

In the morning I felt Lindsey get up around seven-thirty and shuffle about, getting dressed for the funeral. She gave me a wake-up kiss, and I finally rolled out of the bed at eight. As I dressed I stood in front of the mirror and studied myself. I looked decent for a man in his early thirties. I checked my front and side profile—I didn't have a belly yet. I buttoned my dress shirt and cuffs before combing my hair. Every strand had to be in its exact place and then hair-sprayed. My hair was dark with some isolated grays popping in here and there and a persistent area of thinning at my crown. I bent down and studied the top of my head. On the bright side, I knew I was tall enough that most people never got the chance to see this.

I joined Lindsey in the kitchen for breakfast. I had a bowl of cereal while she stood at the stove frying pancakes for us.

She looked over her shoulder at me as I crunched away. "You're quiet this morning."

"I know."

"I'm curious. Anything you want to tell me about?" She peeked under the edge of the pancake to see if it was ready to flip.

"I've discovered things, maybe leads," I said between bites.

"And?" she prodded.

"I found a pair of glasses that probably don't belong to Ralph Meeker. They might belong to the killer. And I got Ralph's pictures back. He had a cat, but it's disappeared."

"A cat? Disappeared?" She flipped the four pancakes in quick succession.

"Yeah, I think maybe the police took it to a shelter or one of them took it home." I drank the leftover milk from the bowl.

"Possibly. We could find out with a call to the police station."

"I know. I have a few calls I'd like to make before we go, but they can wait until after we eat. I'd like to get a complete copy of the police reports and an interview with the coroner, maybe see the autopsy reports for both Ralph and Allan."

"Don't ask for much, do you?" She waved the spatula in her hand.

"Could you help?" I asked. I knew she had all the connections I would need and more.

"I know someone in the coroner's office. I can get you in to see her, and maybe she'll show you copies of the autopsy reports. I can't get the police reports—not without asking Detective Jeffries."

"It never hurts to ask."

"What are you hoping to get from all this?" Lindsey asked.

"Some proof that Allan didn't commit suicide, more leads. I can't help asking myself over and over why Allan would shave if he was going to kill himself?"

"He didn't kill himself." She put our plates and silverware on the table with a thump.

"I know that, but we have to prove it. The reports will help somehow, I know it."

"What are you going to do about the bank you found?"

"I'm not sure. I guess nothing for now. I don't see any way to get the information, legally that is."

"I'm glad you see it that way. I think we should ask the police to look into it," she suggested as she dished the pancakes.

"We can't. I shouldn't even have that information, remember?"

"Oh, yeah."

We ate quietly for a few minutes.

"Oh, I almost forgot!" I said abruptly.

"What?"

"I need to call the bartender at O'Malley's."

"I already did," Lindsey replied.

"And? Did you reach him? Does he remember Allan being there?"

"Slow down, Sherlock. They were closed. It was mid-afternoon, so I left a message. Hopefully someone will call us back."

"Oh," I sighed.

With nothing else serious to discuss, we finished our breakfast. I called Detective Jeffries while Lindsey finished getting ready to go. Instead I got his partner, so I asked her for copies of the police reports, which she said I could come by and pick up. She couldn't remember having seen or heard about a cat during the investigation, but I could check the reports to be sure.

Lindsey gave me the number for the coroner's office and the name of her friend, Betsie, so I called there as well and made an appointment for that afternoon. Betsie would get the reports in order so I wouldn't have to wait, but Lindsey was going to owe her one.

Dressed in our most drab apparel and driving Lindsey's car, a black Saab, we joined the funeral procession after the ceremony. The procession consisted of approximately twenty cars. Margie had decided to hold a strictly private ceremony—no public, no voters, no news cameras. A dozen close friends and all of Allan's family crowded around the grave. A row of chairs sat Margie, Lindsey, and the grandchildren. The smell of fresh earth filled my nostrils. The funeral tent offered some shelter from the hot sun.

The minister's words droned on with the calls of katydids. Pesky mosquitoes, born of stale water, bit into us with an unrelenting passion for blood. Faint rumbles in the distance threatened rain. I felt queasy in the thick, close confines of the tent. There were no chairs, so I swayed on my feet, holding the back of Lindsey's chair, trying not to lock my knees, trying not to fall over.

Everyone wore the same sad, suffering expression. A few cried openly. Lindsey wrung her tissue to shreds. Others fought off tears altogether by staring past the minister and tuning out his words like I was. I wasn't listening. I was thinking about what I was going to do next.

At last the casket was laid to rest. Margie placed her flowers on the casket in the grave. She took the small shovel offered her by the minister and sprinkled the first layer of earth. Ashes to ashes and dust to dust.

After the funeral, friends and family met at the hotel for a luncheon. It always seemed a strange practice to me, eating and talking freely after a funeral. Abundant flowers, food, and condolences were given to Margie. Many guests still cried. Margie appeared to be doing a better job of consoling everyone else than they were for her. People brought her sweets and casseroles. She thanked each and every one profusely and accepted everything, knowing there was no where to keep it all. She insisted we take the meatloaf and apple pie. As we were preparing to leave, she ushered us to an empty corner of the room.

"I need desperately to talk with you two alone." She grabbed Lindsey's hands. "I have a real problem."

"OK, what's wrong?" Lindsey's brow furrowed.

"You know how I had you go get my papers for me?" she asked me.

"Yes. Did I get them all? Did I miss some?" I asked.

"You got them all, but that's the problem. Allan and I had two accounts. One was a retirement investment account and one was our everyday checking." She paused. "Well, the retirement account is empty. It had about a million dollars in it last time I checked, but it's empty now."

Lindsey and I didn't know what to say.

"Allan told me we had plenty in there," she went on. "He was going to retire this year. I was going to retire at Christmas. We have the house paid for, so it would have been enough, but it's gone."

"Gone?" Lindsey asked. "Are you sure?"

"Yes. Both the investment firm and the police are looking into it."

"I wonder why they didn't say anything to me when I called. Have they given you any more information so far?" I asked.

"They said Allan made a large withdrawal about six months ago and had been making steady withdrawals since then. They are going to have a forgery expert check the signature card and the withdrawal slips, but at first glance they seem to match."

"I'm confused," Lindsey said. "Why would Allan take out all that money? What would he have spent it on? Wouldn't there be huge penalties? He'd have to have been desperate to withdraw all that."

"Why wouldn't he have said anything about it?" I added.

"I don't know." Margie began to cry. "I'm going to have to sell the house, or the car, to pay for the funeral. I had no idea we had no money."

"Don't sell anything yet," I insisted. "You'll have insurance money soon enough. I'm going to prove it wasn't a suicide, so don't sell anything," I assured her. "I'll also figure out where all the retirement money went."

Reassured, Margie hugged us both and sent us on our way, laden with food. I dropped Lindsey at home; she wanted to rest and had a terrible headache. My suspicion was that Allan's mysterious withdrawals were directly related to his death, but how I didn't know. At that point I was anxious to get to work on the list of names I had in my possession.

I got out the list I had made of party guests that had also been in Ralph Meeker's Rolodex. I had what I felt confident to be an accurate and complete list of murder suspects. There were thirteen names, not including Allan.

Only Phillip and Sandy Hunt would be easy to question; they were our neighbors. For the others I would need some background information. Then I could determine who would make the most likely suspect and who might have important information—that would be where I would start. I would also need their addresses and phone numbers so I could contact them. I drove over to Lindsey's campaign headquarters to confiscate some materials. On the way, well sort of on the way, I made a stop at the police station for the reports I wanted. I would look at those later.

At Lindsey's office, I was able to obtain from voter records addresses and phone numbers for all the names on the list. If every private eye could only be this lucky! I talked to Jo and got some background information on the names I wasn't familiar with.

Of all the names, Derek Leeds seemed to be a good place to start. Derek was an artist. He and Meeker had art in common. Maybe he would know something. Derek owned a gallery that exhibited his work and that of several other local "starving artists." His apartment and work studio were located above the gallery called Studio One.

Upon arrival, I spent a few minutes outside examining the pieces on display in the front windows. On the left was art deco, lots of shapes, right angles, and bold colors. On the right were sculptures.

As I entered, a chime wildly announced my arrival, but no one approached or greeted me. The gallery space was long and rectangular with a door at the far back wall. At the front on the right side, nearest to where I was standing, was a desk tucked underneath the incline of a stairwell which led up to the loft above. Six artists had work on display, three on each side.

I moved about the room in a counterclockwise motion, examining the sculptures. I couldn't tell what any of the pieces were meant to represent. The metals that formed them were dull and lifeless, but the ends were sharp and protruded in all directions like porcupines. I didn't care for them at all.

I skipped over the display of a still-life painter and went to the left side, where Derek's modern impressionistic works were displayed. Up close they didn't look like anything except a bunch of blobs and strokes of paint on canvas, but from a few feet back images surfaced. Faces and places emerged from the shadows. There were a variety of themes—one was a boat at dock, another was a park or garden in bloom, and a third was of a mother and child.

The other displays were photographs and art deco, which brought me full-circle.

In the middle of the room were a table and a few armchairs, presumably for viewing the art for extended lengths of time. On the table were a guest book, business cards, and some information about the gallery and artists. I signed my name to the guest book, and then I sat down in one of the chairs to wait figuring someone must be there if the door was open. The chairs were scratchy, so I didn't get comfortable.

I glanced at the scattered cards and papers on the table. I picked them all up and sorted them and laid them all back out in neat, evenly spaced stacks. I loved organization.

"Hey," came a soft drawl from behind, acknowledging my work.

"Ahhh" escaped my lips.

"I'm sorry; I didn't mean to spook you. I heard some bells, but I didn't know what it was. I didn't think anyone was here. I was in the back room." She motioned to the back door.

"Is Derek Leeds here?" I asked as I stood up.

"I thought you were him." She knitted her brow and folded her arms.

"Me?"

"Yeah. Mimi's my friend."

"What?" It was my turn to be confused.

"Mimi's my friend. She's the photographer that took those pictures over there." She waved vaguely in the direction of the display.

"That's great, but what does that have to do with me?" I asked.

"Mimi left me here to watch the place. She told me to watch it until Derek got back," she explained.

"So you thought I was Derek?"

"Yeah. I don't know him. I've never met him. I thought he was you." She nodded her head till I thought it would roll off her shoulders.

"I'm Paul Grey."

She shook my hand, without saying a word.

"And you are?" I prodded.

"Oh, excuse me. I'm Sue." She giggled. "Derek should be here soon. His work is over there. You can wait."

"I will, thanks."

We both stood unmoving and silent and uncomfortable with each other's presence, like two people in an elevator without enough personal space.

"He should be here any minute," she repeated and glanced at her watch. I was surprised she could even tell time until I noticed it was digital.

"I'll wait."

I pretended to look at the artwork. She could tell I wasn't interested.

"I'm sorry I don't know anything about art. I can't help you."

"I'm fine, really. I'm not in a hurry," I assured her, and I took my seat again. I twiddled my fingers.

She remained standing but shifted her weight impatiently.

"Well," she began, the wheels turning in her head. I could almost see them at work. "If you're going to wait here for Derek—" she began again, but was at a loss for words. "I'll tell you what. I need to go anyway, so I'll just leave you here. You can watch the gallery."

Yep, wheels turning, but missing some gears. It was obvious she hadn't thought that scenario all the way through.

"How do you know I won't steal anything?" I inquired.

"I have this sense, maybe like ESP or something. Anyway, I can tell you're good."

"I'm good? I don't know anything about art. I don't even know Derek," I protested.

"Neither do I." She rolled her eyes. Then, very slowly so that even a moron like myself could understand, she said, "I told you; I'm Mimi's friend. I gotta go. I have a life, you know."

I followed her to the front door. Ignoring me, she picked up her purse from behind the desk and swung it over her shoulder.

"Go if you have to. Just lock the door, OK?" she asked.

Before I had another opportunity to argue, she was out the door. Great. Now I was stuck babysitting an art gallery. I plopped down in one of the chairs again and rested my head back on my hands. I ran my fingers through my hair and looked up toward the ceiling. From there I could see part of the loft through the railing. Maybe being alone was a good thing. I could do a little snooping. I stood up and backed across the room to get a better look. I could see a table and two chairs, part of a kitchenette, and part of the living room, but nothing interesting.

What are you doing? You're here alone—just go up and take a peak around. What could it hurt? I looked out the front windows to be sure no one was coming. I flipped the lock on the door and charged up the stairs. The loft was one open room with no windows. The walls were covered with art to the point of being dizzying. Other than that there wasn't much to look at. On the left was a small kitchen. Straight ahead was a work area with two easels and paints everywhere and brushes stuck in jars of mineral spirits or turpentine. Empty and painted canvases were stacked against the corner walls. On the far left, near the loft railing, was a futon sofa bed and a television, no cable or stereo, I noted. A single door and a set of closet folding doors were at the back. I immediately headed for the door. It was the bathroom. I checked the cabinet and drawers. Then I rummaged through the closet. I had no idea what I was looking for, or why. I found nothing of interest except that Derek liked cartoon neckties. He had a whole spin rack full of Daffy, Bugs Bunny, Winnie the Pooh, and Mickey.

I turned next to the table. On it were some bills and junk mail. I was careful to replace everything exactly as I had found it. The kitchen was completely lacking a very important item—namely, food. Definitely a bachelor's pad. A large oven took up most of the kitchen space, but it didn't appear he did much cooking because the cabinets were empty except for five or six half-eaten bags of chips and the refrigerator was a void filled only with a carton of outdated milk, a few condiments, and a very old box of mostly eaten pepperoni pizza.

Then I focused my attention on the paintings. All of them appeared to be Derek's works by the signatures, except one—a Manet. An original, not a poster, I checked to be sure. I tried to memorize the scene; then I went back downstairs. Still no one was coming down the street, so I went to the door at the back. On the other side were a restroom and a storage area. To the left was a filing cabinet. I moved to it and opened a stiff, rusty drawer. I had just started flipping through the files, noting nothing of interest, when I heard the front door chime. I quickly, and as quietly as possible, shut the filing cabinet. I looked around for an exit, but there was none.

CHAPTER 8

It had to be someone with a key, because I had left the door locked. It was probably Derek. I knew there wasn't a chance I'd be able to get out without being noticed, so I took a deep breath and stepped out into the gallery.

"Hello," I called. I must have startled Derek, who thought he was alone. He was upstairs already.

"Who are you?" he demanded. "What were you doing back there?"

"Sue left me here."

"Sue?" Derek challenged.

"Um. I don't know her really. She's Mimi's friend, but I don't know Mimi either," I offered. My legs were shaking, so I leaned casually against the wall.

Derek charged down the stairs, his eyes on me the whole time like a bull in a bullfight solely focused on the toreador. He approached me swiftly.

"What were you doing back there?" he demanded, his blue eyes searching mine suspiciously.

"I— I was using the bathroom." I kept my eyes to his. "The photographer, Mimi's friend, Sue. Sue locked me in. She said you'd be right back if I wanted to wait."

"Dumb air-for-brains woman, dumber than a stump," he muttered. "Left a complete stranger in my house."

He shook his head. The explanation seemed to satisfy him, and if angry or suspicious he wasn't going to let his steely eyes tell it. Derek was less than six feet tall, not thin or muscular. His unkempt, wiry hair was all different lengths like it had been last cut with hedge trimmers. By my estimate, he hadn't seen a barber in a few months. He was wearing a pair of faded blue jeans and a green polo shirt.

My heart was thumping so loudly I thought surely he must hear it. He showed nothing if he did.

"Who are you?" he repeated, nicer this time.

"Paul Grey. I came to see you. I wanted to ask you some questions," I stated.

"About what?" The tone was abrupt yet curious.

"Well, about art, sort of. Is that your work?" I didn't completely dodge the question. I pointed to his display. "I must say I like your paintings."

"Yes, those are mine. I am good, aren't I?" He seemed to sadden, to go distant.

"Yes, very," I flattered him. "How did you learn to paint?"

"I went to school at an Art Institute in Switzerland. All the rest I've taught myself. My mother used to tell me I was born with the talent."

I gave him a few minutes of my awe-inspired silence.

"I think you are incredibly talented. Did you happen to know Ralph Meeker?" I inquired.

"How did you know? I just came from his funeral."

My eyes wandered over his ragged attire. "How did you know him?"

"What do you mean?"

"Was he a friend? Or family?"

"He was a friend. I also sold a few pieces of my work through him."

I could now see in Derek's eyes some worry, or perhaps it was only grief. I had this feeling, a sense, like Sue had so aptly put it, that I wasn't wanted there.

"You sold a few things." I nodded. "Did you ever buy anything from him?"

"No. Why would I want to buy anything from him? I have plenty of my own art and talented friends." He motioned toward the walls around us.

"I don't know." I walked slowly around the gallery again. "Your name was in his Rolodex."

"I was his friend," Derek answered.

"He didn't have your number memorized?" I asked.

"What is this really about?" he demanded.

"Do you know of any reasons why someone would want to kill him?"

"No. Are you with the police?" he asked. "Because I've already told you all this."

"I'm just following up. Did he have any enemies or make anyone mad recently?"

"Possibly. I wouldn't know," he replied. "Ralph was a stupid ass. He was always coming up with harebrained ideas for getting rich. No doubt something like that is what got him killed."

"Like what? Can you give me an example?"

"Well, like pyramid schemes and such. I don't know." Derek threw his arms up in frustration. "He was involved in a lot of nonsense—not always on the up and up."

"Did he have any other friends? Anyone else that might know

something? Maybe someone on this list?" I showed him my names.

"You could try Stuart Newsome. He might know something. Ralph had a girlfriend also, but I never learned her name," he suggested. "What was your name again?"

"Paul Grey. I was a friend of Allan Puckett."

"So this is a personal interest. I understand," he nodded. His eyes still held a worried look; perhaps he thought he had said too much to me. "Anything else I can do for you?"

"Yes. I have more questions. Did you know Senator Allan Puckett?"

"Not really. My parents did, so I voted for him."

"You were at his party?"

"Yes." Derek folded his arms across his chest and frowned. "So what?"

"Do you know anything about Ralph Meeker and the Senator knowing each other? Did Ralph ever mention the Senator to you?"

"No."

"Where did you go when you left the Senator's party, and when did you leave?"

"Oh, I don't remember," Derek laughed. "That was a week ago; you really expect me to remember that? I can't even remember what I ate for dinner last night!"

He hadn't eaten here, I thought and then said, "You don't remember?"

"I guess I came home. I don't remember when."

"Were you with anyone? Can anyone support that?" I asked.

"No. Why?" He seemed confused.

"I was just curious," I replied.

Derek caught on without any explanation from me.

"I had no reason to hurt Ralph or the Senator. Ralph was my friend. He provided some of my income. Why would I hurt him?" Derek's answer was straightforward. "For God's sake, I was the only one at his funeral besides the minister. His girlfriend didn't even show up."

"You seem to be doing all right without him." I looked around. The surroundings were not shabby, and I knew how much a space like this rented for.

"Yeah." He laughed sardonically. His eyes narrowed as he spit out the words, "Shows what you know."

"One last thing." I pulled the photograph of the cat out of my pant pocket. "Do you recognize this cat?"

"Yes. It's Charlie Brown." The answer was short and to the point.

"Charlie Brown?"

"That was the cat's name. Unluckiest cat in the world."

"What do you mean?"

Derek was ready to be rid of me; I could tell by the impatient stance. He kept shifting his weight from one leg to the other. He rolled his eyes before giving an explanation.

"He'd been hit by cars probably four or five times, yet he always survived."

"Is he still alive? Do you know where Charlie is now?"

"Charlie Brown," he corrected. "He's got to be alive. He's got nine lives, but I have no idea where he is."

"You haven't seen him?"

"No." Derek blurted the answer with a slight stomp of the foot. His patience with my questioning was worn thin.

"Just one more thing, did Ralph wear glasses?"

"No."

"OK. Well, thanks for your help. If you think of anything, let me know." I handed him a business card. "You can leave a message at Attorney Mayson's office."

"I'll be sure to do that." Derek nodded.

I was certain I'd never hear from him. I departed. I walked to my car and got in. The heat was sweltering. I rolled down all the windows and turned the air on full blast. I made some notes about Derek. His attitude had fluctuated so much that I had found him hard to read. He was helpful, yet something didn't seem right. I chalked it up to grief; I mean, the guy's friend had just died.

It was almost time for me to meet with Betsie Jordan, the coroner. Being early wouldn't hurt. The Medical Examiner's Office was located in a brick building in an area tightly packed with government agencies. I had expected a sterile, hollow, flourescently lit area, but Betsie's office surprised me. It was windowed with ruffled curtains hanging and plants on the sill. Actually, there were plants everywhere—on her desk, on the table, on the floor. The walls were a freshly painted a peach color. Betsie was at her desk, her feet propped up, eating her lunch. I knocked, hesitantly. Her feet flew off the desk. She had dark cinnamon-colored skin, black hair of all one length that gave her head a triangle shape, and deep brown eyes.

"You must be Pawl," she said, with her mouth full. She cleared her throat and stood up.

I nodded.

"I've heard all about you," she said as she hastily wiped her fingers before extending her hand.

"You have? Good things, I hope," I said.

"Oh, yes, of course. Lin adores you." She waved a "don't fret" hand at me.

She cleared her lunch things to the side. It appeared she was eating a peanut butter and bologna sandwich with a side of apple.

"I have your papers here, somewhere." She shuffled. "Ah-ha."

She handed me two extra large file envelopes.

"Should I look at them now or take them with me?"

"You'll need to look at them now. You can't take it with you!" She laughed at her own death humor. "Besides, I doubt you'll understand them. An autopsy can be quite complicated."

I opened Ralph Meeker's file first. It included a typed report, some diagrams and photographs, and some X-rays.

"What were the X-rays for?" I asked.

"To determine the angle and the trajectory of the bullet," she explained. "Do you mind if I eat?"

"No, go ahead." I held the X-ray up to the light and pointed to the stomach area. "Right here?"

"No, no." She smiled at my ignorance. "There, see?"

"Oh, yeah," I feigned.

"See, it entered the abdominal region below the diaphragm, penetrated the liver and stomach, and then exited near the spine." She traced the bullet's path for me. "You'll see in my notes, we call that a perforating shot."

She reached into the folder for the pictures. "See, here's the entry wound."

She handed me a close-up of a small hole where the bullet had gone in.

"And here's where the bullet exited." She handed me the other photo.

"How close do you think the killer was?" I asked.

"Not close. At least three feet, maybe more."

"Do you think there was a struggle?"

"No."

"And there was just one shot? And it killed him?"

"Actually there were two shots. The first one didn't kill him immediately. It appears he bled from that wound for at least ten minutes before the second shot to the head finished him off."

"Is it possible someone was trying to get information from him, like torture?"

Betsie just shrugged as she ripped off another bite of her sandwich. "It's possible, but torture wounds are usually in the arms and legs and genitalia."

I winced. "Anything else about him that seemed interesting or important?"

"No, but the other guy was."

"You mean Allan Puckett?"

She nodded. I replaced all the contents of Meeker's file and opened Allan's. The items were basically the same. She snatched up the photos.

"See this marking, here, where the bullet entry wound occurred? That's called a starburst. It means the gun was pressed tightly against the skin and bone when it was fired. It causes the skin to break open into a star shape."

"And that's unusual?"

"No, not that." She picked up the x-ray. "See here, the bullet entered the front of the cephalic region, that means head. It traveled through the brain and out the back of the skull, right above the neck."

"So that's unusual?"

"Well, the angle and proximity are appropriate for a suicide. The way the body was positioned at death and where it was found in the home both suggest suicide, but—"

"But what?" I prodded.

"It's a little unusual that he shot himself in the forehead and not through the mouth, that's all."

"Have you told the officers on the case?"

"Yes, one of them, Detective Shope, was present at the autopsy."

"But you still ruled it a suicide?"

"Yessh." She chewed thoughtfully on another bite of lunch.

"Why?"

She swallowed hard and looked around for her drink. "Well, we discussed the facts of the case and there was no sign of a struggle. I'm surprised I even got this case, knowing Lindsey is kind of a conflict of interest. I was very careful not to let anything affect my judgement."

"Did it take long for him to die?" I asked.

"Almost instant death." She sighed.

For that I was relieved. I was glad to know Allan hadn't suffered long.

"One other thing that has been bothering me—do you note whether a person is clean-shaven or not in your reports?" I asked.

"Yes. He, ummm, he was clean-shaven."

"That's strange to me," I commented. "Why would he shave?"

"A person in that frame of mind will do lots of weird stuff," she shrugged. "Once we had this whole family in autopsy. The dad had cancer, and so when he committed suicide he killed his wife and two kids first. But before he killed them he made them a nice breakfast in bed, the whole family all in the bed, got them all comfortable and then shot them. Weird stuff."

"I appreciate your time," I thanked her. We exchanged a few pleasantries and I left.

When I arrived home, Lindsey was cooking lasagne for dinner. Again, Italian food wasn't appealing after the autopsy photos I had seen, but Lindsey loved all types of pasta, and if she wanted to cook I wasn't going to ruin her mood. I hung around in the kitchen while she finished up and told her about my meeting with Derek Leeds.

"I've done some sleuthing myself. Do you want the good news or bad news first?" she asked.

"Bad first." I pulled myself up onto an unused section of counter top.

"The owner of O'Malley's called me back this afternoon—"

"That's good news, not bad news," I interrupted.

"No, let me finish," she protested, waving a spoon in my face. "The owner called to tell me they've been closed this week. His bartender has been missing for about four days."

"What do you mean missing?"

"He hasn't shown up for work or called." She shook some Parmesan cheese into the sauce. "The owner went by his place the first night, but no one answered the door. It was unlocked so he went in. He said the place was torn apart."

"Has he called the police?"

"Yes." Lindsey looked defeated. She stopped with the cheese. "They went to the guy's place. They said there were signs of a struggle and there were blood stains in the carpet."

"So what do they think happened?" I asked incredulously.

"They're not sure. They wouldn't give me any details, but they thought it was suspicious that there was a connection to Allan." She carefully poured the sauce over the layer of noodles.

"A connection to Allan?" I stammered. "Surely they don't think he had anything to do with it? Do they?"

"They don't know yet," she sighed. "It's terrible."

"So what's the good news?" I asked.

"Well, now that I think about it, it's not really good news either," she replied.

"Spill it anyway." I snatched a pinch of grated mozzarella cheese from the bag.

"Margie has both the investment firm and the police investigating the problems with her retirement account. They have confirmed the signatures on the withdrawals were Allan's. She called me this afternoon. She wants Mayson to help her, maybe take the firm to court. She was the co-signer on the account. She feels they should have notified her."

"That's good news?" I asked.

She ignored my interruption. "Anyway, Mayson sent me down to the police station after Margie called so I could look at the files. The police already have information from both Allan's and Ralph's bank accounts. When you compare Allan's withdrawals to Ralph's deposits, they match."

"So the money from Allan went to Ralph?"

"It seems that way. Allan was paying off Ralph for something." She reached next to my legs into the drawer for some tin foil.

"Like what?"

"It could be anything—a dishonest political act, an affair, or even drugs."

"You and I both know that Allan didn't have anything like that."

"There must have been something. The proof is in the bank records." She wrapped the foil over the pan. "Allan wouldn't pay all that money for nothing. The police know there was a motive now, even though they don't know specifically what it was. Still, I know he didn't kill anyone. Whatever it was, I'm sure that's what Allan and Ralph were arguing about."

"Derek Leeds said Ralph was into all kinds of schemes to get rich. Perhaps he was into something illegal? What do you think it was?" I asked.

"I don't know. I would never suspect Allan of anything illegal, but the papers speak for themselves." She placed the pan into the oven. "But there's something else interesting which is the real good news."

"What?" I hopped down from the counter and followed her to the living room.

She pulled out a file folder from her tote bag and handed it to me. "Copies of papers from Ralph's safe deposit box at that bank in Alabama."

"Wow!" I was in awe. "Thanks. How did you get these?"

"The police got copies of all the records from the bank, and they confiscated the contents of his box. They retrieved his banking information when they searched his place after he was killed."

"So how did you get it?" I asked.

"I shouldn't have them at all," she confessed. "It's all strictly confidential, not supposed to leave the police station—"

"You stole them?"

"No," she reassured. "Detective Jeffries' partner let me use her office to examine them. I was allowed to take notes, but no copies or anything like that. Well, there I was, alone. She had a fax machine, so—I sent all the pages I could to my campaign office fax machine and voila!"

"Absolutely terrific!" I kissed her.

I opened the file to examine it.

"They were way ahead of me on this," I said.

"Yes, but they saved you a trip," she consoled.

There were about two dozen sheets of typewritten random letters and numbers. The first line of the first page read: S U R N W O E O P T R R G A A A Y T. The letters were evenly spaced and made neat rows and columns, but they made no sense at all.

"It looks like a code," I said and shrugged.

"Yes, the police are working on it," Lindsey said. "They have experts for this type of thing."

I looked at the first page again.

"Obviously the breaks between the words are missing," I commented. "There are three A's in a row in the first line, and it is eighteen letters long. There aren't any words in the English language that have three letters that are the same in a row and that long."

Lindsey's brow furrowed. She was thinking hard.

"You're right. I'm impressed Sherlock," she teased. "I also see two R's in a row. That's a clue to the code, too, right?"

"I would think so. Unfortunately, the only thing I know about breaking codes is what I remember from solving cryptograms in the newspaper. Maybe I could get a book at the library."

We both sat in trance-like thought for a few minutes.

"I'm going to go make the salad and pour our drinks," Lindsey said.

"OK," I replied. I was engrossed in all the papers.

I remembered solving cryptograms for fun in my younger days. First I would have to find the number of occurrences of each letter. The most used code letter could then be replaced by 'E'. The second and third most used letters would be replaced by 'S' and 'T'. But what I discovered surprised me. The most commonly occurring letter in the code was 'E', the second most common was 'S' and then 'T'. How could 'E' be replaced by 'E' if it was a code? And 'S' couldn't be 'S'. It didn't make any sense. I was beginning to doubt my skills at problem solving. Maybe I wasn't remembering the cryptogram rules correctly.

Disgusted with my attempts to solve the code, I gave up for the time being. Dinner was ready anyway. I rushed through the meal. The quicker I ate, the faster I could get to look at the police reports. I helped Lindsey with the dishes and then stole off to the living room.

The police reports were full of technical jargon and abbreviations that with effort I was able to decipher. They dealt mostly with the gun and bullets found and the fact that they matched in both cases. Diagrams and measurements of locations of all evidence found were attached as well as notations that would match up with photographs taken at the scene. Nothing was mentioned about a cat.

"Are you about finished?" Lindsey called out from the bedroom.

"Yeah." I got up and approached. She was already in her nightgown.

"Hey, theoretically, suppose you were going to kill yourself by shooting yourself. How would you do it?" I asked.

"Yuck, Paul. What kind of pillow talk is that? I don't want to think about that."

"Just for a second, if you were going to do it—" I pleaded.

"I guess in the head," she said and shrugged.

"Where in the head?" I asked.

"Paul—" she protested.

"Where?" I repeated.

"I don't know." She crossed her arms.

"I'm not trying to upset you. The coroner told me something, and I have a theory. I just want to see if my theory pans out," I explained.

"What's the theory?" She plopped down on the bed.

"You have to answer me first," I replied. "Where in the head would you pick to shoot yourself?"

"I don't know. I guess in the side or in the mouth." She shrugged, obviously creeped out.

"In the temple or through the mouth," I said. "OK, now what if you were going to shoot someone else?"

"If I was going to shoot someone?" she asked, horrified.

"Yes."

"I— I don't know. I might try the back of the head." She paused. "Or maybe the front, like between the eyes."

"Exactly. I would pick the same places."

"So what's the point?"

"Allan was shot between the eyes. I think that's an awkward and unlikely place to shoot yourself if you wanted to commit suicide." I had stripped down to my underwear and sat on the edge of the bed.

"I agree. It's doable, but it's more like someone killed him."

"Exactly," I nodded. I was also keenly aware that if this was the case, the killer had to have tricked Allan or overpowered him to get him into the tub. "I think I should talk to Detective Jeffries first thing in the morning. It's just too strange."

"I think that's a good idea. Just don't say anything about the papers I got for you. I'd get in so much trouble— " She rolled her eyes.

"Trouble, eh?" I gave her a look she understood. "Might they arrest you? What would you be willing to do to get out of that kind of trouble?"

"If I was arrested, cuffed, I'd be at your mercy." She swung her legs into my lap.

"I'd bail you out." I rubbed my hand up and down her legs, my rough palms on her smooth shins.

"I'd be forever indebted," she giggled and kissed me.

I forgot everything in that kiss.

CHAPTER 9

Next thing I knew it was Sunday morning. It was about eleven when I had gotten showered and dressed. I called the police station with my ideas and the coroner's own statements to back me up.

"That's very interesting, Mr. Grey," Detective Jeffries said, although his monotone inflection told me he found it much less than interesting.

"Will you look into the case again?" I pushed because I didn't get the impression they were going to do anything about it otherwise. Why should they? Overworked, underpaid, and this case closed, so who cares?

"Mr. Grey, you realize that a unique gun like that just doesn't 'show up' in an innocent man's home in his hand," he insisted. "We're still checking on some details, but don't expect anything to come of it."

Disgusted with the police and with my attempts to solve the coded pages, I decided to put off any more work on my "case" and elected to take care of some odd jobs around the house. I had to mow the lawn and fix a drippy faucet that had driven us nuts at night for about a month. I had no idea how to fix it, so I drove to the closest hardware store and got some advice and replacement parts. At the time I thought I had the problem licked. A few hours later when those tasks were out of the way, I decided to go by Stuart Newsome's place of business.

Stuart Newsome owned and ran an indoor shooting range. It was located in the suburbs of Gwinnett County. It was an affluent area that as it grew managed to keep some trees and natural surroundings intact.

I pulled into the parking lot. There were seven or more cars there. It was only a few minutes after 4:00 P.M.

On the outside it was a stone building with gray stucco and bars on all the windows. The door to the inside listed the hours as Monday through Saturday 9:00 A.M. to 9:00 P.M. and Sunday 12:00 to 9:00 P.M. It also warned— "No loaded weapons permitted beyond this point."

Three people were using it—a young woman and two law enforcement or security officials. The rest of the people inside were staff members.

A sign above the door to the practice lanes said "MANDATORY EYE AND EAR PROTECTION AREA. ENTER AT YOUR OWN RISK."

I took in all of this in the few seconds as I entered the building. I even noticed a small camera in the corner of the room near the ceiling. My powers of observation seemed to be keen.

An assistant came to help me. "Hello. Are you familiar with our shooting range?"

"No." I replied.

"Do you have your own weapon or do you need to rent one?" he asked.

"Oh, I'm not here for target practice," I said. "I'd like to see Stuart Newsome. Is he around?"

"Let me see if he's in his office."

The assistant disappeared. I watched the shooters through the glass in his absence. Clumsy clear goggles and bright yellow earplugs intact, each person stood in their own stance, yet they were all similar. Feet spread apart, one slightly in front of the other, helped them maintain balance. Both hands clasped around the gun, arms forward but elbows not locked. As they fired, their arms recoiled from the force. I wouldn't want to mess with any of them. I watched in amazement as the targets were brought back—full of holes.

The assistant reappeared. "He's not here right now. He'll be back around 6:00 P.M. this evening, and he'll be here until we close at 9:00 P.M."

"OK."

Now what? I thought as I drove away. I could go check on someone else on my list. Instead I went to the library to look for a book on codes and cryptography.

This was not the usual library branch I visited, and it was not a good resource when it came to codes. The only book that was available was a juvenile spy book with details on creating your own disappearing ink and making your own codes. The examples were simple, nothing like what I had in mind. I looked at some gaming magazines. A few had cryptograms, but nothing helpful. The cryptogram rules were as I had thought. Fortunately, I didn't leave empty-handed. I found an old art book with a photograph of Derek's painting. The caption didn't specify the Manet's owner. I promptly made a copy. I also found two books written by private investigators on sources of information and how to locate missing persons. I thought they might come in handy, so I checked them out and left.

The shooting range was louder and busier than it had been earlier, and there was a new crowd of people. In particular, an attractive young woman caught my eye. She reminded me of Lindsey, only ten years younger. She was early twenty-ish with long brown hair and smooth skin. She was getting a lesson from one of the staff members. I knew the man was a staff member because he had on the same type of red button-down shirt and black pants as the assistant had been wearing that morning. Judging from her returned target, she must have been a beginner. Although, I could never be one to judge. I'd never shot a real gun before. In fact, I was afraid of guns. I didn't like them.

When I was younger, about seven or eight, I'd been using a BB gun to shoot at tree stumps and empty cola cans. When I began to think it wouldn't hurt anything I started trying to hit squirrels. I was a terrible shot and never expected to really hit one, but I did. It fell out of the tree like a rock. When I ran and told my dad, he got his real gun and followed me out into the yard. My dad sent me back inside the house. I'll never forget the sound of his gun that day. It sent terror through my heart. I felt sick for days about the death of that squirrel. I never wanted to see another gun. I never used my BB gun again.

I emerged from my daydreaming as the staff member who had been giving the lesson came out to greet me.

"Can I help you?"

"I'd like to see Mr. Newsome, please," I answered.

"He's in his office. I'll go get him," he offered. "Let me tell her what I'm doing." He motioned toward the young lady in the booth. She stood awkwardly holding the gun, unsure of what to do in his absence.

"OK," I replied.

He stuck his head into the booth. "Keep practicing. I'll be right back."

She nodded and raised the weapon. He went to the side door. On the wall was an access panel. He punched in a code. A buzz signaled the door was unlocked, and he went through it. While he was gone I browsed. The range offered many types of weapons and ammunition for sale, along with tools for cleaning, safes, and reference books. Targets for use in the lanes were stacked in racks behind a glass display case of rental guns.

The employee reappeared and held the door ajar and motioned to me.

"Mr. Newsome said you can come back," he said. "His office is at the end of the hall."

I approached and went through the door. The assistant went back to his lesson. The heavy door slammed shut and locked me into the narrow and claustrophobic hallway. I felt like I had just entered a prison. I passed a security room where a man inside watched four video screens—one of the front room, one of the shooting range, one of the hallway with me in it, and one of an office; presumably Mr. Newsome was the man behind the desk. The security guard turned and looked at me. I moved on down the hall and under the video camera at the end. I wondered what kinds of activities went on behind these walls.

Through the cracked door I could see a large desk with two chairs in front of it and a filing cabinet on the far side. A large rug hung from ceiling to floor. I knocked and swung the door open.

"Hello there." Stuart Newsome got up to shake my hand. He was a large man, shorter than I was, but wider. He was built like a brick wall.

"I'm Paul Grey," I announced.

"I've been expecting you," he said icily.

"You have?"

"Yes." He smiled, completely comfortable with my uneasiness.

I didn't know what to say. "How did you know I was coming to see you?"

"Word travels fast in this business."

"What business is that?" I asked suspiciously as I took in the rest of my surroundings—a lamp and water cooler in the back corner, a painting and camera behind me.

"My business, running a shootin' range, of course." He stared at me, uncomprehending.

"Oh. How does word travel?"

"I have people in and out of here all the time. People tell me things. Derek Leeds, I believe you know 'em, called and told me you'd be comin'."

"He did?"

"Said you were some kind of do-gooder trying to find out what happened to Ralph. Said you were like a Hardy boy runnin' around trying to solve a crime."

I defended myself. "I'm trying to help a friend. It's purely self-interest."

"It don't matter," he shrugged. "I asked one of my friends to check it out and see who this fella was checkin' up on me. I've had tabs on you."

I felt a shiver run down my spine. "You're keeping tabs on me?" I asked. "You mean like someone is following me?"

"You're a danger to me," was the cryptic reply.

"I am?"

"Yes. I'm extremely important to Samuel Kingman's campaign. As you know, your wife is his only competition. I want to make sure you're not out to ruin him by using me."

"Using you? What do you mean?"

"You're tryin' to pin Ralph Meeker's murder on someone else besides your beloved Senator Puckett. Derek seemed to think you had some kind of list of names."

"I do." I pulled it out to show him. "It's a list of people Ralph Meeker knew. Do you recognize any names on it?"

"Yeah, mine."

"Any others?"

"I think that Jolene woman was an art dealer also, but I don't know. It don't matter anyhow. All I know is that damn list has got my name on it, and

I want to keep my affairs private. I didn't want you broadcastin' it to the whole world."

"Broadcasting what? What affairs?" I asked.

"I don't mean *affairs*, I mean my life. You're tryin' to set me up."

"No, I'm not. I'm here to help the Senator's widow, that's true, but I assure you I would never fabricate anything. You should only fear me if you have something to hide."

"I have nothing to hide."

"Good. Then you wouldn't mind answering a few questions?" I prodded.

There was a long thought-filled silence before he replied. "I'll tell you what I know. You best not get outta line, and then I don't want to see your face in here again, understood?"

"Yes. How did you know Ralph Meeker?" I asked.

"He wanted me to make connections for him. I have all sorts of people in here."

"Connections with whom specifically?"

"With the black market, who else?" He rolled his eyes.

"Why would he want to be involved in the black market? What product did he want or have?"

"I don't know. He had all sorts of schemes."

"Did you connect him with anyone?"

"No."

"Are you sure?"

"Yes." There was no hesitation to his answer.

"Did you purchase some things from him?" I asked.

He pointed to the rug and painting on the walls. "Those."

"They are both beautiful," I commented.

He laughed uncomfortably, his eyes flitted to the painting.

"Why do you have all this security?" I asked, pointing to the camera on the ceiling in the corner.

"All those people out there have guns," he scoffed. "You can't be too careful. Some are everyday folks, some are officers, and some are in the mob. You never know when any one of 'em may snap. Besides, it's good for preventing theft and for insurance purposes. You never know when someone will shoot their toe off at home and try to claim it happened here."

"Has that sort of thing ever happened?"

"Which one?"

"Either."

"No," he replied.

I shook my head in confusion as he laughed. *Laugh it up, butterbean. I'll get you.* "You said you had all kinds of people in and out of here. You must keep your ear to the ground. Perhaps you know what was going on between Ralph Meeker and Senator Puckett?"

He stopped laughing. "I have no idea."

"Ralph never mentioned Allan? He never mentioned what he was into?" I prodded.

"No."

"Where were you the night of Ralph's killing?" I asked.

"I was here, well, actually I was at dinner and then I was here."

"Until when?"

"All night. See, you're already trying to turn this around. You want to point the finger at me, but you can't because I was giving a private shooting lesson, if you know what I mean." He winked.

"With whom?"

"None of your damn business, that's who."

"I need to confirm your alibi."

"You need to do nothing of the sort. You need to get outta my face." Stuart stood up.

"The police are still investigating," I lied and stood up as well. "I talked to Officer Jeffries today about it. He seemed to think of it as an ongoing process. If that's the case, an alibi would be helpful."

"That's crap. I don't believe it. He comes here to practice, and he's said nothin' to me."

"Well then, you'd better talk to your friends more often," I said snidely.

"You better watch yourself or that list of yours is going to get you killed."

"Are you threatening me?"

"I have friends and my friends have ways. Take it however you like."

"I guess I better go." I got up.

"You guessed right."

I wanted to leave, but I didn't want to turn my back on him. I made a dash for the door, shutting it behind me. I headed down that hallway feeling like a whipped puppy with his tail between his legs. My heart was pounding. Maybe I wasn't cut out for this kind of work. Maybe I should get my heart checked if I was going to pursue this any further.

On my way out I passed by the security room, and I had an idea. I stepped into the room. The security officer turned to face me, his hand on his gun.

"Is there a security person here all the time?" I asked.

"Why do you want to know?" he asked suspiciously.

"Just curious. I've been thinking about getting into law enforcement. I was wondering about the hours. What kind of shifts do you run?"

"A guard reports in first to open up and a guard leaves last. It helps deter theft. We run two shifts—the first shift is from 7:00 A.M. until 3:00

P.M. and the second shift, mine, is from 3:00 P.M. until 11:00 P.M."

"Do those videos run all the time?" I motioned to the stack of four video recorders.

"Yep. They run all the time."

"Do you keep the tapes?" I asked.

"Yeah. They're over there." He pointed to a shelf stuffed full of tapes.

"None of them are labeled," I commented.

"We reuse them after two or three weeks. We just throw them over there for a while and then pull them back out and use them again."

"So you would still have tapes from a week ago?" I asked.

"Maybe. Why?"

"No reason," I shrugged. "Do you like your job?"

"Yeah. It's OK. It can get boring sometimes sitting here by yourself watching the screens and no one to talk to."

"What made you decide to get a job in security?" I asked.

"I always wanted to be a 007 type, you know, a little action and adventure, but I don't get much of that here."

"I understand," I sympathized. "Does it pay good?"

"It's OK," he said. "I'd like to get more, but then again this assignment isn't too dangerous, so I guess it's all right."

"Is it easy?"

"Easy as pie."

"Oh. Well how could I get a job like this?" I asked.

"You would have to apply at Security Services & Systems and get trained. Then they give you an assignment. They're listed in the phone book."

"Thanks. What was your name?"

"Bobby. Bobby Kearns."

"Thanks, Bobby." I shook his hand.

"No problem."

I needed to go home and get some rest. If things went as I had planned, I was going to have a long night ahead of me.

I took a nap until 8:30 P.M. Lindsey said she didn't want any part of my plan, so I was on my own. I grabbed a hamburger as I drove back over to the shooting range.

I hadn't forgotten what Stuart Newsome had said about having me tailed, so using a tip or two from my investigation manual from the library, I took a long scenic route. I took three right turns and then backtracked. I watched carefully for anyone who turned when I turned. I made sure that as I backtracked no one followed me. Certain I was alone, I made my way to the shooting range.

Stuart was supposed to leave around nine, according to his assistant that morning. The range was still open. I parked across the street to wait for

Stuart to leave. At approximately 9:15 P.M. he emerged. He didn't look about at all as he got straight into his car and left. I ducked down as he pulled out of the lot onto the road. I was not interested in where he was going; I wanted that he not see me.

Slowly, one by one, the cars emptied out of the parking lot. At 9:25 the last few stragglers left. I watched as the employees locked up and departed. Soon it was just what I presumed to be Bobby Kearns' car alone in the parking lot. I pulled into the lot and parked next to his car to wait.

And wait and wait. Let me tell you—surveillance stinks. This was the first time I had tried it, and there was no glamour in it at all. My legs cramped and my butt went to sleep. It was too dark to do anything. Even the parking lot lights were dim.

I decided to get out of the car and walk around for awhile. If anyone asked me I could honestly tell him I was waiting for Bobby, but no one did. When Bobby came out I approached him. Thinking back, that wasn't a wise idea. I startled him and he reached for his weapon. I could have been shot, but he recognized me and relaxed slightly.

"You! What are you doing here?" he asked, breathless.

"I came to ask for your help," I replied.

"With what? Getting a job?"

"No, I'm conducting an investigation of a murder and Stuart Newsome is a suspect—"

"Oh, no. Not Mr. Newsome," Bobby interrupted. "He's a really nice guy. He'd never hurt anyone. He talks a tough game, but he's not."

"I believe you. In fact Mr. Newsome gave me an alibi, but I need to check it," I said. "That's where you come into the picture."

"Why don't you ask Mr. Newsome? I'm sure he'd help you."

"I did. He wouldn't give me any evidence."

"So you need me? What do I need to do?"

"Let me look at the videotapes in the security room. You can help me prove Mr. Newsome's innocence." I wasn't totally convinced on the innocence part, but the videos could prove conclusive one way or the other.

"How can the videotapes prove anything?"

"Mr. Newsome said he was here at the time of the murder. The tapes should show that."

I could see Bobby was interested.

"I could pay you for your time," I suggested. I thought a little cash might give him the push he needed.

"A bribe?" he asked aghast.

"Not a bribe," I explained. "Just to pay you for your services. I need you to get me inside and show me how all that equipment works."

"I don't know—" He was hesitant still.

"You could be instrumental to solving the case," I prodded.

"I guess it'd be OK," he shrugged. "If Mr. Newsome finds out, I'll be out of a job."

"I won't tell him if you don't," I promised.

"OK," he conceded. "I could use some extra cash. How much we talking?"

"Say, fifty?"

He nodded in agreement. We both parked our cars in the lot across the street to avoid suspicion. Then Bobby let us both in through the front door. He locked it behind us. We strode quickly across the darkened lobby to the hall door. Bobby entered the code. I tried to peek, but I couldn't see what he was doing. At the buzz we entered and went immediately to the security room.

"Now the problem is that none of these tapes are labeled," I said. "How do we know what's what?"

"The tapes are grouped into bundles of four. They will be all the tapes from each of the four cameras for the same time period. They should be rubber-banded together. We change the tapes at 7:00 A.M., 3:00 P.M., and 11:00 P.M. all at the same time and put in new tapes. We just throw the bundle on those shelves over there. There isn't any order after that."

"So like I said, how do we know what's what?"

"Let's put a set in and see," he suggested.

He shut off the current tapes and ejected them. We took the first pack of four and popped them in instead. Bobby hit play.

"Now all four tapes and players are synched," he explained. "That means they show the same second in each location at the same time. If I fast forward, they'll all go at the same time."

"OK. We need to look for the tapes for the 11:00 P.M. to 7:00 A.M. time span. We need the tapes for the evening of July 11th. And there shouldn't be any customers or workers on them because those tapes start after hours."

Bobby nodded in agreement and then explained, "The tapes are embedded with the date and time so we don't need to worry about anything. We'll find them."

The set of tapes that were in the machines were the wrong day, so we got them out and put in another group of tapes. We went through each set in the same manner until we found the tapes that were for the eleven-to-seven time span for July 11th. Almost two hours into the recording, Stuart Newsome came into the lobby, followed by a young woman.

"Who is that?" I asked.

"She looks familiar, but I can't tell," Bobby said.

Stuart led the woman to the firing booths. There he guided her in shooting by putting his arms around her. His hands were on hers as she held the gun. He began kissing her neck and arms. They did that for a while. The clock on the wall in the lobby said it was 2:00 A.M. The tape time was also 2:00 A.M.

Then they headed back to the lobby and then down the hall and into the security room. The video was convincingly real. I caught myself turning to look for them in the room.

"Why did they go into the security room?" I asked.

"It's the only place with no cameras and a big table," Bobby replied candidly. "I guess they wanted a little privacy."

"I think I've seen enough," I said. "Now I just need to know if those tapes could have been faked. Is it possible to change the programming that embeds the date and time onto the tape? Or is there anything else in the film that could give us the time frame?"

"I'm fairly certain the tapes aren't faked. It would mess everything else up—to stop the tapes showing his entry into the building and erase them, then create fake tapes for the date in question, and then go back and make tapes for the missing times. It's not possible. A minute is a minute, he can't alter that!"

"And he wouldn't be able to get rid of the video of himself leaving either."

"Right."

So if we examine all the night-time tapes and this is the only one with him on it and all others are accounted for then we know it's a solid alibi," I said.

We began to examine each set of night-time tapes for their dates, keeping track that there weren't any missing. They were all accounted for. We watched them on extreme fast forward for a glimpse of Stuart Newsome. Only that one night was he on film—the night with the woman.

As we watched the pair enter the range the second time, Bobby recognized her.

"Oh, my God!" he said. "No wonder Mr. Newsome wouldn't tell you who he was with."

"Why? Who is she?" I asked.

"It's Marcia Venuto."

"Who's that?"

"One of the mob boss' mistresses!"

"Oh."

"Do you know what they would do to him if they found out?" Bobby asked, his eyes wide with fear.

"No, and I don't want to know about that. I just want to make doubly sure that the 11th was the day this was filmed."

I turned my attention to the video of Newsome's office. It was like watching a still life. The video was running but everything was stationary.

"The 11th was a Monday. That would have to be a Monday," Bobby said.

"How do you know?" I asked.

"The water cooler is full. It's changed every Monday."

"Are you sure?"

"Positive. Every Monday." He nodded.

"How do you know this wasn't on a Wednesday or some other day and he just hadn't had any of the water yet?" I asked.

"Mr. Newsome is a health nut. He drinks his eight glasses of water a day. I know he does. That was Monday, I'm positive."

I took his word for it, because I had also noticed a day-by-day calendar on the desk. The video was fuzzy, but I was sure the date on the page was July 11.

"That's it then," I said. "We did it."

"His alibi fits?" Bobby asked.

"Yes." I nodded.

We took all the tapes we had been using and replaced them on the shelves. Bobby put all the tapes that needed to be recorded for the night back in the machines. Then he turned the video cameras on. The screens flipped up their views, and we got the shock of our lives. Stuart Newsome was walking through the lobby with the same woman on his arm.

"Is that now? Or is that the old tape?" I whispered. My heart was thumping, again. My adrenaline was pumping.

"It's now. It's on record, not play."

CHAPTER 10

"It's now, now," he repeated.

"Shit," escaped my lips.

"Come on." Bobby grabbed me. "We'll go out the back door."

"What back door?"

"The one in Newsome's office."

"I didn't see—"

He grabbed my arm and cut me off. "Come on."

We raced into Newsome's office. Bobby lifted the woven rug on the wall. Behind it was a door.

"Hurry," he whispered.

We both went through. I let the rug fall back into place as he held the door open. We let it fall shut, and we were standing outside. There was no door handle for the door on the outside and no way to lock it. We were behind a tree and standing in some mildly overgrown shrubbery. As we stepped away, I realized you could hardly see the door. It was the same color as the rest of the building.

"How did you know about that door?" I panted as we crossed the street.

"It's always been there. Mr. Newsome didn't have any place for an office. That area was supposed to be a stockroom, but no one used it for that so he put his office in there and camouflaged the outside. He likes knowing the door is there if he needs it."

"You really saved us," I said.

"Saved me," he said. "I need that job."

"Oh, yeah. Let me pay you." I opened my wallet and gave him a fifty.

"Thanks." He smiled, kissed the bill, and tucked it away. "I hope I never have to do anything like that again."

"Me, too."

We went our separate ways. I went home, and although I was excited and had an adrenaline rush, I crashed in the bed. I think I was asleep before my head hit the pillow. It was late and Lindsey didn't even stir.

I felt her get up for work in the morning, but I stayed in the bed. My misadventures had worn me out.

"How did it go, Sherlock?" she whispered as she sat on the edge of the bed.

"Fine," I mumbled. "I got what I wanted."

"Good. Just be careful," she warned. "Don't do anything stupid."

"Too late," I kidded.

"What?"

"I mean, I will," I promised.

"Gimme a kiss." She leaned into me.

I grabbed her and pulled her into the bed. She smelled good and I nuzzled her neck.

"Come on, let me go," she laughed. "You'll mess up my hair."

"No, you'll mess up my hair." I sat up so she got a good look at my messy ends sticking out everywhere.

"I've got to go." She smiled. "Love you."

"Love you, too."

Without any further motivation to get me going, I went back to sleep. The phone woke me. I groggily reached for the receiver.

"Hello?"

"Mr. Grey?" a timid voice asked.

"Yes." I was anticipating a sales pitch.

"You don't know me. My name is Barbara Warren."

Bells were going off in my head. I didn't know the person, but I knew the name.

"I really need to talk to you. Could I see you?" she begged.

"Me? Yes, but why do you want to see me?"

"Because you're working on that murder case and you're seeing all the people who knew Ralph Meeker."

"Yes, that's true. How did you know that?"

"It doesn't matter. I need to speak to you, and I can't wait any longer."

"OK. How about meeting me this afternoon?" I suggested.

"Fine. Where?"

"How about at noon at Mick's Cafe in Midtown? Is that too far for you?" I asked.

"Noon. I'll be there." Without any "good-bye," she had hung up.

How strange! I wonder what she wants. I scurried about to get ready. I rushed over to DataCOM for a meeting that lasted only an hour. I caught up on phone calls and made out my schedule. My job was flexible. As long as I put in 160 hours a month I got paid. I only needed forty hours to finish out July. Ann Sorrels, another member of my team, stopped by my office, and we chatted. She was getting a promotion and would be leaving my department, and I wasn't happy to hear that. I hated my work. Having Ann to talk with made things easier. I enjoyed her friendly company at meetings and on trips. There were so many business trips. I'd been everywhere, but all my time was spent in corporate offices and airport lounges. Now on top of it all I'd be starting over with someone new.

"Of course, I'll train the new person," she teased. "So they'll be able to put up with all of your anal personality traits like color-coding your files and your perfectly neat cubicle area."

"Thanks a lot," I joked. "I actually prefer perfectionist to anal, if you don't mind."

"OK, perfectionist personality traits, that's a mouthful. Say that five times fast."

"No time." I glanced at my watch. "I've got to go. I have a lunch date."

"A date?" she teased. "I'll walk with you and you can tell me all."

I summarized my case as we walked to the parking deck. I started my car to get the air conditioner going and then stood outside to let it cool and to finish our conversation. A few minutes later I left.

At 11:57 A.M. I was at Mick's Cafe. I had no idea what Barbara Warren looked like, so I waited near the hostess desk. By 12:10 P.M. Barbara had not arrived. After a few minutes a woman in her mid-forties with short, curly, poodle-like black hair and glasses came rushing through the door, breathless. I gathered it was Barbara Warren because she came right up to me. She knew what I looked like. She was not at all what I had imagined. From her voice on the phone I had thought she would look quite different. I expected someone younger and smaller, mousy to go with the timid voice. Her rosy cheeks were flushed and she smiled. She was a large woman, large like a wrestler, and intimidating, until she spoke.

"I'm Barbara Warren," she introduced herself with the same small voice, shaking my hand with wild enthusiasm.

"Nice to meet you. I'm Paul."

"Shall we get a table? Have you eaten?" she blurted, one thick eyebrow raised.

"Yes." I nodded.

"You've already eaten?"

"No. I mean 'yes' get a table and 'no' I haven't eaten," I clarified.

"Good. I didn't eat yet either. I'm starved," she said. "Two for nonsmoking. You don't smoke do you? Good."

She barely waited for my head to shake before following the hostess through the populated restaurant to a table for two.

"Kerri will be your waitress. She'll be right with you." The hostess handed us our menus.

"Thanks," Barbara and I sounded out in unison. I held her chair out for her as she sat down.

"The food here is really good. I like eating here. Actually I like eating." She patted her hips and laughed.

We studied our menus for a few minutes. Barbara's leg was bouncing under the table. My curiosity was killing me. I could barely read the menu I was so distracted by my thoughts. *Why did she want to meet me? How did she know who I was and what I looked like?* The waitress approached.

She took our drink requests and then asked, "Do you need some more time or are you ready to order now?"

"I'm ready," Barbara chirped. "I'll have the Caesar Chicken Salad with vinaigrette dressing and a sweet tea."

The waitress turned to me. I quickly selected the Fried Chicken Salad with honey mustard dressing and a Coke. Chicken is usually a safe choice when dining out. I was an extremely picky eater and wasn't much for trying something new. The waitress took our menus; then she left us to ourselves.

I sat silently. I felt it would be best to let Barbara initiate the conversation since our meeting was her idea.

"Well," she began, "I guess you're wondering why I wanted to meet you. It's a long story. I'll tell it to you and try not to bore you with too many details."

"You have my full attention," I replied.

"I knew you were asking people about Ralph Meeker. I knew it would only be a matter of time until you got to me. So, I decided to go ahead and get it over with. I might even be able to help you and save you some time." She waved her arms about and gestured with her hands as she spoke.

"How did you know I was asking people about Ralph Meeker?"

"I just did."

"How did you know how to find me and what I looked like?"

"I've seen you before, and I remembered you were tall. You stick out in a crowd. Your wife is so well known that it wasn't hard to find you," she explained.

"What do you want to talk to me about?"

"About Ralph, of course! That's what you want, right?"

"Yes. I just wasn't expecting this."

"I can tell you all you want to know about Ralph Meeker," she claimed.

"OK. Go ahead and tell me everything," I encouraged.

"He was born here in Atlanta in that same little house where his shop was. He went to school at North Carolina State and flunked out first semester. He never knew his father and his mom died of cancer when he was in his early thirties, and left the house to him so he moved back home. To make some money he started buying items at yard sales and selling them to antique shops. Later he opened his own shop at the little house where he lived and worked. It was a mediocre shop—a few great items and a lot of junk. You know, because you've been there."

I nodded in agreement. *How did she know that?*

"Anyway," she said and swung her arms around, "he was always just breaking even. The city taxes on his place just kept going up and up." She gestured higher and higher with her thumb. "But his sales stayed the same. He was living month to month, just dollars away from bankruptcy."

She interrupted as the waitress set down our drinks. We both took a sip, or rather I took a gulp and she took a sip.

"So his sales stayed the same. Then what?" I prodded. *Where was this going? How would this help me?*

"He started looking for ways to get rich quickly. He got into stuff like pyramid schemes, selling insurance, and the like, only none of it ever worked." She leaned forward and said in a whisper, "Then things got really weird. All of a sudden he had money to burn. He started buying new clothes and going on trips."

"All of a sudden?"

"Well, within a few months. He had more money than ever before, but his sales were still the same."

"Yes—" I leaned forward in anticipation.

"He was blackmailing his customers for stolen paintings," she concluded.

"He was blackmailing you," I further deduced.

"What makes you think so?" she asked.

"I don't know. I was just guessing," I confessed.

"Anyway, you have a list of the people he was blackmailing," she said.

"I have a whole list of customers, that's true. But I didn't know any were being blackmailed. Do you?" I showed her the list.

"No." She shook her head regretfully.

"Do you know any of these people? Someone that might know something?" I asked.

She showed keen interest in the list, scanning it quickly yet thoroughly. She shook her head again.

"Were any of the people on this list friends of Ralph?"

"Friends?" She crossed her eyes. "Ralph didn't have friends. That Benton fellow is a lawyer, his maybe."

"Do you know where he got his stolen paintings from? Any names or anything?"

"Not really. I know he sold a total of ten stolen pieces. I know he bought them all from the same source. Ralph always called him 'Rembrandt'. I know that's just a nickname or an alias."

"Do you think he might have backed out of paying 'Rembrandt,' and that's who killed him?" I proposed.

"No way; he paid the guy."

"How do you know all this about Ralph Meeker and about me?" I asked.

"I've done my own investigation. I started gathering information on Ralph right after he began blackmailing me—"

"So you were being blackmailed?" I asked.

"Yes."

"What did you buy?"

"Some stupid painting. I mean, it's really beautiful and it's a classic, but I was so stupid to think it could be legitimate."

My thoughts went to Stuart Newsome and Derek Leeds. They both had paintings. Were they all being blackmailed?

"How did you pay for it? How did he get payments from you?" I asked.

"I'm independently wealthy, so I just paid him cash whenever he came calling. Then I started following him, checking up on him. I wanted to get something on him. You know, turn the tables and give him a taste of his own medicine. Then after he got killed I kept my eye on things for my own protection."

"Did you ever follow him to see whom he collected money from or whom he bought the paintings from?"

"I tried more than once, but I always lost him. It isn't easy and I got discouraged," she confessed.

"Why didn't you go to the police? Wouldn't that have been easier?" I asked.

"I might have, but I'd have lost all my money. I was so angry. I wasn't thinking straight. I just wanted to get even, and I ended up sinking to his level," her waving hands came to rest in her lap, she hung her head shamefully.

"Were you angry enough to kill him?" I made a stab, hoping to catch her off guard.

Her eyes flew up to hold mine in their gaze, but any further reaction or response was cut short as our meals arrived. We both began eating, but I didn't wait too long before I got back to the conversation.

"Tell me again how you got all this information on Ralph Meeker," I demanded after clearing my mouth.

"Well, he told me some of it himself, like how many paintings he sold and about his past. I got his sales records from his store. I had to sneak a peek."

"I don't suppose any of his sales records indicated blackmail activities."

"No." She crunched on her salad. "He covered himself well, but I knew that's what he was doing because he did it to me."

"Did you ever see anything about a code? Did he ever say anything about a code to you?"

"No."

"Did Ralph Meeker wear glasses?" I asked, pulling the pair out of my pocket.

"I don't think so; where did they come from? His shop?"

"Yes. I see you wear glasses. Would you mind putting them on and see if they work for you?"

She took her pair off and put on the ones I had brought.

"They work pretty good for me." She smiled.

"Are you nearsighted?" I asked.

She nodded. "And I guess whomever these belong to is also nearsighted and probably not getting around too well these days!"

She folded them up and placed them next to her plate then put her own glasses back on.

"Where were you the night of Ralph's murder?" I asked.

"Well, let's see. I was at the dinner party for your wife. It was absolutely lovely, by the way. Then I went by my daughter's house, but she wasn't home. I stopped at a twenty-four-hour grocery store and did a big food shopping. I get munchies at night and you should never go grocery shopping when you're hungry. Anyhow, I have my receipt that shows I was there. I saved it because, well, because I usually save them anyway, but I was particularly careful to hold onto this one once I found out Ralph had been killed. I figured it was best to keep it, given our past and all."

She fished around inside her purse. The contents looked like a grenade had gone off inside.

"Well, I can't seem to find it just now," she dug a little longer, then shrugging gave up.

"Did you buy any cat food?" I asked.

"Excuse me?" She furrowed her brow.

"Do you have a cat?"

"Um, yes."

"What's his name?" I prodded. I knew where I was going now.

"His name? Um, actually I have several cats."

"Do you have Ralph's cat? Do you have Charlie Brown?"

"Yes." She smiled sheepishly. "When I heard Ralph had died, I went and got him, the poor thing."

"How did you get him?"

"I took him. I had a key to his place."

I was beginning to feel like she was playing with me. She knew so much. I knew so little. She seemed to have access to Ralph, his shop, even personal information. Yet she kept leading me astray with little tidbits, juicy facts to my minor questions, but I was missing something important here. By sharing all her information, was she hoping to put herself above suspicion?

Was she luring me to the belief that she was just an amateur investigator like me?

"Why did you have a key? Why would he be telling you all of this stuff, like the name of his supplier? Tell me how you know all of this."

Barbara's rosy cheeks flushed to an even darker red. She lowered her eyes.

"I started sleeping with him," she whispered.

So she was the girlfriend Derek Leeds had spoken about. I felt a shudder creep up and down my spine. The thought of her and Ralph Meeker together was disgusting. She must have seen in my eyes my aversion to the idea.

"I had to." She waved her fork around. "He stopped blackmailing me then. I made a different kind of payment to him. I just did it until I could find something on him, only I couldn't find anything."

"What do you mean 'find' something on him?" I asked.

"You know, something I could hold over his head like he did to me—sort of a blackmail tradeoff," she huffed. "Only that didn't work, so I killed him."

CHAPTER 11

Her hands flew to her mouth as if to prevent the words that had already escaped her lips. Tears welled up in her eyes. In my surprise I choked on my drink. Coca-Cola up your nose, is not a pleasant feeling, and it doesn't go away for a long time. After regaining my composure, I didn't know what to say. Some detective I was. I stared at her mute and dumb for what seemed like an eternity.

Finally, the only question I could think of was, "You shot Ralph Meeker?" I spoke in hushed tones. "How could you? You just told me your whole alibi that would prove you weren't there. And if you did it, why tell me this now and not right away?"

"I wanted to check you out a little, see if I could trust you. You see, I couldn't get Ralph to stop blackmailing me unless I was with him, and I couldn't stay with him forever," she replied.

No wonder she hadn't attended the funeral. She was glad to see him go.

"So you shot Ralph Meeker and made up an alibi?"

"No." She shook her head. "I hired someone to kill him. I knew when it would be taken care of, so I made sure I had an alibi by going to my daughter, except like I said she wasn't home, so then I went to the store."

"Hiring someone to do him in is the same as killing him yourself. Whom did you hire?"

"I don't know. We never met," she answered curtly and wiped the tears from the corners of her eyes.

"So you hired a murderer?"

"Yes." She resumed eating.

"How did you do it?" I was dumbfounded.

"There are ads for this kind of thing in those military magazines. I put an ad in and arranged for an information drop so they could get the name and address of the person I wanted killed and when. The next week an ad was addressed to my code name, and it set up a meeting place. There were instructions at the meeting place for me to leave the money at a park bench trash can at Piedmont Park. I don't know who did it."

"You never talked to or met the guy?"

"Nope."

"Are you even sure it was a guy?" I asked.

"No, I don't know either way." She wiped her eyes again before the tears could roll.

"How do you know this person really carried out your instructions?" I asked.

"Ralph's dead, isn't he?" she snapped.

OK, so there is such a thing as a stupid question. "Good point," I said. "Do you have copies of the ads?"

"No."

"Have you told anyone else this?" I pushed my plate of food to the side. Eating was last on my mind now.

"Are you kidding? No. You're the only person I've told."

"We— we need to go to the police. Now, right now, so you can turn yourself in."

"No way."

"You hired a killer. You killed Ralph Meeker."

"You don't know that for sure," she rebutted.

"You just told me you were sure," I said.

"Anyone else that was mad at him could've done it, too. Maybe I hired your friend Allan Puckett and I didn't know it. Ralph deserved to die. Allan is dead."

"Why tell me if you're not prepared to pay the consequences?"

"I wanted to try to convince you to drop the case—just let it go. Can't you let me go? Just let it go. Having me arrested won't change anything. It won't bring them back."

"It will change things. Allan may be dead, but his wife suffers under the idea that her husband killed someone else. I'm a firm believer in justice; you need to be punished for what you did."

"OK, OK," she shrugged. "I'll go to the police and tell them, but I want a lawyer first. Can you get me Mayson?"

"Yes." I was confused at her sudden change.

"It's settled then. I'll turn myself in tomorrow morning. You get Mayson for me."

"Why not go now?" I asked.

"My last night of freedom?" She laughed. "I want to live a little."

I didn't know what to say. I didn't want to let her out of my sight, but what choice did I have? She might run. *I wish I had a tape recorder. I wish a police officer was eating lunch in here.*

"OK," was all I could say.

We were finished with lunch around 1:00 P.M. The first thing I did was call the police from the restaurant pay phone. They said they would bring her in tomorrow for questioning if she didn't show up as planned. I wasn't satisfied with that, but there wasn't anything more I could do. I wanted to be at the station in the morning when Barbara Warren arrived, but I had an installation scheduled.

I went back to my office, gathered my things, and called my customer to announce I was coming over to do their installation right then. Why put off til tomorrow what you can accomplish today?

I wasn't done until after 6:00 P.M. The client and his staff had left more than an hour prior. When I left I locked the door and took the key to the security office. Then I went home.

Lindsey had dinner ready, and she warmed it up. It was take-out fried chicken with mashed potatoes and gravy. Messy but good. As we ate, I told her about Barbara Warren.

"I couldn't believe it. She sat right in front of me and confessed," I said.

"So Columbo, you think this is the solution to the case?" she teased.

"Well, maybe."

"I didn't want to be the one to rain on your parade, but there's something you need to know about Barbara Warren—"

"What?"

"She's certifiably nuts. I mean that literally, the woman has been in and out of more mental institutions than she has bathrooms. She used to be married to Stan Warren, of the Atlanta Braves, until she had an affair. When they divorced she had a breakdown. It was her third mental breakdown. She takes all kinds of medications for depression."

"How do you know all this?" I was even more amazed at my wife's talents.

"Because I work with the police. They like to share their crackpot stories, and occasionally they slip with the names."

"She sounds like the type of person who might go off the deep end and kill someone," I said.

"She's not credible. You can't take anything she says seriously. She's been known to take drugs—both prescription and illicit. She sees, hears, and imagines things. I don't know her diagnosis, but it must be something scary like multiple personality or schizophrenia or something. A few months ago she had a vision that she'd killed a prostitute, but when she tried to lead the police to the body, there was none, so they let her go."

"Then the things she told me may be the truth or lies or fantasy," I said.

"Or a combination of all three. She's just plain crazy," Lindsey offered.

"If she's guilty, she sure created an elaborate cover up," I proposed.

"Well, in any case, at this point it doesn't help any." Lindsey got back into her chicken dinner. "It still doesn't explain Allan's death."

"It might. Her hired assassin must have killed Allan as a cover up. Allan was being blackmailed, so he'd make a good cover-up. It was the same gun in both deaths."

"For now Barbara is our only lead. Let's hope she turns herself in like she promised. The police can get to the bottom of it."

We finished dinner without much more conversation. Then we cleaned up our take-out boxes and paper plates. I went to the living room to watch television.

"I think I'd better go to bed," Lindsey said.

"I'm right behind you. I just need a minute to clear my head of all this."

Something was bothering me. Something didn't fit; I just didn't know what. The phone rang and I reached to answer it, but Lindsey had already picked up in the bedroom. A few seconds later she called out to me.

"Paul, get in here." There was tension in her voice, the same way she calls me when there is a spider on the ceiling and she needs me to get it.

"What?" I rushed into the bedroom.

She held out the receiver. "Listen."

The line was full of static and the voice was garbled; however the words were clearly understood. It said, "YOU'RE GOING TO DIE."

After a few seconds the message repeated. "YOU'RE GOING TO DIE."

Lindsey grabbed the receiver back from me. "You bastard, leave us alone. We'll have this call traced," she shouted.

The line went dead before she could slam down the phone. Her hands were shaking. Her face was flushed.

"Th- this ha-has never happened before," she stammered.

I couldn't decide if she was scared or angry. I pulled her into my chest and held her for a few seconds. She pulled away, stomping her foot.

"The nerve!" She stormed about. "Idiot. Creep. I can't believe this."

Angry, I decided, definitely angry.

She threw her hands up in the air. "What am I going to do?"

"What do you mean, what are you going to do? That call wasn't meant for you," I said. "It was for me."

"You?! What for? I'm the one that got a death threat in the mail at the campaign office."

"You know about that? I thought Jo—"

"She hid the letter, I know, but I found it under your car seat when I was looking for the umbrella this morning."

"Why didn't you say something?"

"What's to say? There's nothing to be done, nothing to say. Jo's already notified the proper authorities." She sighed. "Now we need to report this, too."

"On that I agree. We're calling the police, but I'm still not convinced that call was for you. It might have been for me, because I've been snooping around, asking questions about Ralph Meeker's death. The word is out. Maybe I've got somebody scared."

Lindsey tried to hold back her laughter—she really did.

"What? What's so funny?" I demanded.

"You," she giggled. "You're so cute when you're on a mission. You've got someone scared, you think?"

"You never know. You're not the only one that can get death threats. I could get one if I wanted to." I folded my arms, but then relaxed when I realized the silliness of our current argument. I began laughing, too, the sinister phone call diffused.

"Let's get a third opinion from the cops," Lindsey suggested.

So I placed my second call to the station for the day and I got Detective Shope. She thought the threat was most likely a prank, having little to do with either of our activities. I thought perhaps the detective was just saying that to calm us. Detective Shope suggested that Lindsey vary her daily schedule so she wasn't so predictable and that I stop prying and let the police handle everything, just in case.

"I'm sorry you have this to worry about on top of everything else, but don't worry too much. Most threats, even when they're not pranks, are never acted upon," she reassured us. "You should still come by in the morning to fill out a report. We'll go ahead and pull the call records for your number with the phone company."

"We appreciate that. Could you also send a patrol car by our house during the night to check on things?"

"We always have patrols in that area, but we'll put someone in your neighborhood tonight. Be sure to keep your doors and windows locked."

"We have an alarm system."

"Even better." She seemed satisfied.

The call into the detective left Lindsey and me with no clear winner in our argument. Both feeling a little insecure, we didn't sleep much that night, tossing and turning. We left the hall light on and the bedroom door locked. Lindsey rationalized that if someone was in the hall, we'd see a change in the light under the door and no one could get in without making some noise.

At about 3:00 A.M., after unsuccessful attempts to sleep, I went downstairs. I poured myself a big glass of milk. Milk usually made me sleepy, but not that night.

When I arrived at the police station the next morning, I was surprised that Detective Shope was still there.

"You work long shifts, don't you?" I asked.

"Twelve hours at a time," she said, smiling.

Detective Shope was a large black woman. She was big in all the right places. She had large muscular arms and legs that made her look like a formidable adversary, but she was still curvaceous and feminine.

"Thanks for coming down to the station. Here are the forms I need you to fill out." She handed me a clipboard and pen.

I took a few minutes to fill out the complaint form. When I was finished, I handed them back to her.

"Did you get the call traced?" I inquired.

"Yes, but unfortunately we found it was made from a pay phone. There's no way to tell who placed the call." She shook her head in regret. "I'm sorry."

"I can't say I'm not disappointed, but I have another issue I want to discuss—Barbara Warren. Has she come in yet?"

"Yes. She was here bright and early this morning, but she's already gone."

"Gone?!" I felt like I choked on my own tongue as I said it.

"Gone. We didn't have any reason to keep her here."

"No reason? Didn't she confess to you? She told me she hired someone to kill Ralph Meeker."

"She told us that, too. She's confessed to other crimes before. We'd spoken with her about Ralph Meeker already once right after he died and got nothing. Then today she comes in with a story, which we've checked out and it was a sham."

"A sham—" In my heart I hadn't believed her story, but I had held out hope.

"We checked the personal ads where she said she had contacted the hired hit man, but we came up with nothing. There were no ads. We checked her bank records as well. She hasn't paid out any large sums of money in over a year. She said she contracted the killer two months ago and paid with cash straight out of her bank account. We had no evidence and no reason to hold her."

She continued, "However, now we know that Ralph Meeker was involved in blackmailing some of his clients because he provided them with stolen art pieces."

"Ralph Meeker was blackmailing Barbara Warren. She must have been pulling money out for that," I insisted.

"Until the two of them started dating and Ralph didn't ask for money from her anymore. We're also checking into a name she gave us— 'Rembrandt.'"

"I can't believe you let her go. So she wasn't telling the truth, but why would she lie? What purpose could the lie serve? There must be something more," I pleaded.

"Personally, I think she's crazy," Detective Shope responded. "About two months ago she was in here confessing to the murder of a hooker."

"Two months ago. Everything with her was two months ago."

"I know. I've suggested she seek counseling."

"Maybe the craziness is an act, a part of her plan. Maybe *she* shot Ralph Meeker and Allan and all this stuff about an assassin is just to cover it up. Maybe she confessed to all these crimes to make it look like she's nuts, but in reality she's a brilliant criminal."

"Maybe you need some counseling, too," she muttered.

"What!"

"What I mean is the death of someone close can really be an emotional strain," she offered.

I nodded my head in wary agreement.

"Face the truth, Mr. Grey. Barbara Warren's story is a red herring, as you self-made detectives like to call it. Our minds, in an attempt to make sense out of something that is senseless, will sometimes trick us. None of our evidence points to Barbara Warren. It all points to Allan Puckett. We now have a motive. He was being blackmailed." Detective Jeffries appeared in the doorway. Shope quietly added, "We found a stolen Degas in his home early this morning."

I was speechless.

She continued, "I have a duty to warn you. Last night I wasn't worried about that phone call, but now with blackmail we have a different story. I like you and your wife. I don't want to see anything happen to either of you. Take my advice. Murder and blackmail are police business and extremely dangerous to investigate."

"Why should I worry?" I asked. "According to you, the murderer is already dead, so this shouldn't be a problem."

"Mr. Grey, I'm not your enemy. We had evidence against Senator Puckett, but that doesn't mean he was guilty. If he was alive, a jury would have to decide that. Since he is dead, we have no trial, nothing more to go on."

"I'm aware of that," I said.

"Let me explain something," Detective Jeffries interjected. "Even if we have a suspect in custody for a crime, our investigation isn't over. Evidence needs to be processed. Sometimes new evidence comes in. In the case of the Senator, our evidence points to him. This doesn't mean someone else couldn't have done it. We operate by different rules than you. You operate on conviction. You are convinced the Senator was innocent. The police can't work that way. The other day I pulled into a bank parking lot because I saw a suspicious car. I knew the two men were going to rob the ATM, but

I had interrupted. I had the conviction, but I had no evidence."

"I understand."

Detective Shope attempted to guide me out of the office. "If new evidence comes up that points the other way, we will certainly reopen the investigation and follow that avenue. Right now it is not cost effective to do so because we already have one dead suspect and evidence. Speaking of evidence, there is another issue I must warn you of."

"What's that?"

"You don't have a license to conduct an investigation. If you destroy evidence, either wittingly or unwittingly, or impede the police in any way, you can be prosecuted. This also means that if you find anything you must report it as well. Did you know that?"

"No, but thanks for telling me." Thinking about the burnt up ID badge in my ashtray, I looked at my watch impatiently. "I've got to go."

"I know it's hard to accept, but this case is now closed."

Her words were final. They rang in my ears. The case may have been closed according to the police, but not to me. Threats or no threats, I wasn't done yet.

CHAPTER 12

There was a definite connection between Ralph Meeker and Allan in life; however, their connection in death existed only because the motive for killing Allan was he would make the perfect suspect for Ralph's murder. Allan's motive would take suspicion off of anyone else since he had bought a stolen painting and was paying blackmail to Ralph for it. That's why there was no money in his retirement account. In my investigation I needed to focus less on persons that would want Allan dead and more on those that would want to kill Ralph Meeker. There seemed to be a lot more people in the latter category —Barbara Warren, Derek Leeds, Stuart Newsome, and who knew who else might have been blackmailed and wanted Ralph dead. The suspect would have to know about the blackmail, that was key.

I had several leads I needed to wrap up, including checking to see if Derek Leeds' Manet was in fact a stolen piece, deciphering the coded pages, and deciding whom to interview from the list of twelve people. I also wanted to look again at the film I had developed. Some of the pictures were of paintings; I was sure there was a connection.

I decided to check on Mark Benton next. He was a British attorney who lived to the north of Atlanta. He was a criminal defense lawyer, fresh out of college only a year or two ago. He had been given top position in his father's law firm right after graduation. Already he was rich from representing important and affluent clients in various civil and criminal aspects. Why would Ralph Meeker need an attorney like that?

I looked at my watch. It was almost noon. Since it was a weekday, I wasn't certain he'd be home. But I decided to risk it. I got in the car and drove over, following the real estate map. I wondered what I would ask him when I got there.

Mark Benton's house was located in Dunwoody, the playground of the rich. The house was set far off the road, surrounded by a wooded lot. Scattered leaves and pine straw covered the grounds. They did not appear to be well kept; the gardener had been away for a long time. The trees' branches above the drive leaned into each other as if they were holding hands. Bushes closely hugged the sides of the house.

The two-story home was European in architecture, built of stacked stone, probably slate. There were large soaring windows and a large wooden double front door with stained glass. I pulled my car around to the parking area. The three-car garage was left with one bay open. I hungered after the beautiful Mercedes parked inside. Above the garage were double verandas overlooking the three or four acres of woods. It was a slice of heaven in the midst of the city.

I glanced through each window that I passed on my way to the front door. There was a living room, a dining area, and a room with the blinds drawn closed. I reached the front steps. I took a deep breath and rang the bell. I took a step back. There was a very long wait, but at last I felt footsteps vibrating down the interior stairs. On each side of the door were small vertical rows of windows with sheers. I could see the figure coming down the stairs and toward the door. The deadbolt retracted and the door swung open.

Inside stood a young, athletic man. He was about five foot eight and in his late twenties. He was wearing a cantaloupe-colored T-shirt and khaki shorts with loafers.

"Hallo," he said. "Can I help you?"

There was only a hint of British accent in his query.

"Yes. I'm Paul Grey. I'd like to speak to Mark Benton."

"That would be me." He gestured toward himself. "You're not a solicitor, are you?"

"Oh, no," I said. "I'm a, uh, I'm working for attorney Robert Mayson. I'd like to ask you a few questions."

"Really?" His green eyes pierced mine, and he looked me up and down. "You're a lawyer?" There was doubt in his voice.

"Actually I'm just part of his legal team," I answered as truthfully as I could. I knew I did not look like a lawyer. I was dressed in khakis and a DataCOM polo shirt—not the typical lawyer's suit.

"Well—" He paused to debate my credibility. "I don't know what I could possibly say that could help you."

"I just have some questions," I said.

"All right." He opened the door fully and invited me inside.

"Thank you," I said. I felt a few niceties would go a long way with him. "I appreciate it."

"Not a problem." He led the way to his study. "Would you like a drink?"

He was playing the part of a gracious host.

"No thank you, " I said.

As he poured his drink, a plain club soda, I studied the contents of the room. You can tell a lot about someone from his house. It is an outward reflection of what that person is like inside.

The spacious room was papered in thick hunter green stripes and decorated with paintings of landscapes dominated by the same rich, dark green color. There was a heavy oak desk, hardwood floors, a fireplace with mounted prize buck, and built-in oak bookshelves on each side, displaying volumes of the Classics. Whether he actually read them or just collected them for show I couldn't tell. They were arranged in alphabetical order, reminding me of my own meager book collection, which I arranged by size. This man was organized and neat like me. He also liked comfort and elegance.

"What would you like to know?" he asked, plopping down into an overstuffed chair. He leaned forward and put his elbows on his knees. His hands cupped his glass. He rolled it between his hands, the ring on his finger making a rhythmic clicking on the glass, almost hypnotic.

"Are you a sportsman?" I asked, motioning to the antlered head on the wall.

"My father taught me how to hunt when I was a lad. That was his," he said and sighed. "I'm out of practice right now, but I was never very good in the first place."

"Do you like hunting?" I inquired. I personally disliked the idea.

"No. Actually, I don't like guns, but they keep me in the attorney business so I can't complain." He flashed a win-the-jury-over smile at me, then fell silent.

"Did you know Allan Puckett?" I began to question him.

"I know, knew of him and I had met him. We were never friends, just acquaintances."

"He sent you an invitation to Monday night's dinner, right?"

"Yes. I am a well-known lawyer and a Republican supporter. Rightly so that I should have been invited," he responded.

"I don't doubt your right to be there," I explained. Already he was challenging me, and I hadn't even gotten to the tough questions yet. I took a step forward and looked right into his eyes.

"When did you leave the dinner and where did you go?" I continued.

"I left around ten because I had other plans." He looked at me sheepishly, green eyes sparkling. "I went to Monday Night Madness bowling. Several of the lawyers in my firm go every Monday night."

"Oh." Mark Benton participated in that kind of commonplace activity? It seemed shocking to me. I felt a tinge of guilt for asking personal questions, but I pressed on. "Did you know Ralph Meeker?"

"No."

"Your name appears in his Rolodex in his office. You're listed as an attorney, perhaps his attorney? Maybe you defended him? Maybe you bought something from him?"

"I may have bought something, but I don't recognize the name."

"His name has been in the paper. He was an art dealer," I prodded.

Mark Benton stared at me blankly and continued rolling his glass in his palms.

"I find it difficult to believe you don't know the name." I stood up and circled behind him. "You know Senator Puckett died because you corrected yourself when you began speaking of him in the present tense. If you knew he died, surely you must recognize the name Ralph Meeker, the man he supposedly killed. You're a lawyer and a good one. You don't miss facts like that. There are connections here. I want to know how you fit in."

Mark lost the rhythm with his glass. His arm and leg muscles tensed involuntarily.

"I knew him," he answered slowly, thoughtfully.

I felt a surge of power run through me. I had hit gold. He refilled his glass and then returned to his chair.

"Was he blackmailing you? He was blackmailing lots of people."

No response.

"The police know about the blackmail. If I mention your name and they discover illegal dealings couldn't you be disbarred?"

"Are you threatening me?" He scoffed.

"Well, yes and no. I need to know and I'll get the information any way I can, but I also understand you were the victim here. I can help. You can tell me."

He sighed heavily. "I don't think you can help."

"I can't help unless you tell me what happened." Using my most sincere tone, I continued, "Ralph Meeker was a terrible person. He blackmailed his own girlfriend. I'm trying to get the whole picture. Can't you help me out?"

"I guess." He paused to think. "About six months ago I met Ralph Meeker. I was looking for a unique treat for myself. I'd won a really large case, defending this guy on an arson charge. A friend suggested I go to Mr. Meeker's shop. So I went. It was a small place stuffed with trinkets and junk. I was not impressed with anything on the showroom floor and was about ready to leave when Mr. Meeker asked what I was in the market for, and I told him I really didn't know, but I needed something special. He said that if nothing he had struck me, possibly he could get something else. He said he could get some rare pieces, but he kept them elsewhere for fear of theft. He asked me if I liked Vermeer, or Picasso, or several others. I thought he meant copies, you know, like you can buy at a museum. But he said no—the real things. Then I laughed at him because I thought he was joking.

"Mr. Meeker got huffy when I didn't believe him, like I was insulting his pride or abilities. He insisted he could get the real thing for a price. I told him I had always admired Willard Metcalf's landscapes. His paintings aren't as popular or as well known as people like Picasso, but I was interested and I asked how much a Metcalf would be. He took my name and number and said he'd call if he found one, and he'd give me the price.

"Three days later he called and said he'd found one for me—a real Metcalf painting. He wanted three hundred thousand dollars. I should have known then that something was wrong. I asked him why so little money for that piece of art. He said that no one can spend millions on a piece of art and explained art is always worth far more than it was bought for or could sell for even at auction. At that point I had suspicions that it might be stolen, but I was so excited that my judgement was clouded. He told me to bring cash. I used some savings to buy it. I thought it was an investment, a once-in-a-lifetime opportunity.

"When I saw it I knew for certain it was hot. On the back of the canvas was a mark that said 'Property of Weider Private Collection.' I immediately asked him if it was indeed stolen. He laughed, saying what on earth did I think? Did I really think I could get an original Metcalf legitimately? I was livid. I shouted for him to get out. He just shrugged and left claiming he'd be seeing me.

"Then I was scared. I had participated in, if not arranged, an art theft. I felt like running through the house and closing all the blinds. How could I ever hang that painting on the wall? But then I realized no one would ever know that it wasn't just a fake. Metcalf isn't well-know like some other painters. There was no proof, no trail, no one to suspect me. So I framed it, put a backing on it, and it's hanging right over there."

He pointed to one of the landscapes on the wall.

"That?" I asked in disbelief, "I never would have known."

"I know. That was the beauty of it. No one even suspected it was real. People have visited and studied it. No one knew—until now." Mark ran his hand through his ash brown hair which seemed to be having a calming effect.

"So what happened after you decided to keep it and hang it up?" I asked.

"One day Mr. Meeker called me out of the blue," he continued. "He said he was a little short on cash, and he knew he could count on me to help him. He said I knew where to bring the money. At first it was sporadic. He would call every three or four weeks and hit me for a couple thousand dollars. Then it became more often, every two weeks, and for more money. I convinced myself I was better off to pay him. I had already lost my savings. I wasn't going to lose the painting, too. I paid him another seventy thousand dollars above the cost of the painting. He threatened to report me to the FBI and the local authorities if I didn't pay. If that happened the painting would be confiscated, I could lose my job, be disbarred. I could be disbarred and I've just gotten started in law. I'm not good at anything else."

Mark Benton fell silent. I waited. I knew if I was patient he would fill the silence, the way Sue had at Derek Leeds' studio. Quiet is uncomfortable between two people. Someone always feels it is necessary to talk.

"Of course, I could afford his petty demands," Mark said and shrugged.

My thoughts went to the unkempt yard. No servants here.

"Ralph was a petty thief, an obnoxious, sniveling creature," he continued.

I shuddered, remembering my own experience with him. I couldn't help but agree.

"So you were paying him whatever he demanded?" I asked.

"Yes. And I would keep on paying him if he were still alive."

"But he's dead." I paused. "Did you kill him?"

"NO!" Mark jumped up, spilling his drink. "Damn—"

I jumped up as well. He quickly surveyed the mess, ranting and cussing as he wiped his shirt with a napkin.

"How dare you sit in my home and accuse me." His eyes were so angry they seemed to glow. He lunged across the room and grabbed me by both arms. I wasn't expecting an attack, and I didn't have time to react. His talons dug through my shirt.

"Get the hell out of here—" His breath heavy and hot in my ear as he whispered this warning.

"I'm going." I threw his hands off me.

I may have had a size advantage, but I wasn't ready to test it in a brawl with someone who could sue me and win, so I was out the front door and into my car, pulling down the drive in no time. Mark stood in his front door, his hawk-like eyes watching me angrily as I left.

As soon as I was away from the house, I pulled over to the side of the road to jot down some notes before I forgot the information.

Despite his show of force, it seemed that Mark Benton was in the clear. It would be a simple matter to check his alibi.

I drove back to the freeway and took the Ashford-Dunwoody exit. There was a small dessert shop close by where I could grab a bite to eat and check the phone book. I parked the car and went in. *Mmmm, the smell of chocolate.*

The lady behind the counter was small and overweight, no doubt from taste-testing her own concoctions. She spoke with a heavy accent, German maybe.

"May I help you?" She smiled.

"Yes," I said. I looked up at the sign where the daily specials were written out, and I pointed. "I'll have a piece of raspberry cheesecake and a coffee."

I paid her with a ten.

"Here is your change." She placed it in my outstretched palm. "I'll bring your cake to you if you'd like to pick a booth."

I turned and looked around. There were only three other customers in the shop. There were two young teenagers who looked barely old enough to have reached puberty, much less hold hands and kiss over an ice cream sundae. And there was a businessman with a briefcase and portable phone in tow.

I turned back to the counter.

"Do you have a phone and phonebook I could use?' I asked the woman.

"Yes." She offered me the white and yellow pages from under the counter. I took the yellow ones. "The pay phone is down the hall," she added.

"I'll be sitting over there." I motioned to the table closest to the phone.

As I settled in, the woman appeared with my cake and coffee.

"Thanks," I said.

She hovered near the table, superficially wiping a table that didn't need wiping. She glanced surreptitiously toward me as I took my first bite of cake.

"Very good," I said, nodding.

She nodded and with a satisfied smile she went back behind the counter. She had known all along that the cheesecake was delicious, but she still desired each customer's approval.

I doctored my coffee with cream and two sugars. It was bitter compared to the sweetness of the cheesecake. I ate a few more bites, sipping the coffee in between. Then I flipped open the phone book to BOWLING. There were three bowling alleys in the area. I fished around in my pocket for change, but all I had was one quarter, a few pennies, and some dryer lint. I went up to the counter and asked the woman for change for a dollar. She smiled and gave me four quarters.

First I called home and left a message for Lindsey. Then I called the first alley.

"Fastlanes," a man answered.

"Do you have late night bowling?"

"Yes. Thursday, Friday, and Saturday."

"But not on Monday nights?" I inquired.

"No."

"Thanks," I said and hung up.

I called the second alley. The line rang only once and was picked up by a machine. A voice listed the hours, prices, and an alternate phone number.

I hung up and called that number.

"Perimeter Bowling, can I help you?" a woman answered.

"Do you have Monday Madness bowling?"

"Yes we do. It's the second Monday each month from midnight till 3:00 A.M."

"Thanks."

I mentally checked a calendar. The night of the murder would have been the second Monday.

I called the third bowling alley just to be sure that they didn't have Monday bowling also. The call confirmed it. I realized however, that had I asked Mark Benton, he'd have probably told me which alley and saved me some time. I'd have to remember that.

I would have to check now to see whether Mark Benton had actually been there that night. I could wait until the next Monday Madness bowl night to question people, but that might be too late. Witnesses would be subject to forgetfulness by then. I could question Benton's fellow lawyers, but they might cover for him. The best witness would be an employee of the alley.

I jotted down Perimeter Bowling's address and phone number on my notes about Benton. I would need a picture for positive ID when I questioned the staff. I mulled over this newest dilemma as I finished my cheesecake and coffee.

CHAPTER 13

By the time I was finished eating, I had come up with an idea. I could get a photo of Mark Benton from the newspaper. He said he had defended someone on an arson charge. I remembered vaguely some rich fellow had gone broke and thought he'd torch his multimillion-dollar home to collect the insurance and be rich again. Only he got caught. I couldn't remember the suspect's name or even the outcome, except that Benton reminded me he'd won, so the defendant got off. I hoped that Benton's name would be all I'd need to find a picture in the paper's archives.

At three I was at the library. The parking lot was almost empty. The librarian, a petite, middle-aged woman, appeared startled as I burst in the front door. She was extremely courteous and even more helpful. Her dark eyes took in every word and movement as I explained what I needed. She took me back to the reel-to-reel and microfiche room. I followed her obediently. She walked quickly. Her skin was pale compared to her dark hair which shone, iridescently, like a crow's feathers, under the fluorescent lighting.

The research room was small. A computer contained the database or catalog of information. The other machines were for viewing and printing from the filmstrip reels and microfiche.

She typed in my clue words—Mark Benton and arson—her fingers pecking quickly at the keys. The words "Searching, Please Wait" flashed across the screen and held for a few seconds. The system found three matching articles. Beside the listings were reel numbers, and I wrote them down. The librarian explained their significance.

"The reels are alphabetical in the cabinets over there. Microfiches are in those." The librarian pointed to a wall lined with four cabinets; her short, styled hair ruffled as she turned her head. Her lips pursed as she spoke. "Viewing instructions are on the machine. Let me know if you need any help."

"Thanks," I said, and she left me alone. Her feet made no noise as she left the room.

I found the reels I needed, *Atlanta Journal-Constitution*, December 18 and 20. I took them over to one of the machines. I threaded the reel according to the diagram, a time-consuming process. The pages all came up backwards. I took it apart and tried again, but it was still backwards. All I needed was a photo, so I looked at the reel anyway. The page numbers were all backwards and forward/reverse controls on the machine made the situation worse, however I found the photo I wanted. I pushed the print button, and presto! I had a black and white mug.

I heard the alarm at the front door go off, signaling a possible book theft, as I put away the reels in the "Re-shelve" box and went to the front desk to pay for my copy. A second librarian was rechecking a young girl's books for the culprit that set off the alarm. I thanked the librarian and scooted past them.

It was 4:08 P.M. by the clock in my car. I headed home. When Lindsey got there I would try to convince her to go out for Chinese and bowling. In the meantime I spent some time examining Ralph's photographs. I originally assumed the pictures were taken at an art museum somewhere, but now I was more convinced that they were photos of a private collection, pieces for prospective theft. Perhaps Ralph went and checked out private collections, photographing those he thought he could resell. Then he could give his pictures to the fence of whoever was actually going to steal them so they would know which ones to snatch. I didn't recognize any of the paintings in the photographs as any I had seen before, but they were of well-known artists like Picasso and Monet.

I heard the familiar purr of Lindsey's car as she pulled in the drive. I met her at the door.

"How did your day go?" she asked.

"Great, " I enthused, giving her a hug and kiss.

"Really?" she asked, one eyebrow raised. She knew I disliked my job. "Then you must not have worked."

"No. I didn't have anything today."

"All right, Sherlock, what did you get into?" She put her hands on her hips in a fake display of disapproval.

"Why don't we go out for Chinese and I'll tell you all about it?"

"I don't know," she said and shrugged. "I guess we could. I don't feel like cooking anyway. When we sit around the house I get to thinking about Allan and get depressed. Bowling might occupy my mind."

"Sounds like a yes to me. Go change out of your dress clothes."

She agreed. We went to The Happy Wok down the street. It was a college hangout, but it had great food. I told Lindsey all about my meeting with Mark Benton.

"So now you want to go down to the bowling alley and check out his alibi?" she asked.

"Yes." I grinned ear to ear.

She shook her head in disbelief.

"I suppose it won't hurt anything," she said. "Besides, I like to bowl. It's one sport I think I can beat you at."

We finished our Mandarin chicken and went to the Perimeter Bowling Center. We rented our shoes, picked an alley and bowling balls, and got started. We played a whole game. Lindsey beat me 95 to 91. She went to the snack bar for a Coke, so I went to do a little sleuthing.

I found the young man who had rented our shoes to us. He was hunched over the counter with his back to me.

"Excuse me, " I said.

He turned around from where he was disinfecting a pair of returned shoes with a foul-smelling spray. He stood upright. He was tall and thin like me, only younger and blonde. He looked directly at me, attentively. I pulled out my mug photo.

"Did you work last Monday night?" I asked.

"Yes. I work every weeknight," was the reply.

"Do you recognize this man?" I prodded. "Was he here last Monday night?"

He thought about whether he should answer for a moment.

"Yes, I do." He was sincere. "He was here, but he didn't rent shoes. He had his own."

"Are you sure he was here Monday?"

"Yes. He played a very good game for a non-leaguer."

"How do you know he's not in a league?"

"Well—" The boy paused. "Well, he's not in our league because they play on Wednesday and Friday. I'd have seen him there."

"Do you remember how long he was here? When he came in and how long he stayed?"

"I don't remember when he came in. But I remember watching him and his friends play. They all played two or three games. He was here until late."

"When was that?"

"Around 2:30, maybe. I don't wear a watch, but we closed only a short while after he left."

"Thanks." I turned to walk away.

"Oh, um—" The youth regained my attention. "Are you with the police? Should I call if I see him?"

"No," I said. "This is just personal interest."

I could see the boy rethink his previous decision to talk to me. Then he shrugged in a too-late-now manner.

"OK, " he said.

I rejoined Lindsey and we played another game. She beat me again 105 to 96. At least I was consistent.

Wednesday morning I got up and worked out with some free weights for a half-hour before shaving, showering, and getting dressed. Then I sat down at the breakfast table with my collection of evidence and materials and the phone. The evidence seemed to conclude that Mark Benton was telling the truth, so I decided to tackle another name on the list—Jolene Harris. I dialed the number. It rang and rang.

"Hello?" a gravel-like, sleepy voice answered.

"Hello, Jolene Harris?"

"Who wants to know?" she said gruffly.

"My name is Paul—"

"I don't want any," she said and slammed down the phone.

I sat there a moment stunned and stared at the receiver. The dial tone came back on. I hung it up. At least I knew she was home. I located her address on the real estate map I had confiscated from Lindsey's headquarters. Lindsey appeared in the kitchen.

"Who were you talking to?" she inquired.

"No one really," I said.

"Into your case again *already?*" She pretended disgust.

"Yes." I looked at her sheepishly.

"Who are you after this time?"

"Jolene Harris."

"What's the plan?"

"I don't know. I guess I'll drive over to her house, and maybe I'll think of something on the way."

"Great plan," she teased.

"I know." I couldn't help the grin on my face. "Do you want to go with me?"

"I guess I'm up for some adventure." She winked.

"Let's go then."

"I'll get the keys."

We both headed out the door. Lindsey drove. She loved to drive on beautiful days. She had a relatively new convertible Saab. It was black with gray leather interior. It was only a few years old, and we practically stole it from the guy who sold it to us a year ago. We paid only a fraction of what it was worth. He worked with me at DataCOM, and he transferred out of the country. He had to sell it quickly; with me ready to buy a car, it was an easy sale.

We rode along with the top down. The wind ripped through my hair, disregarding the hair spray I had tediously placed there. Lindsey's hair was even worse. When we came to our stop I laughed at her despite my attempts not to.

"You're no Don Juan yourself," she said. She pulled down her visor with the vanity mirror and fixed each strand.

I saw in my mirror what she meant and combed my hair as well, then grabbed my notepad and pen.

"Here goes nothing," I said.

We stepped out of the car. We were parked by the garage. There were two walkways. One led to the front, and it looked less used than the one to the back. Lindsey and I walked the front way and approached the door.

The home itself was a two-story with a long front porch, which had been painted white but now looked speckled gray where the paint was worn and mildewed. Two completely overgrown ferns were on each side of the steps leading to the door. A bird flew out of one of the nearby bushes, and it startled Lindsey. When the house was new it had probably been well landscaped, but now it was overgrown.

I pressed the doorbell, but nothing happened. I tried again and decided it must be broken. In order to knock I had to open the glass door. It was not locked and creaked horribly as I pulled it. I heard a scrambling on the wood flooring on the other side of the door. What I assumed to be a very large dog started barking and sniffing under the door. I knocked. When I stopped, the dog stopped also. His large furry face appeared in a nearby window, and he began barking again.

I heard footsteps. The dog disappeared from the window, leaving a fresh, wet nose print. The person inside was talking to him.

"Shut up, Maxx. You stupid dog. Enough already."

The dog stopped barking, but was now growling.

"Who's there?" the person asked. The door remained closed.

"Paul and Lindsey Grey," I said. "Are you Jolene Harris?"

"What do you want?"

"We are from Attorney Robert Mayson's office. We'd like to speak to you for just a minute."

She cracked the door. She was short and looked to be about our ages—early thirties. Lindsey offered her a business card, which she took.

"May we come in?" Lindsey chimed in.

Jolene grumbled something unintelligible, but it must have meant "yes" because she opened the door and stood aside.

"Back, Maxx." She reached down and shoved the dog. "I said get back!"

I could then see it was something of a Rottweiler mix. The hair on its neck stood up like a brush, and I could clearly see its teeth. However, he obeyed and retreated into a side room.

She walked down the hall, beckoning us to follow. I realized then she was in her bathrobe, a bright rainbow pattern that reminded me of Mrs. Roper from the old 70's television show, and big fuzzy slippers.

I glanced into the rooms as we passed. All the walls were completely bare; no curtains hung in the windows. There was very little furniture. The den had only a coffee table and sofa. The television was on the floor. The dining room was completely bare. There was a dinette set in the dim kitchen area. This is where she led us to and sat down. I offered to turn on the lights, and she waved me off.

The inexpensively decorated kitchen gave off a dark, peachy glow. On the table were a dirty glass and paper napkins in a wooden holder painted to look like an apple. A bottle of Jim Beam whiskey made the centerpiece.

"Recently divorced." She spoke softly, waving her hand across the room in an explanatory manner.

"Really? That's too bad," said Lindsey, trying to get her empathy going.

"Nah." Jolene shook her head. "He was a bastard."

"Oh!" Lindsey was surprised at the response.

"Prenuptial agreement." Jolene rubbed her forehead and motioned for us to sit at the table.

"I'm sorry, I don't follow," I said, as Lindsey and I each took a seat.

"I was married to Michael Harris for fifteen years. I put up with all his crap. Then he leaves me with not a penny more than when he found me."

She reached into the pocket of her robe and pulled out a cigarette and a lighter. She lit the cigarette. The first puff seemed to soothe her.

"He's a multimillionaire, you know," she added.

At that point Jolene Harris was way off the track I wanted to take. I cleared my throat.

"Anyway, about why we are here," I said. "I— we wanted to ask you a few questions."

"Shoot." She looked at me point blank.

"What do you know about Ralph Meeker?"

"Nothin'." She took another long drag on her cigarette.

"Were you aware that he was murdered?" I had my notepad and pen in hand, ready.

"Yeah, the son of a bitch deserved it." She winced as her own voice level rose.

"So you did know him?"

"Of course I knew him. How could I forget him? He screwed me out of ten thousand dollars," she whispered. "You tend to remember people like that."

"But you just said you didn't know him," I said, perplexed.

"I said I didn't know anything *about* him," she clarified.

"Was he blackmailing you?"

Jolene laughed. "Whatever would give you that idea? I don't have any money."

"Yes, but you did. You just said he took your ten thousand dollars."

"He was a competitor in the antique business." She explained further, "I used to go bid on auctioned estates and abandoned self-warehouse units. He outbid me on this one unit that was full of antiques. It was worth a fortune. I would have made about ten grand off their sale, so that's why I say he took my money. There was one item I just loved, a Dutch estate box, full of secret compartments, and very old. I wanted that. He was such a bastard; he wouldn't even sell it to me afterwards. And there were these two chairs—"

"So you wouldn't have wanted to kill him?" I cut her off from her rambling.

"Hell, no!" She shook her head. "If I'd murdered anyone, it would have been Michael," she said emphatically, puffing on her cigarette.

"Well, just to make things airtight, for your benefit," I said. "Can you tell me where you were on Tuesday, July 12 at 2:00 A.M.?"

"Geezz, you really want specifics, don't you?" Jolene thought for a moment. "I think that was the night I went to a campaign party, I think I was on the list only because I used to be married to Michael and he has money, he could contribute, you know. I don't have any money—"

She trailed off and looked up at Lindsey.

"Now I know who you are. I knew I recognized your face and your name—Lindsey Grey. I never expected to see you here."

"That's me," Lindsey admitted.

"I'm voting for you," she said. "Us women have to stick together."

Lindsey nodded and looked back toward me. I understood the meaning of the look. "Don't ruffle my supporters," she was saying with her eyes, but Jolene took it as a signal to get back on track.

"Oh, right." She got up to retrieve the ashtray from the kitchen counter and put out her cigarette. "Let me think. Afterwards I went to a friend's house."

"Till when?"

"Until the morning." She picked up a paper napkin and began folding it precisely.

"Who was your friend?" I asked.

There was a long pause. I wasn't sure she was going to answer.

"Johnny," she said.

"Johnny who?"

"Heck if I know. I met him at the dinner at the hotel. I didn't think it was important." She shrugged. She was wringing the napkin now. "I'll admit I don't live a pretty lifestyle, but I pay my bills. I work. I deserve not to be lonely."

Lindsey and I were silent.

"I could tell you where the guy lived. It was on the east side of town toward the Peachtree Corners area." Jolene got a devilish look in her eyes.

"If you really want to investigate someone, why don't you go see my ex? He knew Ralph Meeker on a more personal basis than I did. He also has a motive."

CHAPTER 14

"We already planned to go see Michael," I said, "but what was the motive?"

"I'm sure he'd rather tell you himself," she smirked. "As much as I *hate* to send trouble his way."

"So what was the motive? Blackmail?"

"Then I guess that settles it," she said, unresponsive to my question, her eyes gray and misty, like a possible storm cloud brewing as she looked at me. I wondered what was hiding behind those eyes.

"Settles what?" I was puzzled. "You didn't answer my question."

"You can let yourselves out," she said, almost as if we weren't even there.

Maxx eyed us suspiciously as we left the room. As we walked down the hall, I turned and looked at Jolene. She had uncorked the bottle of whiskey and was pouring herself a stiff drink into last night's glass.

I realized I hadn't written a single thing while we were inside, so I jotted down some notes in the car while the conversation was fresh in my mind.

"What do you think?" I asked Lindsey as she drove along.

"I think she was telling the truth. She's bitter and depressed, and quite possibly in the mental state to have killed someone." She paused. "But if she was going to go to all the trouble, why kill two people who don't seem to have given her any cause? Why not just kill Michael?"

"I don't know. I'll check her alibi. She was so calm about everything. It seemed a little suspicious to me."

"I think she was just hung-over. But go ahead and check her out. I don't see how you can. You don't know the Johnny guy's full name."

"I shouldn't need it. He was at the dinner. How many Johnny's could there be?"

"Are you going to check that now?" Lindsey asked.

"No. I think I'll see Michael Harris next."

I pulled out my list of addresses and phone numbers. I looked him up on the real estate map.

"380 Charleston Way, Alpharetta, Georgia," I read aloud.

"That's in north Fulton County. It is a long drive from here. There will be lots of traffic." She paused, waiting for me to respond. "I better not go. Michael Harris is a big supporter of mine and a contributor. I don't want to throw accusations in his face."

"What is the difference between him and Jolene?" I asked, astonished.

"Money," she said. "And money makes the difference between winning and losing a campaign."

"They both have a vote," I said, not understanding the difference.

"I don't want either one of them angry at me, money or no money. But I know Michael Harris' reputation, and he plays rough. He's got money and connections. He could easily spread a bad word about me. I've already got enough bad press. Jolene doesn't have connections like that."

"Isn't the truth important?" I asked.

"Discovering the truth is extremely important. I'm not saying to leave Michael Harris alone. I think you should go, but drop me off first. Besides I have my own work to catch up on."

"That way you can pretend you had nothing to do with it if I ruffle his feathers?"

"Exactly," she said and grinned.

"You're a true politician, Lindsey," I teased.

"Is that a compliment or a slur against my person? Never mind, don't answer that," she said. "You'll want a place to come home to tonight."

We arrived at Lindsey's office around noon. I left her there and took the driver's seat. Within the hour I was at Michael Harris' home, or rather his subdivision. It was a subdivision surrounded by a tall brick wall and a cast iron electronic gate. The name of the community, Suffolk Hills, was spelled in Old English print on a large brick monolith. There was an intercom and identification scanner at the front of the gate. I pulled up and looked at the list of residents. There were about one hundred listings. I found Harris, Michael and dialed his code number. It buzzed his home.

"Hel-woe?" a female voice answered, as garbled as any fast-food intercom. *How cheap. The least they could do is install a decent system.*

"Hello. I'm Paul Grey. I'm here to see Michael Harris."

"Well woo can't. S'his golf day. Come back nuther time."

"But—"

The connection was cut off. I buzzed the house again, but no one answered. There was an area for U-turns, so I pulled through. I drove across the street and parked in the grass. I looked up on the gate and nearby poles and trees. There were no visible surveillance cameras. I wasn't sure exactly how tall the wall was. I thought I might be able to scale it. I got out of the car. Looking both ways, I crossed the street. The wall was taller than I thought, probably ten feet. I looked in all directions to be sure it was safe. There was no one around. I stood on tiptoe and tried to reach the top. I tried jumping, but to no avail. Even with my six-foot-three height I couldn't do it. There was nothing to stand on and no overhanging trees to climb. *Very secure.*

Discouraged, I got back in my car. Then another car approached. The occupant reached out and slid his passkey through the reader. In a few seconds the gate opened. The gate was fairly slow, probably operated by pulleys or gears. The car pulled through and took an immediate left. A few seconds later the gate began to close. That gave me an idea. I could just wait for the next car to come along and then follow them inside. There was enough time for two cars, but I'd have to wait for the first car to get out of sight in order to avoid detection. Now I had a plan. All I had to do was sit and wait for another car to come along. I started my vehicle and pulled it into position. I left it running and put it in park. Then I sat and waited.

I waited. And I waited some more. Thirty minutes or more passed, and no one came along—in or out. My thoughts wandered to potential dangers of what I was doing—not just going into a subdivision uninvited; the whole investigation was fraught with perils. *How would Lindsey support herself without me? Was our life insurance policy paid up? How much was I insured for? Would it be enough?* I thought of ways to protect myself—always talk with others present, make a written record, make sure the suspect knows I'm telling others about the information I collect, stay aware. Had anyone followed me today? I wasn't sure. These thoughts of risk and death were making me uncomfortable. Actually, I was uncomfortable for a variety of reasons. I was stiff from sitting still so long. I was hot since the air conditioner was not running. I was hungry and thirsty, but worst of all nature was calling. The movies never depicted surveillance like that. The cop always had a hot cup of coffee and only had to wait a few minutes before their prey came along. I decided I'd just run into the woods for a second. As soon as I did, my opportunity came along. A black Porsche pulled up and went through the gate.

"Damn it!" I said aloud, zipping up hastily.

I was determined I wasn't going to sit anymore. I pulled out the map and examined the boundaries of the subdivision. Maybe it wasn't walled or as well protected all the way around. I started driving a slow circle around the perimeter. Eventually the brick gave way to plank wood walls, but they were still too tall for me. The trees had been meticulously trimmed back from the wall all the way around. I could see no way in except the front gate.

I was back where I had started from, so I decided to give my gate-rushing idea another chance.

I sat and listened to the radio. Eventually a car came along from inside the community. Magically the gate opened. The car pulled through the gate and took a right turn. I was in position. I pulled up to the intercom. As soon as the car was out of sight I rushed through the U-turn area and in through the exit way. I clenched my teeth as I did it. The gate was closing and I expected to hear crunching noises as my wife's Saab was cut in two, but miraculously I was on the other side, unscathed.

Now what? I was in, but I had no idea where to go. I needed to find the golf course or the clubhouse, and I couldn't very well ask for directions. From distributing thousands of Lindsey's campaign flyers, I had learned that as long as the streets are not set up like city blocks, if you keep going to the right you will eventually traverse the whole thing and come full circle. So I took the first right. It was a cul-de-sac. As I exited the cul-de-sac, I turned right again. Then right again. I continued the pattern until I'd found the clubhouse. I parked and went inside.

It was a large sprawling complex consisting of tennis courts, racquetball and basketball courts, several pools, a children's playground, and, most important, the golf course. Inside the clubhouse was also huge, so huge that it had a directory. There was another racquetball court, a sauna and spa, a weight room, an aerobics room, and a beauty salon. An arrow to the left pointed out the tennis pro shop. The arrow to the right was the golf pro shop and course entrance. Straight ahead were a bar and a restaurant overlooking the eighteenth green. Every other doorway was an entrance to a veranda overlooking the golf course or the pool. I could see where a person who lived here would never have to leave.

I headed to the right. When I reached the golf pro shop, I could see two clerks busy arranging merchandise like polo shirts and expensive accessories promoting their association. Beside the shop was an archway that led to an area enclosed by white lattice and rose bushes. It was the parking lot for the golf carts.

"Can I help you?" a youth asked, jumping to attention from his lawn chair. Beside the chair was a portable television on which he was watching a baseball game.

"Is Michael Harris playing today?" I asked. "I'm a friend of his."

The boy looked at the day's schedule.

"Yes," he said and nodded. "His tee time was at noon. He should be more than halfway done by now. There were only two in his party."

"Which way to the eighteenth hole?" I asked.

"To the left."

I started off, but then turned back.

"You wouldn't by chance remember what he was wearing today?" I asked, realizing I had no idea what Michael Harris looked like.

"I think he had on a red cap today," the boy said and shrugged.

"Thank you," I said.

I took the stairway that led to the course instead of the cart driveway. I briskly walked the course in reverse, and as I went I couldn't help but notice how lush and green all the vegetation was. It was so perfect it was almost unnatural. I tried to concentrate on looking for a red-capped man yet remaining aware of flying golf balls around me.

I guess it would have been too much to ask for me to locate Mr. Harris on the eighteenth hole, or even the seventeenth hole. I'd walked so far and for so long I was beginning to worry that I'd missed him somehow or other along the way. The course was very busy.

I'd worked up a tremendous sweat, and I'm sure I smelled absolutely delightful. My legs were tired, and my lungs were begging for a break. Somewhere along the fifteenth hole I found a bench in the shade. I sat down to rest. A few moments later a young woman in a golf cart came tooling along selling beer and soft drinks. The answer to my prayers. The expensive cola was well worth it. At that precise moment it would have been worth its weight in gold to me. The young woman smiled, pocketed the money, and went off in search of other parched victims. I bet they loved days like that day.

I decided I'd had enough walking for the day. I figured I'd stay there and let Michael Harris come to me. Perhaps I could then get a ride back to the clubhouse. Somehow I must have drifted off to sleep. When I awoke, ten minutes had passed, and I was hot and thirsty again even though I wasn't moving. I was more worried about Mr. Harris. I might have missed him while I dozed.

A pair of middle-aged women came driving down the fifteenth fairway.

"Excuse me," I hollered to them. I leapt off the bench and out onto the course.

"Can we help you?" the older of the pair asked.

"I hope so." I was out of breath from my short sprint. I would have thought my weekly bout at the gym would have cured that by now. "I'm looking for Michael Harris. Do you know him? Have you seen him today?"

"Yes, Michael. I know him." She glanced at me with what I thought to be a disapproving look.

"We played through his party back at the twelfth, I believe," the second woman said, looking at the first for confirmation. "I believe everyone has played through his game today."

"Yes, he's a terrible golfer." The first woman laughed.

Both ladies laughed and proceeded on their way. I sat on the bench again to wait. No matter how bad his game was, Michael Harris would have to come through the fifteenth hole eventually.

The heat was unbearable, my clothes were drenched, and I was tired. I wanted to stretch out on the bench and sleep, but instead I occupied myself by studying shapes in the clouds and by identifying all the wildlife around me, from the mockingbird in the tree above to the ants below. About twenty minutes later a golf cart came bouncing up the path. It was steady on course, but going quite fast. There were two men on board—one with a red cap stuck over one of his golf clubs.

"Michael Harris?" I yelled as they passed.

The driver slammed on the brakes, lurching to a halt. With difficulty he put the cart into reverse and backed up. He stopped next to me. He was a short, stocky man with a spare tire that went all the way around. He was balding, but his remaining hair was curly and long, pulled into a ponytail. He wore expensive mirrored sunglasses.

"Yes," he said. "Who wants to know?"

"I'm Paul." I extended my hand for a shake.

Michael reached to accept and in doing so took his foot off the brake. The cart lurched backwards, but he caught it quickly. He and his companion laughed hysterically. I didn't think it so funny as he had narrowly missed running over my foot.

"I met you last Monday at a party," I explained.

"Oh, yes." He nodded as if he remembered and shook my hand heartily.

"I wanted to ask you some questions," I said. "I'm working on Allan Puckett's murder. You know he was murdered, don't you?"

"Murder? No. I thought it was suicide, but never mind that. His death was a darn shame. I always thought he was a good guy."

"Yes, me too. May I ask you a few questions? I could ride along and ask as you go."

"Sure." Michael motioned toward the back of the cart. "Hang on."

And he wasn't kidding around. He took off down the course. He drove like he was insane. He totally disregarded tree roots, rocks, cracks, and holes along the path. We drove right past the fifteenth green without stopping.

"Aren't you going to finish that hole?" I asked, bewildered.

"Nah, we're already par for the course," he explained. He turned to look at me. I must have looked confused, so he elaborated. "Par for this course is 72. I'm two under par and Bill in right on the money."

Bill laughed some more.

"You mean the par for all eighteen holes, right?" I asked.

"Yes."

"But you didn't play all the holes—"

"I know that." Michael looked at me perturbed. "Are these the questions you wanted to ask me? Stuff about how lousy a golfer I am?"

"No," I reassured him. "You're a better golfer than I am."

"Flattery will get you everywhere!" Michael's friend piped up.

"Get to the point," Michael said.

I cleared my throat. "I wanted to ask you about Ralph Meeker's death."

"I thought you said you wanted to talk about Allan Puckett." He looked back over his shoulder to where I hung tenuously on the back.

"It's all related," I insisted.

"So, what about it?" Michael asked.

I was blunt. "I know Ralph Meeker was blackmailing you, just like he did Allan."

Michael practically ran off the path into the woods. After successfully steering until he could stop, he jumped off the cart as if to run away from the confrontation. I stepped off the back of the cart. Checking his impulse, he turned to look at me.

"You've got nerve," he said indignantly. "You've come here to accuse me? Do you know who I am?"

"Yes. You are a multimillionaire, owner of a Fortune 500 company, recently divorced, no children, and avid, but poor, golfer," I continued, "All I've accused you of, unless you are hiding something, is that you are a victim of blackmail."

"No." Michael was firm. "I've read the paper. I know why you're here. You've come to check if my being a victim led me to murder Ralph Meeker and Allan Puckett so I could get off the hook. Well, you can forget it, because I didn't kill anyone."

He jumped back on the cart and left with a jolt. That hadn't gone too well. His use of my word "victim" led me to take his statement as a confession of motive, but that was all I got out of him. Resigned to a long walk back, I set off to the clubhouse.

When I finally arrived, I walked back through the complex with the intent of going directly to my car; however, as I passed the lounge I caught sight of Michael and his friend. I paused to listen for any conversation. There was none. I approached the bar tentatively. Michael must have sensed my presence because he turned on the barstool to stare me down. He was feisty, small man, only about five-foot-five. At this point my height worked to my advantage. Looking up at me, his stare softened and he averted his eyes.

"I'm not going to answer any questions," he said, staring into the bubbles of whatever it was he was drinking.

"It would be to your benefit. At this point you're already a suspect," I said.

No response.

"Ralph Meeker blackmailed lots of people. You're not alone. I'm not with the police, so you can tell me because your secret is safe with me," I reassured him.

"Secret? You mean you're not working with the police?" Michael was taken off-guard and pulled from his stony silence. "I thought you worked for them."

"No."

"Well then, who the hell are you, and how did you get in here?" He jumped up from his barstool.

"I told you. My name is Paul. I'm working directly for the Senator's widow. I have nothing to do with the police. And I came in through the front gate," I retorted.

"This is a private subdivision and club. You have no right to be here." He waggled a finger in my face.

"That's true," I said and shrugged. "I was just leaving anyway. I only came because your ex-wife suggested you might know something about or actually be responsible for Ralph Meeker's death."

"Oh, she did. She suggested that, huh?"

"Yes. She said you had a *real* motive," I prodded. I knew I had hit his weak spot—his ex.

"Yeah." He was angered. "And I've even got a *real* alibi."

"I'd like to hear it," I said.

"I was on a plane flight to Denver on business. It was a red-eye. At the time of the murder I would have been in the air." He spiraled his pointed finger up at the ceiling to simulate flight.

"You are lucky to have such a perfect alibi," I said. "Very well prepared."

"What's that supposed to mean?" He was defensive.

"What airline were you on?"

"What?" His lips turned sour like I had caught him in a lie.

"Your flight. What airline did you use?" I repeated.

"Delta." His response was quick that time and firm. "Our company always uses Delta."

"Well then," I said, smiling and turning to leave, "I guess that's all."

"Wait!" He grabbed my arm. "What do you mean about a perfect alibi and being prepared?"

"Nothing really. It's just that most people need a minute or two to think about where they were, but you spit it out right on cue, almost like it was rehearsed or prepared."

"I had time to think about it the whole time you were walking back," he insisted smugly.

"True." I turned and walked out.

Michael ordered the bartender, "Make sure that he leaves."

"Yes sir," the bartender responded.

The bartender probably called the security personnel. I never saw them, but I'm sure they watched me as I got in my car, drove to the gates, and passed through. Once outside I pulled over to make some notes on Michael Harris.

I didn't have time to get started before I looked up to see a red Jeep

pass me. It was Michael. I thought for a split second, and then on impulse
I decided to follow him.

CHAPTER 15

I'd never followed anyone before, and it was not as simple as it might seem. I remembered what Barbara Warren had said about tailing. It wasn't as easy as following someone who knows you are there and will wait for you. You can ride right behind them. With my suspect I tried to stay at least two cars away so he wouldn't recognize me. I was lucky his car was bright red and tall. We were on populated roads, so it wasn't obvious when we both turned the same way. I prayed the traffic lights would stay green. However, green lights were the least of my worries. Michael drove like a maniac, the same as he did with the golf cart. He was weaving in and out of traffic and cutting people off—a definite candidate for road-rage.

When we got to the highway, he headed south. I followed him there for several miles. Traffic was racing along at a hectic pace, and Michael fit right in. I matched his speed about four cars back and one lane to the right. When his exit approached he zoomed across all three lanes of traffic, nearly wrecking into a bus. I, on the other hand, missed the exit. I couldn't get over fast enough. I went up a mile and came back to that exit, hoping to catch a glimpse of the red vehicle somewhere. I drove for blocks looking to the left and right, but it was a lost cause. I was disappointed. My first attempt at tailing had been a dismal failure. And I had no idea where he had been headed. *Where was he going in such haste?*

Depressed, I turned the car around and headed to Lindsey's office to pick her up. I made a mental note to practice tailing. My only solace was that I would have time to check Delta Airlines and Jolene's alibi when I got home.

Lindsey was alone in her office. When I approached she couldn't see me in her faraway eyes. She looked lost.

"Lin—" I tapped on the door. "You OK?"

"Oh, yeah," she weakly answered. "I'm just about done."

"Looks like you've had too much time alone." I indicated the scrap of paper twisted into submission in her hands.

"I've been thinking too much," she admitted, dropping her melancholy expression for a half-smile.

"It's good to think about Allan," I reassured her.

"I was just remembering the time we took him to the lake to go water-skiing, and he nearly drowned when he didn't let go of the rope." She smiled again. "But every time I think of something like that which makes me laugh, then I remember he's gone and I want to cry. I'm so mixed up. Am I OK? Am I crazy?"

"You're not crazy. I think that's perfectly normal. I miss Allan, too."

"How come you don't get sad and cry like me?"

"I haven't let myself. I'm trying to be here for you. I don't think we can both be miserably sad at the same time and survive."

"I'd cheer you up if you were sad," she offered.

"I know what would cheer you up," I teased.

"What?"

"I'll let you mess up my sock drawer."

My organization drove Lindsey nuts. My underwear and socks were folded and placed neatly in rows in my dresser. All closets were neatly organized. I even kept the pantry organized into sections for canned goods, boxed goods, and things that came in bottles. She loved to go behind me and rearrange to see if I'd notice. It was our little game and I thought it might lighten her mood.

She laughed, crossed her arms, pretended to pout. "Sock drawer and the pantry."

"OK. Deal."

Once Lindsey had satisfactorily rearranged my things and eaten almost a half-gallon of chocolate ice cream, her spirits were lifted. We spent the evening in the living room scanning the guest list for John, Jon, or Jonathan.

"This is going nowhere," I said. "There are no matches."

"Maybe he wasn't a guest," Lindsey suggested. "Maybe he was a waiter or staff member of the hotel. Let's check the police files."

We both jumped up from the sofa to go for the police reports. In our race Lindsey got there first. She flipped through them.

"Somewhere there should be a whole list," she muttered. "Ah-ha! I've got it."

She played a quick game of keep-away as I tried to snag it from her.

"I'll look," she insisted.

I watched her eyes intently scan the page.

She looked up at me and smiled devilishly. "What will you do for me if I give you the clue you've been looking for?"

"Anything you want."

"Anything?"

I nodded.

"I'll remember you said that. And rest assured I will collect." She ran her fingers across the nape of my neck. "I have here in my hands the name of a hotel waiter," she said and paused for full effect, "Jonathan M. Tate."

She pawed through the stash of papers again.

"What are you looking for?" I asked.

"His statement to the police," she answered. "Here it is."

I looked over her shoulder as we both read it to ourselves.

"This can't be right," she protested.

"What? What can't be right?" I asked. "I'm not done reading. Let me see."

"Right here, he claims he arrived at 8:00 P.M. for the beginning of his work shift and stayed until 3:00 A.M. when the staff had cleaned up and was dismissed. It says his time card was punched for 2:58 A.M."

"If this is the same Johnny that Jolene spoke of, then she must be lying." I felt a surge of excitement.

"Or else the waiter is lying," Lindsey countered.

"Why would the waiter lie?" I asked.

"I don't know." She shrugged. "We should call him and find out."

"Do you have the number?"

"No, but we can call the hotel and talk to him. Tell them you work for Mayson."

I called the hotel. I was connected to the manager. Lindsey was trying to listen in the receiver with me. We each had half an ear on the phone.

"May I help you?" the manager asked.

"I hope so," I said. "I am working for Attorney Mayson on a murder case. I need to speak with Jonathan Tate."

"Let me see if he is working this evening. Hold on."

Piped music came over the receiver until she returned.

"I'm sorry. He's not here tonight."

"Oh." I paused. "Well then could you give me his home number? I really need to speak to him."

"Our employee's records and files are confidential. I'm not sure I can do that."

"I'm sure you have already given it to the police, right?" I asked.

"Well, yes."

"Well, then what is the difference? Either you can give me the number now, or I can call the station tomorrow. However, I hate to delay until tomorrow. After all, this is a murder case and lives are at stake."

"A little flair for the dramatic," Lindsey whispered as she moved away from the phone and went into the kitchen.

There was a long delay. The hotel clerk was debating whether to give the information to me or not.

"I guess it would be OK since you're working with the police and all. I'll look it up."

"I got it!" I hollered for Lindsey after hanging up.

"That's great." Lindsey appeared grinning. "But next time you should try the phone book first."

She held open the page for me to see. He was listed.

"Oh, well," I said. "You learn something every day."

"Call the waiter," she urged.

"Why don't you call him? You're the lawyer's aide. You could be more convincing."

"Yes, but you want to be the detective. If he is lying, you can make him talk. I don't think I could do that."

I dialed the waiter's number. I got his tape machine. I decided not to leave a message.

"Too bad," Lindsey empathized.

"I'll try again later."

"So what are you going to do now?" Lindsey asked.

"I don't know. It's getting late."

"Yeah." She came up close to me and put her mouth to my ear, breathing heavily. "I'd like to collect my anything now."

I had to get up early the next morning for a 6:00 A.M. installation. I made some calls from my office cubicle. I scheduled a preliminary meeting for Tuesday and an installation for Wednesday. I checked my e-mail and messages and was back home by one in the afternoon. I decided to try calling Samir Chander at home. There was no answer. I figured I'd have to try to reach him at his work. The office was closed until two for lunch.

Then I called Delta Airlines. There was a long series of messages about pushing one for this and two for that and three for something else. I just pretended I had a rotary phone and held on the line. A message informed me that my call was being transferred to the next available customer service operator. I sat on hold for twenty minutes listening to a series of prerecorded messages telling me to please stay on the line to keep my priority status and that my call would be answered shortly. I just wanted to speak to an actual person. Finally, a customer service representative picked up.

"Thank you for calling Delta. This is Robert. Can I help you?"

"Yes. I need to know if there were any flights heading out of Atlanta to Denver late last Monday night or early Tuesday morning?"

"Last Monday? What was that date?"

"Umm, it would have been July 11th late at night or early morning on July 12th."

"Let me check. Bear with me a moment."

I waited.

"Yes. There was a flight that left Atlanta at 11:45 P.M. It was flight number 921," he said.

"Can you tell me if there was a Mr. Michael Harris on that flight?" I asked.

"No. I'm sorry we can't give out that kind of information."

"Who can give me that information?"

"No one. We can't give that information out unless you are with the police, and then only if you file the appropriate application and paperwork."

"Oh, OK." I sighed. "Thanks anyway."

I took out my note cards and added one on Michael Harris.

I called Lindsey and asked her to have the police check with the airline and get the information. She seemed to feel that they wouldn't do it.

"Why not?" I asked.

"Well, because they don't think that Michael Harris is a suspect. If he isn't a suspect then they don't need to collect information on him," she explained. "It's a waste of time and money."

"That's crazy." I shook my head in disbelief. "Michael Harris was being blackmailed also."

"There is no real proof to that—only your conversation with him and the fact that his number was in Ralph Meeker's Rolodex."

"They should still check every possible lead," I complained. "Try to get them to apply for the airline information anyway."

"I'll try," she promised.

I had been off the phone for only a few seconds when it rang. I fully expected it to be Lindsey.

"Yes?" I answered.

"Hey. Somebody there called me," a man's voice said.

"They did?" I questioned the unexpected voice on the line.

"Yes. You didn't leave a message, so I did a call return."

"Who are you?" I asked.

"This is Jonathan Tate."

"Oh, yes," I replied. My heart began to race. "I called, but I was looking for Jolene."

"You must have the wrong number," he stated.

"No, no—" I stopped him so he didn't hang up.

"I called because I thought she said she was at your place."

"I have no idea who you're talking about." The answer was emphatic. "You have the wrong number."

He hung up. I called him back immediately. His machine picked up. This time I left a message.

"I know you're there. You just called me. I'll keep calling back until you pick up." I paused and then taking a more condescending tone I said, "I know Jolene was at your place the other night and you lied to the police. Did you know she was a murder suspect?"

The sound of the line changed as Jonathan Tate picked up.

"Jesus! Who the hell are you and what business is it of yours?" he asked.

"Answer me first, was Jolene Harris at your place on Monday night or not?"

"Why should I talk to you?"

"Just answer the question," I demanded.

"I— I—" he stammered. "I don't know who you think you are, but I don't have to answer any questions." His voice trembled as he spoke.

"If you're not going to talk to me, then why did you pick up? You're curious about this, aren't you? You don't know her very well. You're not denying knowing her, right?" I asked.

"Yeah. I know her."

"Well, either you or Jolene has lied to the police about your whereabouts on Monday night. Did you know she could be a murder suspect? If you lie you could be charged with perjury or worse you may end up becoming a murder suspect yourself."

"Perjury? Murder? Whose? That ain't gonna happen," he said. "No way man."

"It could happen," I asserted. "Your statement to the police says you left the hotel at 3:00 A.M., yet Jolene says you were together at your place. That makes you both suspicious because they can't both be right, can they?"

"No," he muttered and with a sigh, "I know I just met her, but I really like her. I wouldn't want her to get in trouble."

I cringed at the thought. They don't even know each other's last names. How can you care about someone like that? It didn't matter what I thought, though; a confession was forthcoming.

"Did she say she was with me?" he asked with careful curiosity.

"Yes."

"Well, she's right. She was with me. We left early to go to my place, but my shift wasn't over until 3:00 A.M. I had another worker punch my timecard when he left. We do it all the time."

"So you left and went home? Did you drive together or separately?"

"She followed me home," he said.

"Who was your friend that punched your time card?"

"I don't know who actually punched it for me. We're all buddies and they said they'd cover for me, but please don't tell the hotel. I could lose my job."

"I won't say anything, unless it becomes necessary, but I hope you change your statement to the police."

"I will, man," he said. "Hey, who is this anyway?"

I hung up. He didn't call back. I wrote down the gist of our conversation in my notes about Jolene Harris. Jonathan seemed reluctant to tell me Jolene was with him until he was sure that was her story as well. Could Jonathan Tate be covering for Jolene? It was an interesting idea. I hardly thought those two knew each other well enough, or did they? I began to wonder if more than one person could be involved. Maybe they already knew each other. Maybe they pretended to "meet" at the party. Then they killed Ralph Meeker. Then they killed Allan to divert suspicion and used each other for alibis. What crazy thoughts I was having. A conspiracy theory for goodness sakes! I needed a break.

CHAPTER 16

I didn't have the time to take a break, though. Lindsey's election, Margie's insurance check, our family's reputation, my ego—all hung on the line. I decided to try to reach Dr. Samir Chander.

"Northside Internal Medicine."

"I need to see Dr. Chander."

"Have you been to the Doctor before?"

"No."

"OK. Do you have a referral?"

"No. I don't need one. I just need a consultation. I want to talk to the doctor."

"The earliest appointment I have is September 15th at 9:00 A.M."

"September, Geezz! Isn't there anything sooner?" I pleaded.

"No."

"Are you sure I can't fit in somewhere?"

"No, sir. September 15th is all I have."

I sighed. I would have to catch him at home. I couldn't wait two months.

"The only other thing I can do is put you on a waiting list for cancellations. That way if someone calls and cancels their appointment we can call you and you can take it. Usually there is very little advance notice," she offered.

"That's fine. Put me on the list."

I gave her all the pertinent information and then it was back to the drawing board. The next names on my list were Philip and Sandy Hunt. Lindsey and I knew them from our subdivision pool and tennis club. They were about our same ages. They lived only a few houses from us, but we didn't know them well. We had lived there for a few years and had met lots of people on a superficial basis while campaigning but had gotten to know only one or two couples on what I would call a friend level. The Hunts were only acquaintances.

I figured I could drop by to see Sandy anyway. She would be surprised to see me. She was a stay-at-home mom. They had five children, approximate ages eight, seven, five, three, and less than one year. I didn't know their names, but I knew she was almost always home with the children because she home-schooled them. Even though it was now summer break I felt she would be there because she rarely took all five of them somewhere by herself. Who could blame her?

I'd seen couples walking through the mall with children in tow from every possible appendage and older ones pushing younger ones in strollers. I had always watched these families in awe, knowing full well I was not capable of such. Philip and Sandy didn't seem to mind having so many little ones underfoot, and the children appeared happy.

Our child for many years had been our dog, Oreo. She was black on both ends and white in the middle. She was a mutt, but probably had some Border collie in her. When Oreo died a little over a year ago, we got an alarm system to replace her bark, but nothing to replace her love. There was still time left for us to have children, but it was fleeting. Lindsey was 33 and I was 32. We had never made a plan to have children. We had been so busy with work and careers that we had never made time for kids. Judging from what Sandy Hunt had told us, it takes up a lot of time to raise children. She was joyful when she explained this, not regretful. I placed my bet that they'd both be regretful when all five became teenagers. I also bet Lindsey and I would be regretful later on if we never had children at all.

These thoughts aside, I figured it would be best to drop by a little later in the evening when Phillip would be home as well. In the meantime I decided to take a nap since I'd had an early rising. As I lay in the bed, thoughts stampeded through my mind. I didn't feel like I was getting anywhere because I hadn't gotten anything solid. Everything was turning up dead ends or at least roads to nowhere. At this point detective work was not looking at all attractive or easy. Truthfully, right at that moment it was boring, and I was tired of it. However, I knew I had to keep going. I was not a quitter just because something became difficult. Nonetheless, I was hoping for the breakthrough clue you always read about in detective novels and mysteries. I needed that one clue that ties everything together and makes the puzzle whole. I was also hoping that if the clue was out there that it wouldn't take too much longer in getting to me. I napped fitfully.

When I awoke, it was 5:32 P.M. I decided to drive by Sandy and Philip Hunt's house. I left a note for Lindsey to let her know where I was.

As I pulled up their U-shaped drive, I noticed the two oldest children, both boys, in the side yard tormenting a pile of fire ants. They stood in awe as the critters scurried to repair the damage done by these two giants. One has to admire an ant's instinctual commitment to doing for the good of the group. The human species will never comprehend that simplicity. We are much too focused on individuality, and there is no room for self-sacrifice. I stood for a moment transfixed, watching the boys watching the ants.

"Hello Paul," came a voice. It was Sandy. "I thought I heard a car pull up."

She approached me from the other side of the house. She was a wispy creature. She had a small, thin frame with long arms and legs. Her sleeveless shirt and shorts accentuated these features. She had been working in the yard. Her knees and palms were covered with dirt. The five- and three-year-old were with her. They hung behind her, unsure of my presence.

"Hey Sandy." I stepped through the grass to meet her halfway. "I'm sorry to bother you. I know how busy you are."

"Nonsense. What can I do for you?" She pushed her short curls of red hair back off her face. She was hot, flushed, and sweaty.

"I need to ask you some questions about a criminal murder case that Lindsey is working on."

"Me?" Sandy looked shocked. "Why do you need me?"

"Well, actually you and Philip." I felt awkward.

This undertaking was going to require tact, and I wasn't sure I was capable of that. How do you come right out and ask your neighbor about their possible involvement in blackmail and murder? I was going to be living near them for several years to come as far as I knew. I would see them at the pool and on the tennis courts. It wasn't going to be the same when I asked them questions. The other people I might never see again. And even though they were only acquaintances, I had a gut feeling they were completely innocent of any wrongdoing. It was a feeling I couldn't ignore. If a store clerk *undercharged* them for a product, they would report it. They were a quiet, honest, churchgoing family.

"Maybe we could go inside?" I suggested. I was not afraid of the Hunts, so it would be safe to conduct my investigation indoors.

"Sure, let me just grab the portable monitor. The baby's down for a late nap." Sandy was entirely baffled, but probably happy to go in where it was cooler. "Don't look so serious. Is it serious?" she queried.

"Yes," I admitted.

We took the stone path which led to the back screened porch, then proceeded through the porch and into the kitchen. The five- and three-year-old followed. At the kitchen door they both sat down and took off their shoes without any cues from Sandy. She smiled at them proudly.

"Brian, Julie. Go wash up and play in your room with your toys," she commanded.

Without a peep they disappeared, hand in hand.

"Wow!" I exclaimed, "If I ever have kids I need to get some lessons from you."

"There's really nothing to it," she said and shrugged as she fixed two ice waters and offered one to me. "You have to establish control and discipline right away and the rest just follows."

"Wow," was all I could reply.

"Anyway, why are you here?" She sat down at the kitchen table and took a sip of her beverage.

I sat across from her. Her deep blue eyes filled with interest and concern.

"Did you hear the news about Senator Puckett?" I inquired.

"Yes. I was so surprised. He was such a nice man. I don't think he did it," she blurted. "You can just tell about some people, you know?"

"Yes, I know." I paused. "Which is what makes this so difficult."

"What?"

"Well, if Senator Puckett was innocent, then someone else is guilty. I'm trying to find that someone."

"And you think Philip and I could help?" She seemed excited by the prospect.

"Well, sort of." I took a deep breath. "The man who was killed was Ralph Meeker, an art dealer."

"I knew him." She shook her head in pity. "God have mercy on *his* soul."

"Why do you say that?"

"That man had no morals about him." She shook her head. "And he didn't know the Lord."

"I agree. He was blackmailing some of his clients that had purchased stolen artwork. I think one of them killed him."

"I'd be glad to help, but I still don't see how I can. I don't know anything about art."

"Your names came up on Ralph Meeker's Rolodex as clients. Did you know anything about him?"

"Not really." She shrugged.

"Neither one of you bought anything from Ralph's shop?"

"Oh, sure, we bought stuff," she assured me.

"If you don't mind telling me, what did you buy?" I asked.

"I collect teacups," she replied and pointed to the ceiling.

All around the kitchen were shelves filled with antique teacups. I chided myself. I hadn't noticed my surroundings until then. What a blundering detective I was. The kitchen and the areas of the living room and dining room that I could see were decorated in what I considered to be bad taste—French provincial-style floral furniture, probably vintage, and antique trinkets, probably expensive.

"You didn't buy anything else? No pictures or anything?" I asked.

"No, why do you ask?" She frowned at my repetitiveness.

"Ralph Meeker was blackmailing people. Senator Puckett was tricked into buying stolen art," I explained.

She gasped and covered her mouth. "I don't know why I'm so surprised, I mean, about Ralph selling stolen art and blackmailing people. He wasn't much of a Christian."

"I know." I nodded. "I'm not saying you would do anything wrong intentionally, but are you sure you didn't buy anything stolen?"

"I'm sure." Sandy smiled. "If I had I would tell you, especially if I thought I could help solve a mystery."

"What about Philip? Could he have bought something?" I asked.

"No, well, I don't think so. You can ask him when he gets home if you'd like." She glanced at the clock. "He'll be here soon."

"Where did you go after the dinner party Monday night?" I tried to be casual, like it was unrelated, but she caught on.

"I'm afraid we don't have much of an alibi. We came home. We don't like to leave the kids with a sitter more than we have to. I think it was a little after one, maybe later. We stopped twice, once at the all-night drugstore because Willie was sick and then for some ice cream at the grocery. I'm expecting again." She patted her tummy. "And the cravings have started already!"

I congratulated her. I wasn't sure if congratulations or sympathy would have been more appropriate. The baby woke up and she fed it a bottle while we conversed at length about child bearing and rearing, waiting for Philip to come home. I was ill at ease, but Sandy seemed relaxed. She continued in her normal routine, checking on dinner and the other kids. I don't know how she did it all. Sandy greeted Philip outside when he arrived, and they talked for a minute.

"Hello Paul." Philip entered the kitchen and placed his briefcase at the end of the counter. He and Sandy stood side by side. Even though he was smaller than I, his overall size dwarfed Sandy, who was tiny enough to get sucked up by a vacuum cleaner.

"Hey Philip," I greeted him. "Did Sandy tell you why I was here?"

"Sort of. You need to know if we bought anything from the Atlanta Arts shop, right?" Philip twirled his mustache. I knew it covered a large scar on his lip. I could barely see it, but I remembered it was there. He had been clean-shaven the summer before.

"In particular I need to know if you bought any pictures or paintings."

"Well, actually, yes I did." He stopped twirling his moustache.

"You did?" Sandy couldn't believe her ears.

We were both shocked. I was expecting an absolute "no" and then I could have politely excused myself and left.

"Yes, I bought a painting a few months ago," he said and nodded.

"Where is it then?" Sandy was shaken.

"At work, in my office." Philip was smiling. His brown eyes sparkled devilishly. "Don't worry dear, it's not stolen. If it was, I wouldn't have it."

"Who painted it?" I asked.

"I don't know." He shrugged. "Miguel something, no one famous. What are you looking for?"

It was my turn to shrug.

"No painting in particular, probably one by someone famous like Monet or Degas. Anything that might be stolen," I replied.

Philip was still smiling, "If I wanted one of those paintings, I could buy it legitimately, so why would I risk my home and family for it?"

Philip was right. I didn't know the fine details of their financial standing, but I did know his father had been a multimillionaire, Philip himself was a CFO of a major firm, and they owned property all over the country. Philip and Sandy lived in deliberate simplicity, probably for religious reasons. But they had enough money wrapped up in real estate to buy a famous artwork outright. I assumed they were stashing away their money for retirement, or for their kids.

"You're absolutely right," I assured him. "I apologize for bothering you."

I stood up to leave.

"Not a problem, Paul." He extended his hand and shook mine. "You're just trying to get to the truth. That's admirable."

He walked me through the house to the front door. I glanced at the pictures on the walls and in the rooms we passed. Nothing seemed unusual. I felt relieved.

"Thanks for coming by," he dismissed me. "No hard feelings."

I nodded in acknowledgment. I truly believed he wouldn't hold a grudge. They weren't the type.

It was almost seven when I got home. Lindsey wasn't there yet—my cue to make dinner. So I ordered pizza. I straightened up and started a load of laundry, mostly towels. Almost everything we wore got dry-cleaned. I folded my shirts and her dresses to take to the cleaners. We were hardly ever home, so the place had little opportunity to get dirty, but I vacuumed the living room anyway. Even when we were home our activities were generally confined to three rooms in the house—the kitchen, living room, and bedroom.

I had just shut the vacuum off when the doorbell rang. The pizza had arrived. I paid the delivery boy and tipped him. As he pulled out of the drive, Lindsey pulled in.

"Hey," I called to her as she got out of the car. I held up the pizza box. "I made dinner!"

"I see that," she laughed. She got her papers out of the backseat and came inside.

"I really wish we could get all that stuff out of our garage so we could park in there. It's so hot to be walking around outside!" she complained as she unloaded her armful in the foyer. She had been out campaigning.

My Great-aunt Susan had gotten wild in her old age and sold her house so she could tour Europe for a year. In the meantime all her furniture was stored in our garage awaiting her return when she planned to purchase a smaller home outside the city. I could sympathize with Lindsey's complaint. We'd been parking outside for over six months and it was ruining our cars' paint. We always had to dash for cover in the rain, and in the summer heat the inside of the car baked like an oven by ten in the morning. Personally, I couldn't even look in the garage without having my stomach turn in knots—disorganization like that, ugh!

"Are you ready to eat now?" I asked.

"Yes," she gasped. "I'm starved."

We both sat and ate the whole pizza like pigs. We were done in less than ten minutes. Then we both complained that we had eaten too much.

"I need to ask you to do me a favor," I said as we cleaned up our paper plates and napkins.

"What's that?" she asked.

"Do you know anyone who works with the FBI?"

"The FBI! What on earth for?"

"I need to ask about a painting I saw in Derek Leeds' loft apartment. I need to know if it was stolen or not." I pulled the photocopy I had made of the painting out of my papers.

"Not to crash your party, but the FBI has bigger problems to deal with than stolen paintings."

"They would be the ones to ask though, right?"

"Well, yes. They cover cases of art theft, but they also have lots of bombers and rapists and murderers to catch."

"I know, but you haven't answered my question," I said. "Do you know anyone that works for the FBI?"

She huffed. I could see she didn't want to tell me, but she finally let it out.

"Charlotte."

"Charlotte?"

"You don't know her. She works in the hair analysis section."

"They have a section just for hair analysis?"

"Yes, and she's an expert."

I really was stunned. I guess I'd never thought about all the things investigators must examine from fingerprints to blood to fibers. You would have to pick a specialty; there's just too much otherwise.

"Maybe I could call her." She took the paper from my hands. "But don't get your hopes up!"

"I won't." I gave her a hug, "Thanks."

"No problem." She folded up the page. "Who's left to check on your list?"

"Dr. Chander, Megan and David Rawlins, and the two Wells brothers," I said.

"Rawlins?" she said. "They would be a good choice to check next."

"Why?"

"Megan Rawlins is Barbara Warren's daughter."

"That's a strange coincidence. I didn't know they were related."

"Both Megan and David work at Georgia State University. She's an associate professor and her husband is a Ph.D. They both work in the English department."

"How do you know that? You astonish me."

"When you're in politics it pays to remember names and information about your voters. That way if you see them, you can impress them with remembering their work or hobby or something." She smiled devilishly. "It's the personal touch."

"I'm hoping to finish the list tomorrow."

"You're doing just fine. No one expects you to find the murderer anyway." She was trying to make me feel better, but that made me feel worse. It was a vote of no confidence.

"You don't think I can do it?" I asked.

"I didn't say that." She changed her story. "I think you can do it. Anything is possible."

We sat in silence. I was depressed. Lindsey was right. How could I have ever thought I would be able to solve a murder? It had seemed so easy at first. Now it seemed complicated and never ending. I wondered if it would end. How would it end?

Later that evening I called the house of the girl down the street. She was the neighborhood babysitter. She confirmed that Mr. and Mrs. Hunt had gone out last Monday night. She claimed they came back around 1:00 A.M., but that she had stayed and went over the evening's activities because one of the kids had been sick. She said it was around 1:30 A.M. before she was paid and Mr. Hunt drove up the street to take her home. She said they usually came back early and that night was unusual, that's why she remembered it. I believed her. I also felt that I could safely clear the Hunt's from any wrongdoing. Since the police had pointed out the time of the murder to be around 2:00 A.M., one or both of the Hunt's would have been hard pressed to get to Ralph's shop from their house in time to pull the trigger. I made an index card for them and added it to my file.

Lindsey and I made a plan to get up around eight and drive down to Georgia State University (GSU) to talk with Megan and David Rawlins the next morning. As we were walking out the door, the phone rang. I debated about whether to let it ring or go back inside and pick it up. I dashed back inside to grab it. It was Dr. Chander's office. If I could be there at 9:30, they had an open appointment. The office was in town, but the roads would be clear of morning traffic. I was going to try and make it. Lindsey and I made a plan to meet for lunch and visit the Rawlins' later. I jumped into the car and took off.

I didn't usually speed, but this constituted an emergency. When else would I get another opportunity to see Dr. Chander? I was flying along. I zoomed right past a cop, but he didn't even look twice at me. I sighed with relief. My reaction was to slow down; it's the same even if I'm not speeding. He didn't turn to follow me either. I hated being followed by a police car, even if I wasn't doing anything wrong. I knew they were just doing their jobs, but they made me nervous.

It was 9:29 when I arrived at the physicians' complex. The offices were located on the fifth floor and it wasn't my lucky day, because the elevators were under repair. I ran up the stairs. I counted down each flight as I went. One more to go. I would probably regret this exercise the next day.

I arrived at the front desk of the doctor's office at 9:33, huffing and puffing. I was young; I was physically fit. Why did sprinting up the stairs still affect me this way?

"Are you OK?" the receptionist asked.

"I'm fine—" I panted, huge breaths between each word I spoke. "I'm here, for my appointment, 9:30."

"Sign in and have a seat."

I signed in dutifully.

"Is this your first time to see Dr. Chander?" she asked.

"Yes."

"I'll need you to fill these out." She handed me a clipboard.

I took a few minutes to complete the form. Then I ended up sitting there in the waiting room, which deserves the name, for forty-five minutes. Why bother having an appointment at all? I took the time to catch up on current events. I skimmed *TIME* and *Newsweek* for interesting articles.

At last, the nurse came out and called my name. She escorted me to the back to their mini lab center. There she recorded my weight and height. She took my temperature and blood pressure.

"What are you here for today?" she asked.

"A consultation."

"So, you don't need any blood work then." She made a note on my chart.

"No, no blood." I cringed at the thought of needles.

"Follow me." She led me through a maze of patient rooms. "Wait here."

She motioned inside the room. On the exam table was a paper gown which I had no intention of putting on. I entered and she shut the door. It was the typical exam room with the padded table, complete with plastic pillow and paper sheet. On the counter were jars of disinfectants, cotton swabs, and tongue depressors. There was a small sink and roll-around chair for the doctor.

I made myself comfortable on the exam table. I was tempted to lie down and take a short nap. Soothing music was playing over the intercom. I knew there would be another wait, so I spent the time reading the charts on the walls and the pamphlets of information. Dr. Chander was a doctor of internal medicine and gastroenterology. There were some disgusting-looking pictures of the inside of the large intestine insitu and another of an aggravated ulcer in someone's stomach. The pamphlets were not bestseller reading materials.

I heard Dr. Chander's pending arrival, the sound of his footsteps getting closer. I heard him take my chart out of the rack on the exam room door. He knocked lightly, then entered the room.

Samir Chander was a petite man of Indian descent. His name clearly gave him away. He had dark hair and eyes, but was fairly light skinned. His skin was a light brown, perhaps somewhere along the genetic line he'd had relatives of other ancestry, Hispanic, maybe?

He had good posture. His stature was straight and dignified. He was about forty years old, healthy and sturdy as I suppose a doctor should look. I wouldn't go to a doctor that looked weak and sick all the time. He wore glasses, a stethoscope, and a white lab coat over his suit. He approached me and shook my hand.

No telling where that hand has been I thought, reflecting on the posters and the type of work he did.

"Hello, Mr. Grey," he addressed me. There was no discernable accent.

He sat down in his roll-around chair opposite where I sat on the exam table.

"You need a consultation?" he asked. "What seems to be the problem?"

I knew he meant medical problem, but I launched into the reason for my visit.

"It's about Allan Puckett." I smiled ingratiatingly. "It seems the only way I can get to speak with you is to make an appointment."

"I'm sorry, I do not understand." He shook his head.

"I need to ask you some questions about Senator Puckett."

"Questions about what?"

"About the murder of Ralph Meeker," I said. "What do you know about him?"

"Which man do you refer to?"

"Ralph Meeker, what do you know about Ralph Meeker?" I clarified.

"Nothing. Nothing that I can tell *you*." The doctor folded his arms.

CHAPTER 17

"What do you mean you can't tell *me*?" I asked.

"There is strict confidentiality between a doctor and his patients."

"So you were his doctor?"

Dr. Chander nodded.

"You did know he was murdered, right?"

"Well, yes. I know that."

"Did you know he sold art?"

"Yes, such was his occupation." Dr. Chander furrowed his brow.

"Did you know he was selling stolen art and blackmailing people?"

"Yes. That was Senator Puckett's motive was for killing him. I have read all of this much in the paper."

"Well, Allan Puckett did not kill him. That's why I'm here."

"I feel that is a matter for the police, not you." Dr. Chander was unemotional.

Some doctors have a way of speaking that is completely factual with little compassion. Dr. Chander was one of them.

"You're right. It is a police matter. They refuse to investigate it, so I have been investigating on my own. I just want to talk to you and get some facts."

"You are a very precise, organized person, are you not, Mr. Grey?"

"Yes." I was taken by surprise at the change of topics and the accuracy of his description.

"Would you say you are a perfectionist?"

"Yes. How did you know?"

"I am a doctor. I pick up on these things," he said and shrugged. "You are a Type A personality."

"What does that mean?"

"It means you stress about everything and focus on every detail, therefore you are prone to ulcers and at a much greater risk of having a heart attack."

"Oh."

"When was the last time you had a physical?" he asked.

"I don't know. I don't get sick much," I explained. "Probably when I was in college."

"Great stars above!" was his expletive. "You are overdue. Stress can have tremendous negative affects on the body."

"But, I feel fine."

"We will just see about that." The way he said it scared me. "I'm going to step outside, and you are going to put on that gown."

His tone was authoritative, made me feel like I had to do as instructed. I figured I could use a checkup. I was going to be paying for the visit anyway, and Lindsey had been bugging me to go, so I put the gown on. When he returned, he washed his hands thoroughly then proceeded to check my heart and breathing with the stethoscope. It was cold and made my chest hair stand on end.

"When was the last time you ate?" he asked.

"Last night."

"Perfect," he exclaimed, pressing a nearby buzzer. "I'll get my nurse to come in to take blood."

"No, no!" I jumped up from the patient bench and backed away. "No needles." When the nurse came in, I felt like a preschool child avoiding a spanking by keeping the table between the nurse and me.

"When is the last time you had blood taken?" Dr. Chander asked.

"At least ten years."

"Techniques are much improved," the nurse said. "You will hardly feel it." She took my arm and coaxed me back to the table. "Trust me."

The nurse then proceeded to cut off my circulation with a huge rubber band. I couldn't watch as she swabbed the skin. I gritted my teeth as she punctured the skin. Soon the vial was filled. It wasn't too bad, but they had lied. It still hurt. She put on a cotton ball and bandage.

"Bring in the EKG machine, please," Dr. Chander instructed her as she left.

"Does anyone in your family have heart problems, cancer, or prostate problems?" Dr. Chander asked.

"No."

"What about kidney disease or gall stones?"

"Not that I'm aware of. That's not the kind of thing we talked about at family get-togethers. Besides all that was on my paperwork I filled out."

Dr. Chander ignored my implication that he could read it for himself and went right on with his questioning.

"Do you ever suffer from indigestion, reflux, or gas?"

"Not really." I felt this was getting a little personal.

"Do you ever experience hesitancy during urination?"

"No."

"How is your sex drive?" Dr. Chander asked, just as the nurse wheeled in the EKG test machine.

"Fine." I was astonished. Now that was it. I refused to answer any more of these personal questions.

"Are you getting enough fiber? Are you eating well?" Dr. Chander attached the wires and began running the test.

"I guess."

"Give me an idea of what you eat each day," the doctor ordered.

I told him about all the healthy foods I eat, but I must say I neglected to tell him about the fries, hamburgers, and pizzas. He made a few notes on my chart. *What is he writing? He's probably noting that I'm a pathetic liar and have no poker face.* He saw me straining to take a peek and he stopped writing. He disconnected the EKG monitor which the nurse took away.

"Test is good," he noted.

"Uh-um," I cleared my throat. "Anyhow, the questions I wanted to ask—"

"Open your mouth and say ahh."

"Ahhhh," I submitted.

"OK, go ahead."

"Did you ever buy any art from Ralph Meeker?" I asked as he examined my eyes and ears one by one.

"No. When is the last time you had an eye exam?"

I shrugged.

"I am going to give you the number for a friend of mine who is an ophthalmologist." Dr. Chander jotted down a few notes.

"You never bought anything?" I asked.

"No," he answered. "Take this cup to the bathroom. We need a urine specimen."

He practically shoved me down the hall. I was beginning to worry there might be something wrong with me the way he was acting.

It took me a minute to complete the task. It's difficult to go in a plastic cup on demand, knowing everyone outside is waiting on the result. However, I emerged triumphant. I was ushered back to the room. I will spare the details of what happened next, suffice it to say I spent a few uncomfortable and unnatural moments with the doctor. He then gave me instructions for getting my test results, a drug sample, and the eye doctor's phone number scribbled on a sheet of prescription paper.

"Doctor's orders," I commented.

"Is there anything else?" he asked.

"Yes. About Ralph Meeker—"

"Oh yes. I almost forgot. What else do you want to know?"

"You never bought a painting from him?" I asked.

"No. I have already told you, I bought nothing."

"I'm sorry to keep repeating myself. Your name was in Mr. Meeker's Rolodex, so I thought—"

"You thought I was a client. If you had done your research, you would have known that Ralph Meeker was obese. He had many health problems and many doctors. I am sure there were other doctors and phone numbers. What makes me so special?"

"You were at the Senator's dinner party. You are connected to both dead men. The other doctors aren't."

"So you are a man on a mission?"

"You could say that." I shrugged.

"And what is the mission exactly?"

"To find the person that killed both Allan Puckett and Ralph Meeker."

"So you are using lists of contacts of both men and checking on any matches."

"Right," I replied. This man was smart. He knew precisely what I was up to.

"You are here because my name appears as a contact for both. I am a suspect!?" His voice quavered indignantly.

"Well, yes."

"I am an upstanding citizen of this community. You are investigating me?" He pointed at himself. His eyebrows lowered with anger. "No wonder there isn't any police investigation. This is ludicrous."

I made the decision to go ahead and ask, knowing it would be the last straw. "Where were you after the campaign dinner party on the night of Ralph Meeker's murder?"

"None of your business. Get dressed." Then addressing the receptionist through a call box, "Get security."

Dr. Chander yelled at me with a good grasp of the English language, including most four-letter words and derogatory slang. For a moment I felt like I was an army recruit late for roll call as I struggled to pull on my jeans.

"How dare you come in here and accuse me in front of my colleagues and employees," he hollered and shoved me down the hall, not waiting for me to put on shoes or shirt.

We were near the front counter now. I hopped on one foot, putting on a sneaker as Dr. Chander half-chased me and half-pushed me out. As he came in for another shove, I turned sharply toward him and said, "Stop!"

He stumbled to a halt.

"I did not accuse you in front of anyone, we were alone in the room. You're the one creating a scene and I will leave if you will give me the opportunity," I insisted.

Dr. Chander remained still and quiet. I put on my other shoe. I was gathering the nerve to ask him for his alibi again. Dr. Chander must have read my mind, and I saw the frustration gathering in his brow.

"Get out already! I do not have to stand for this."

The door to the sitting area flung open, and to the astonishment of waiting patients, an armed security guard grabbed me by the elbow and escorted me out.

"You will be getting my bill!" Dr. Chander slammed the door behind us.

Once downstairs I was not so politely shoved out the front door. I stood half-dressed on the sidewalk, a little embarrassed, my ego deflated. I can't believe I let that little guy shove me around, and he didn't even answer my question. I made a move for the door. The guard stood in the doorway to bar any re-entry. He was not to be messed with.

It wasn't lunchtime yet, but I decided to find Lindsey and see if she still wanted to grab a bite to eat. She was at her office. I caught her in the hallway.

"You took a long time." She sounded exasperated. "Where have you been?"

"At Dr. Chander's office. I got a physical and then I got thrown out," I laughed. "What's the matter? We said we'd meet for lunch and it's not even noon yet."

"I need to talk to you. Remember that bartender we thought might have seen Allan the night of Ralph's murder?" she whispered as she ushered me into her office and shut the door.

"Yeah, the one who's been missing."

"Well, he's not missing anymore," she continued in hushed tones.

"They found him! That's great."

"No, it's not. He's dead."

CHAPTER 18

"Dead?" I was stunned. The words hit me like a ton of bricks. "How? When?" I asked.

"He was cut up by a knife or something. They found his body in a dumpster somewhere downtown near his apartment," she replied.

"Do they have a suspect? Do they know who did it?"

"They don't know," Lindsey said. "The bartender had been missing ever since he left the bar early Tuesday morning. They think someone ambushed him in his apartment that night. There was a struggle and the intruder stabbed him to death."

"What was the time of death?"

"It's not an exact science, but forensics thinks it could have been anytime from when he left the bar up to twenty-four hours later."

"So, do you think it's related?" I asked.

"I don't know." She shrugged. "But I'm worried about your, our safety."

"You think whoever killed Ralph and Allan had to kill the bartender to keep from being exposed?"

"I don't know. If that's the case, then we're in way over our heads," Lindsey replied.

"With the bartender dead, there is no way to know if Allan was at O'Malley's or not. If the bartender were alive, he might be able to report the murder-suicide was a cover-up."

"I'm going with you from now on," Lindsey declared.

"To investigate?" I asked.

She nodded.

"Why?"

"It would be a lot harder for the murderer to get rid of both of us than just you or me if we were alone. I think we should stick together. If both of us disappear or get killed, it would look very suspicious to the police, especially since they know what you've been up to."

"You're right. I'm already taking precautions," I assured her. "You don't need to worry about me."

"I still think we should stick together," she insisted.

"Did you call Charlotte at the FBI about the painting?" I deliberately changed the subject. In one way I would be glad to have Lindsey along for her company and intelligence. She could be useful. On the other hand, I felt it might cramp my fledgling detective style.

"Yes, but Charlotte's very busy. I doubt we'll hear back from her. I left her our home number just in case," Lindsey replied.

"Why wouldn't she call back?"

"They have more important cases right now. A stolen painting is only a drop in the bucket to them."

"You ready to go get something to eat and help me track down Megan Rawlins?" I asked. Style or no, I knew she wouldn't let me get away alone.

"As ready as I'll ever be." She grabbed her purse up and followed me out.

We stopped for lunch at the Varsity, a semi-tourist attraction and college eatery downtown. The food was extremely grease laden, but good. It was a heavy meal, not intended for dieters or those with cholesterol problems. While we were eating in the restaurant, a thunderstorm brewed outside. As we finished up it turned into a torrential downpour. We waited for the storm to break before venturing forth.

Our bellies full, we walked over the wet, steamy sidewalks to the general classroom building on the GSU campus. The temperature outside had dropped to a blissful 85 degrees, and there was a slight breeze. The school is in the heart of the city, where traffic is all too common and cheap parking is scarce. Once you have a good parking spot, it's best to leave your car there and walk or take the MARTA subway to wherever you need to go.

The first thing we had to do was to find someone who knew Professor Megan Rawlins or where her office might be located. We wandered until we ended up in the library. The librarian was busy, but helpful. She had a list of personnel and offices. I wrote down both the Professor's and the Doctor's office numbers. Once we had directions, Professor Megan Rawlins wasn't hard to find. She wasn't in her office, but her schedule was posted.

She was due back at 1:30 P.M. It was about ten after one, so we both sat down in the hall to wait. The building was one of the oldest on campus, converted from one thing or another to serve a purpose as the school had grown and aged. Industrial strength blue carpet ran the length of the hallway down to a tiny window. I felt like I were a student again waiting to be advised, only without the anxiety of exams and schedule arranging hanging over my head. I remembered spending many mornings at crucial times of the year waiting outside a teacher's door for a meeting.

It wasn't long before another student came along and took position outside a door halfway down the corridor from us. The student didn't seem affected to see two thirty-something adults waiting in the hall. GSU was mostly a commuter school and many older people went to school there to complete or achieve a degree they hadn't received in their younger years. Classes were offered year-round for all ages.

A teacher came down the hallway, acknowledged our presence with a nod, and unlocked the door across from our positions. I figured classes must have just let out and, depending on how far away her class was, Professor Rawlins should be along shortly. When she did arrive, she was loaded down with a satchel, books, and stacks of papers.

"Sorry I'm late," she apologized as she balanced her weight to let herself into the office.

The keys jingled as she unlocked the door. Lindsey and I stood up.

"I got held up in class with questions," she explained further.

She dropped all her things on the floor behind her desk. Her office was a mess. It looked like a bomb had exploded. There were bookshelves, but the books were strewn every which way, on the floor, stacked in corners. She desperately needed a filing cabinet. The table behind her was filled with folders and stacks of papers. A room like that would drive me insane.

"Come on in." She waved her arms emphatically and then began to rummage through the stuff on her desk.

I wasn't sure I wanted to go in. I might not ever get back out. She stood upright as I approached. I could see her resemblance to Barbara Warren. She had dark hair and eyes and rosy cheeks, but she was small, unlike her mother.

Lindsey hovered near the door. The disarray bothered her somewhat as well. I took a seat in the chair in front of the desk.

"I'm Paul Grey," I introduced myself.

"Now, you are not one of my students." She lifted a stack of papers to look beneath them. "Are you new for fall quarter?"

"Actually, no," I said. "I came to speak to you about the death of Ralph Meeker."

"Oh." She stopped rummaging. "I don't think we should discuss matters like that. That should be strictly for the police."

"Did you know him?"

"Yes, I knew him, but I'd rather not discuss it." She was abrupt.

"I'd be glad to meet you after school," I offered. "Just name when and where."

"Never and nowhere," she retorted. "I don't want to discuss it. Now kindly step out of my office."

"It's extremely important I discuss some things with you. Had you ever done any business with Ralph Meeker?" I didn't move from my seat.

"I told you. I will not discuss this."

"Did you know your mother confessed to Ralph Meeker's murder?"

"My mo—" She stopped. "You have no business disturbing my mother or anyone else. She isn't well. She didn't kill anyone and you know it. Now kindly remove yourself from this office."

"Do you know why she would confess like that? Perhaps she was trying to protect you? Or maybe you're trying to protect her?" I rattled off the questions.

"Frankly, I don't know my mother all that well. I don't know what she does or why and I really don't care."

I had hit a sore spot. I had Megan Rawlins talking. Now if I could just get her to answer some questions about her whereabouts.

"Doesn't sound like you two get along," I prodded. "Why is that? Would she still try to protect you or you her? Or are there bad enough feelings—"

"Just stop. Stop it right there." She slammed her fist down on the desk. A stack of uncontrolled papers slid to the floor, scattering like leaves before the wind. "You have to go."

"But we just got here," I protested.

She placed her hand on the phone. "I *will* call campus security."

"I'll go." I got up. I didn't want to start a habit of being thrown out of places all over town.

She followed me to the door. I turned in the hallway to face her. She stood in the doorway, one hand on the framing, one on the door handle.

"Just one more thing. Did you know Ralph Meeker was blackmailing your mother over a stolen painting?"

"GET OUT!" Megan slammed the door in my face. The rush of the air forced my eyes shut.

Lindsey was standing in the hallway. She turned to the left and chuckled, then began walking, and I followed.

"OK, now what?" Lindsey asked.

"Now we try Dr. David Rawlins," I said, my voice a little jittery. "Maybe he's more talkative."

Luckily his office wasn't on the same hall, so we didn't have to worry about Mrs. Rawlins seeing us. He was hunched over his desk, grading papers. He looked the part of a college Ph.D. He was in his thirties, much older than Megan was. He had the complete set of immaculately trimmed facial hair—beard, sideburns, and mustache—which made him extremely distinguished looking. I rapped on the door, my adrenaline in overdrive, prepared for another onslaught.

"Come in. Megan told me you'd be here." He didn't look up.

"What?" I was flabbergasted. The excitement rushed out of me like air out of a balloon. "How did you know?"

"She called me from her office. She said you would be over here next."

He looked up and grinned. "Are you a private investigator?"

"No. I'm just working on my own."

"I see." He rubbed his beard with his hand.

I stepped into the office. It was completely the opposite of Megan Rawlins' office. Everything had its own special place. The books were organized on the shelves. The papers were grouped, held together by bog black gym clips and stacked in individual stationery boxes on the table. I liked it.

"You may ask me anything you like. Megan and I have nothing to hide. I must apologize for the way she acts."

"That's OK."

"She's a lot like her mother." He pointed a finger at his head and twirled it in circles. "Crazy."

"Really?" I commented. "I—"

"She thinks everyone is out to get her. She's delusional, probably schizophrenic," he interrupted.

"Really?" I repeated. I wasn't totally disinterested in her personal problems. That kind of knowledge could actually help me.

"Yes, well anyway, how can I help you?" he asked.

"Tell me what you know about Ralph Meeker," I said.

"Megan's mother was seeing him for a while, but I think she had motives besides forming a relationship with the man. He owned an art shop over off Peachtree. That's about it."

"Have you ever been to the shop or met Ralph Meeker?"

"I met him once. I was with Megan and her mother, and we stopped by his shop. We met him then. We ended up buying a rug for our new house there, but Megan did that on her own."

"Do you remember what you did the night he was killed?"

"Not really. We were out of town. We didn't know what had happened until we got back a few days later."

"You were out of town?" I asked.

"Yes. It was our five-year anniversary, so we went to Mexico for the week."

"How great! Where did you stay?"

"The Plaza Hotel in Cancun."

"That's fabulous. I'd like to travel more often. But weren't you also supposed to be attending a campaign dinner for the Republican Party the night of the murder? You were listed as a guest. You couldn't be both places at the same time."

"We were in Cancun. We had bought the dinner tickets before we decided to go on vacation. The tickets had our names on them, but we gave them to two of our students majoring in politics. We thought it would be good for them to have the experience and make some contacts. As far as I know, they went."

"Who were the students?"

"Alicia and Mark."

"Do you have their last names and phone numbers?"

"I'm afraid I can't give you that information. It's confidential. I'm sorry." He shook his head in regret.

"Well, thanks anyway." I stood up and shook his hand. "You've been very helpful."

"No problem."

It felt like a very successful interview. I learned insanity runs in the family. I learned the Rawlins' whereabouts. I just needed to make a confirmation. A call or two would prove or disprove his story.

Back at Lindsey's office, I had her do some sleuthing for me. I had her call the social studies department of the college claiming to need the two students who has been at her dinner party to help her with her campaigning and for them to get in touch with her. She left her number for them to call.

With the ball in their court, she gathered up some files, and I walked her to her car, which was still parked there from that morning. She had some work to do at the courthouse.

"Promise me you won't do any work on your case while you're alone." She stared me down.

"Lin," I complained. "Come on. I can't stop now. I just have the two Wells brothers and I'm done with my list."

"Will there be other people around?" She put her hands on her hips.

"I'll make sure there are," I reassured her.

"OK," she conceded and gave me a kiss. "Be careful."

"I will."

Russell and Steven Wells were professional bodybuilders. They ran a gym and club called The Powerbuilders in Roswell in Fulton County. Upon arrival I glanced around to check the safety factor. The gym was densely populated. Satisfied, I asked to see the Wells brothers. They came to greet me. They were twins. I didn't know that going into it, so it took me by surprise when they appeared tanned and sweaty, smiling. They were both about my height, which is unusual. I didn't run into many people my size. And they were muscular; their arms and legs were so large that they looked painful. I couldn't stand to look at them—arms so big around they couldn't lay them down to their sides. They could have crushed me if they had so desired, except that I could have outrun them. Their large leg muscles hindered movement. Both men were handsome in the face. Their bodies shaved and oiled. Russell was wearing red and Steven was in purple; at first that was the only way I could tell them apart.

"What can we help you with?" Russell asked after I'd introduced myself and explained the reason for my visit.

"I wanted to know about Ralph Meeker," I said.

"I didn't know anything about him personally," Russell said and then addressing Steven, "Did you?"

"No," Steven replied.

"Did you know him professionally?" I inquired.

"We bought things for the gym there. He had some Oriental art, antiques, and artifacts," Steven said.

"We got a Samurai sword and some reed paper scrolls from him," Russell explained. "We love the Oriental culture."

"Do you know karate?" I asked purely to satisfy my own curiosity.

"Yes," both responded.

"Do you think any of the art you bought could have been stolen?" I asked.

"No, I think it came from some storage unit foreclosure place," Steven said.

"Do you remember the dinner party last Monday night?" I asked.

"Yes," Russell replied and Steven just nodded.

"Where did you go afterwards? Where were you both at about 2:00 A.M.?" I inquired.

"Two A.M.!" Steven shouted, "Who in the world would be anywhere except in their beds at 2:00 A.M.?

"I take it you were asleep," I responded.

"Yes, I was in bed."

"Me too. We went home afterwards. We usually go to bed around 10:00 P.M."

"Even that night?" I prodded.

"Oh, yes. We follow a very strict schedule in order to stay in shape. We are in bed by 10:00 P.M. every night," Russell responded. "And we get up every morning at 4:30."

"Four-thirty!" It was my turn to be surprised. "Can anyone support your statements?"

"I can," Steven said.

"No, I'm afraid it doesn't work that way," I explained. "I need someone other than yourselves to verify your story."

Both men set to thinking very hard.

"Oh! I know," Steven said. "The doorman at our apartment building knows. He's kind of a guard. He knows our schedule. He'd remember."

"That's a good idea," Russell congratulated him.

"Do you mind if I go talk to him?" I asked.

"No, go ahead," Steven said and Russell nodded in agreement.

I got directions to their apartment, thanked them for their time, and left. Despite their size and gruff looking exteriors, they had been extremely nice and accommodating, considering the circumstances of our meeting.

The apartments were only a short distance away. I was there within fifteen minutes time. I parked in the side lot. As I approached, the doorman looked up from his position from inside the building. Not recognizing me, he turned on the intercom by the numbered entry keypad.

"Which apartment?" he asked.

"None, actually," I replied. "I came to talk to you."

He frowned, probably suspicious of some sort of trick.

"What do you want?" he asked.

"Are you the doorman?" I inquired.

"Sort of. I'm retired," he explained. "I live in this first apartment, but I suffer from insomnia and boredom, so I usually spend my time out here. The neighborhood has gone downhill and the landlord cuts my rent in half if I sit out here and answer the bell. That way he doesn't have to pay for a guard."

"I see." A lengthy explanation for what I had anticipated to be a yes-or-no answer. "Would you say you see most everyone come and go around here?"

"Oh, yes. I see many people and things—things people probably don't want me to know. Like Mrs. Leary. She's married but having an affair with a young executive. And Mr. Burns—he smokes even though he told his wife he quit."

He stopped, seemingly waiting for me to respond.

"Aren't you going to buzz me in?" I asked.

"What's wrong? Can't talk from there?" He grinned from ear to ear. He was easily in his eighties. His entire bald head was wrinkled; his eyes had crows' feet, which led me to believe he was amicable. "I'm just kidding you, son. Come on in."

He pressed the buzzer. An obnoxious mixture of tones signaled I could open the door.

"Thanks." I went in a took a seat near him. "The Wells brothers sent me to see you. I'd like to know what time they usually come home."

"I don't think I should tell you that."

"They sent me here to talk to you," I explained.

"Now, son, how do I know that?"

"Good point, OK." I could understand his reluctance. "Then tell me this—if they came in at, say 10:00 P.M., would you know if they tried to leave?"

"Of course! I'm out here almost all the time. Nothin' better to do and insomnia and all. Did I tell you that already? Anyhow, I leave my door open even if I just go into my apartment for a second."

"Couldn't someone leave without being seen?" I asked.

"No. I'd see them. This is the only way out."

"Could someone sneak in or out if they wanted to?" I pressed again.

It's just one doorman he couldn't possibly see everyone all the time.

"I guess it's possible to get out if I was in the restroom or something, but I'd have to have heard someone coming in no matter what. That buzzer sounds even if you use a code. It's not a key door. I check every time there's a buzz in of any kind."

"There aren't any fire escapes? Or back doors from the stairs?" I asked.

"There are only stairs, no elevator. So I'd see them. And there are no fire escapes because it's only three stories. I guess they'd jump if they needed to."

"What floor do they live on?" I asked.

"The top," he answered.

"If someone did jump or climb down from the top, could they get back in without being seen?" I questioned.

"Only if they had a ladder or a rope or something. I'm pretty sure someone would notice that. Their apartment faces the street," he said. "In fact I'd see them through the glass."

"True." I thought about that for a minute. "What about the roof?"

"Nope, no access. It's locked and as far as I know only the management has a key to it. Why do you want to know all this? Are you a cop or something?" he inquired.

"No, I'm just doing my own investigation."

"What did they do? Did they rob a place or something?" He was getting excited.

"No, they didn't do anything. So, what time will they be here tonight?" I tried again.

"Probably around seven."

"Would you say they're usually here the same time almost every night?"

"Yes, most of the time."

"How long have they lived here?" I asked.

"About six years or so now, I think. A long time anyhow."

"In that time, how many times have they ever been later than seven?"

He thought for a few minutes, staring off into space. I thought maybe he'd forgotten the question or lost what he was trying to think about.

"I'd say at most ten times. I could count it on two hands for certain. They're usually here pretty regular," he said.

"What is the latest you've ever seen them get home?" I inquired.

This time he thought for only a few seconds.

"Around midnight. I remember it so well because it was Steven that was so late, and Russell was worried to death. They're never out that late. Turned out Steven was with a lady friend—" he winked "—if you get my drift. Russell was ready to call the police and start a manhunt when Steven showed up all sheepish."

"That helps a lot. You've been a great help," I said.

Satisfied with his participation he shook my hand as I departed. His eyes followed me to my car and watched me leave.

Russell and Steven Wells seemed clear. What could the strange, old doorman get out of lying for them?

CHAPTER 19

I made notes on the Wells brothers when I got home. I sat in the living room and contemplated calling Dr. Rawlins' hotel. Mr. and Mrs. Rawlins may not have attended the party, but they could have been in town and still had opportunity to commit the murder. I didn't know for sure if they had the motive.

I had to call the operator and get the number for international information. She gave me the number. The hotel was listed—a good sign. I dialed the hotel, but I immediately hung up. How would I get them to tell me about a guest? I needed a plan.

At that precise moment Lindsey arrived.

"How's it going?" she asked. "Everything OK?"

"I'm fine, but I've got something else you could help me with," I coaxed.

"Oh, no." She frowned.

"This is minor compared to everything else. I need to call the hotel to check on Dr. Rawlins' story, but I don't know how I'm going to get the information I need," I confessed.

"Why don't you just pretend to be Dr. Rawlins? Maybe you could get some information that way," she suggested.

It was simple enough that it might work.

"Good idea. I could say I lost something," I continued the thought.

I dialed the number. I wasn't sure what language they spoke in Cancun, since I'd never been there.

"Hello?" Thankfully, the man answered in English. "How may I help you?"

"This is David Rawlins. My wife and I stayed at your hotel last week."

"Yes, Mr. Rawlins, what can I do for you?"

"I seem to have lost my copy of our bill. I will need another copy with the dates of our stay and all charges."

"Certainly. We can do that. Should we mail this to you at home?" he asked.

"Umm." I was thinking. I had to think fast. "No."

"Where should we send it?"

"Umm. Do you have a fax machine?" I inquired.

"Of course we do, sir. You used it, remember?"

"Oh, yes. How could I forget?" I asked. "Will you fax it to me, please?"

"Certainly, sir. What is the fax number?"

I gave him the number to the fax at Lindsey's campaign office.

"We will do that right away, sir."

"How soon is right away?"

"I'm pulling it up on the computer and printing it right now. I'll fax it as soon as I get off the line."

"Fabulous. Thank you very much."

"Thank you for staying with us. We hope you'll come again soon." He sounded like a travel agent or a commercial.

When I hung up, I jumped up from my chair.

"Let's go!" I said triumphantly.

"Where are we going, Columbo?" she asked coyly.

"To your fax machine, of course."

"Of course, how silly of me." She rolled her eyes.

My heart was thumping all the way over to her campaign headquarters. The shopping center was all closed down for the night, except for the grocery store. The lights in her office were all on.

"Why do you leave the lights on?" I asked. "Doesn't that run up our bill?"

The rent was expensive enough. I was very cost conscious.

"Yes, but it's better this way," she explained. "This way the police can see in and make sure everything is OK."

In a heated campaign yard signs and flyers had ways of just disappearing from yards and posts. I guess she was worried someone might go after the whole stash. Or else she was worried about the person that wrote the nasty threats to her.

"Better safe than sorry." She unlocked the door and swept it open. The chime kicked in.

I raced to the fax machine. There it was in black and white. I was a little disappointed. The Rawlinses had been in Cancun from July 8th until the 15th. They were telling the truth. They had a solid alibi. I didn't want them to be lying, but I was desperate for a break. I needed a clue or a lead, or something!

"Look on the bright side," Lindsey said. "At least you have narrowed down the list. You know some people are innocent, and you still have some suspects that could be guilty."

"That's true; not everyone is turning up roses."

We drove home in silence. I was thinking. I was finished with my list. What next? When we got home, I made an index card with notes for the Rawlinses. Then I got all of my cards on each person from the list, laid them out on the coffee table, and sorted them into piles based on opportunity and the information I had gathered. I had three piles. I had Mark Benton, the Huntses, and the Rawlinses as suspects that had no opportunity to commit the murder and were clear. Then I had those that maybe had the opportunity and could be clear if I could confirm the alibi—Jolene and Michael Harris. And the last remaining three—Derek Leeds, Barbara Warren, and Dr. Samir Chander—had the opportunity or hadn't offered an alibi. Their statements left them open to suspicion of guilt.

At this point I took a major step and crossed the definite "no's" off the list. I was left with five suspects. There was still plenty of time left in the evening, so I decided to call Margie at the hotel. I hated to bother her, but I thought she might know something about these suspects.

"I'm worried," she professed.

"Me too," I replied, "but I'm working on it. I'll get it straight. Let me tell you what I've figured out so far."

I had my cards spread out on the table. I summarized my meeting with each person for her.

"I wanted to get your opinion on each person. Allan was their elected official for years. I thought maybe you might have had contact with them or know of contact Allan had," I said. "For instance, you might know a reason one of them would want to kill Allan. Maybe you know a piece of background information about them that could help me?"

There was a long pause at Margie's end; I imagined she was deep in thought. "I can't think of any reason any of them would want to kill him, but let's go over them all one at a time," she said.

"OK. Let's start with Jolene Harris."

"I've never met her or talked to her before," she said. "But her name is familiar because Allan knew her husband Michael, but only since they've been separated."

"Aren't they divorced?" I asked.

"I don't know. I don't like to stick my nose into all that stuff."

"All right. What about Michael Harris?" I asked.

"He knew Michael, but only since the last six months. He met him at a New Year's Eve party. Allan told me very little about him, just that he hates his wife, or ex-wife rather. They missed playing golf together at a celebrity tournament because Michael was in jail for assaulting someone at a baseball game. They had golfed together before in tournaments and that's all. Allan never did anything to him, with him, or for him. I know some other people in his company, but I don't know anything or anyone that could help."

"What about Barbara Warren?" I asked.

"I may have met her once at a function, but that would be it."

"OK. What about Dr. Samir Chander?"

"He's a well-respected doctor. I've heard others talk about him. I've never met him, but he used to call Allan on the phone all the time."

"About what?"

"Well, let me think. He would call about legislation or write letters. Allan was his Senator, and he knew how to use the system to help himself. Most people won't write or call, and then when things don't go their way they complain."

"What did he contact Allan about most recently?"

"It was something about the state healthcare system and the way it affected his practice," she replied.

"A law or bill? Did it affect his practice in a good way or bad?"

"I don't remember the specifics. I probably could if I really thought about it. Allan would talk to constituents and lobbyists all day long and then tell me all about it, but I can't remember every detail," she continued. "But whatever it was I'm sure it wouldn't have affected him enough to want revenge on Allan."

"Are you sure?" I asked. "Think hard. Try to remember all you can."

"Whatever it was, I'm positive the problem was resolved, and I think he was happy."

"You don't suppose any of the legislation was enough to make Dr. Chander angry enough to try to take revenge somehow?"

"No, definitely not."

"What about Derek Leeds?"

"Allan knew Derek's father. Derek was about five years old then. He hadn't seen the boy since. However, he was in the news a few years ago when he was arrested for drugs."

"That didn't have anything to do with Allan, did it?"

"No," she replied.

"Did anything happen when he was younger that he might have blamed Allan for?" I asked. "Would he even know who Allan was?"

"No, I don't think he knew who Allan was when he got older. Allan and his father had a falling out, but it didn't affect Derek at all. His father died later when he was in high school."

"How did his father die?"

"Heart attack, such a shock because he was very young."

"What about his mother?" I asked.

"Oh, she's still around, and she took great care of Derek. They got a lot of insurance money when his father died, at least five million. She used some of it to send him to an excellent art school. She bought a huge house in Alpharetta and bought him his art gallery—"

"So his gallery is paid for?" I interrupted.

"Oh, yes. He's got tons of money."

"He wouldn't need to work or have a business if he didn't want to?" I asked.

"No, not unless he wasted all his money away, but I don't think he has. He was too smart for that, even as a child. Does that help?" Margie asked, hopeful.

"Actually, yes," I said. "I think I'll arrange a meeting with my five suspects."

"Be careful," she urged. "I wouldn't want anything to happen to you because of me."

"I will, and don't worry," I reassured her again, "I'll figure this out yet."

I decided I should call all five suspects, just like in the movies, and invite them to meet with me. I could accuse them one by one, until hopefully someone would confess. I needed a public place to minimize any risk of harm. I settled on Denny's Restaurant. I called each of them and asked them to meet me for lunch at Denny's near Perimeter Mall at 11:00 A.M. I made no mention that it would be a group meeting. I told each of them that I knew who the killer was, but that I needed their assistance. I paid careful attention to each response. Most were surprised. Dr. Chander was annoyed that I was bothering him again. Barbara Warren was aloof. With the phone calls out of the way, I had the rest of the evening to make my plan of action.

That night as I tried to sleep, I couldn't sleep. Even after sex, which usually knocks me down for the count like a cold medicine, I couldn't sleep. I tried to watch some late-night television, hoping to drift off, but thoughts were spinning in my head. I shut the television off, hoping to let the dark and silence take me, but all I could hear was the shower still dripping. I thought I had fixed that.

A little after 3:00 A.M. I went to lie on the sofa and watch television. I was afraid I was keeping Lindsey from a comfortable night's sleep as I tossed and turned. As I lay on my back staring at the shadows on the ceiling, I thought I saw the shadow of a person rush past our living room window. It must have been my imagination, but I got up to look anyway. I cracked the curtains and peered out into the dark. The yard was illuminated by a streetlight a few houses away, but I didn't see anyone.

I decided to check out front. In my robe, quietly, in the darkened house, I made my way to a window that looked out at the street. Nothing. Satisfied, I decided to return to the bedroom. I turned off the television. When I got there, Lindsey was sitting up in the bed.

"I heard a noise," she said.

"It was just me," I said.

"No," she denied. "It was outside."

"I just looked out the front and back and there is nothing out—"

WHOOP, WHOOP, WHOOP. The house alarm went off.

"Oh my God!" Lindsey screamed. "I told you I heard something. Someone is trying to get in."

"It's OK." I grabbed her and the cordless phone from the bed stand and took her to the master bathroom. "The alarm is tied into the police emergency line. They'll send someone. Go ahead and call 911 anyway. You lock yourself in. I'm going to go look around."

"No, don't," she urged. "Just wait for the police."

"I'll be fine. It may be a false alarm," I yelled over the racket.

"Wait." She ran to the shower and grabbed her shaving razor. "Take these." She handed me the razor and a can of hairspray.

"OK." I took them from her.

She shut the bathroom door and locked it. I made my way from the bedroom, poised to pounce with hairspray and razor. The alarm continued to sound. All the neighbors were probably awake by now. I checked the spare bedrooms and the office before heading for the living room, which had the main alarm panel. I exited the safety of the hallway cautiously. I slowly crept across the room toward the alarm panel and shut it off.

"Freeze!" someone yelled.

My hands flew up automatically, and I halted dead in my tracks. My heart stopped for a second. The figure of a man was silhouetted in the doorway to the kitchen. He had a gun trained on me.

"Drop your weapon!" the man's voice commanded.

I dropped my "weapons" immediately. The razor clanked on the hardwood floor and the can of hairspray clattered and slowly rolled to a stop.

"Identify yourself!" came the command.

"I— I'm Paul Grey." My voice was trembling like my body. "I— I live here."

"Slowly," the man continued, "and I *mean slowly* lower your right hand and turn on the lights."

I did as instructed. The lights were blinding to me, but the police officer never blinked.

"OK, you can put your hands down," he said. "I recognize you from the police station."

"You scared me to death." I put my arms down. "I'd like to see some identification and how did you get in?"

"The front door was open when I arrived," he explained, showing me his police badge. "My partner and I were only a minute away when I got the call. I thought the intruder might still be in the house, but I guess he got scared off."

"So you think there was someone here?" I asked.

"Most definitely. The door was open and the alarm was activated. Good thing you had an alarm."

"Yes, good thing," was all I could say as I surveyed the room, making sure we were alone.

"You'll need to come down to the station tomorrow at noon to fill out a report," the officer instructed.

"Oh, I can't at noon," I said.

"Then come at your earliest convenience," he insisted.

"OK, I'll come in early."

"We're going to check your house now to make sure the intruder isn't still inside," he informed me. They checked all the customary places—closets, under the beds—and a few unusual places, like in the dryer. I had completely forgotten that Lindsey was still locked in the bathroom until the search reached our room.

"My wife's in there," I told them. "Lin, you okay?"

"Yes," she called and stuck her head out the door.

"OK, we'll patrol the neighborhood every hour for the rest of the night unless we get a call."

"All right."

"You have a good night, sir," the officer said as he was leaving. "Don't forget to reset your alarm in case the intruder tries to come back. My feeling is he's probably long gone."

"Yes, probably long gone," I said, although I wasn't so sure I agreed.

I reset the alarm and then went to get Lindsey.

"It's OK," I told her through the locked door. "The police have been here. You can come out."

She opened the door and peeped out. Seeing I was alone she came out.

"What was it?" she asked.

"False alarm," I reassured her.

"Paul, are you sure?" she asked. "I'm scared."

"I'm sure. The police searched the house and are keeping an eye out just in case, but it was a false alarm," I answered. It could have been the truth. No one actually saw an intruder. No need to worry her.

I didn't sleep any, but Lindsey curled up close. She told me my arms encircling her made her feel safe, and she dozed. First thing in the morning I went to the police station and filed a report. When I was finished, I went to Denny's.

I arrived early enough that I could watch the others' arrivals. I picked a round table that would seat eight near the front windows. I sat in a seat where I could have a clear view of the breakfast bar, front door, and parking lot. The first of my guests to arrive was Jolene Harris. She was driving a dark blue Volkswagen with a bashed-in front panel with a poor bondo and primer job. The windshield was cracked. When she got out, she gave the car door a heave and it slammed shut. Slinging her purse over her shoulder, she headed for the restaurant entrance.

As she was entering, a black BMW with tinted windows pulled into a parking place, followed by a Dodge van. A family of five got out of the van. Dr. Chander was in the BMW. From where I sat, I could see in the front windshield. He was talking on his cell phone. When he stepped out of the car, I noticed it had black leather seats, a color you mistakenly pick only once in the Atlanta heat. He adjusted his glasses before approaching. He was wearing a black suit and tie, a dark shirt, Mafia-like, totally out of place for the normal Denny's crowd.

At that moment Jolene arrived at the table. She was wearing a sleeveless, pink sundress, no bra, and sunglasses. She removed the glasses. She looked different from when I last saw her; she had her face done with heavy makeup.

"Hello," she said.

"Hello. Have a seat." I motioned to a chair.

As she sat, she glanced at the other six chairs, puzzled.

"I'm expecting some more people," I explained.

"I wasn't expecting anyone else," she said.

Dr. Chander approached.

"I'll introduce everyone once they've all arrived," I announced to them both.

"How many more people are we waiting on?" Dr. Chander asked impatiently. "I am a very busy man and on call this weekend. I cannot spend all day here."

"I'm surprised you even came. I expected the rest to show up, but not you," I replied. "Why did you?"

"What and miss all the fun? You said you needed my help. I am in the helping profession. However, I was not expecting a party." He indicated the empty seats as well. I looked at the clock on the wall at the front register. It was 10:55 A.M.

"I'm waiting on three more people. It's not eleven yet. If they aren't here by five after, we can start without them."

Satisfied, Chander introduced himself to Jolene, and they began to converse on superficial terms about work and weather. Several more vehicles arrived, none of which were my suspects. Then a cream-colored Chrysler arrived, driven by Derek Leeds. He got out and brushed himself off. He was in blue jeans and a tee-shirt, almost identical to what he had worn the other day.

The next arrival was Barbara Warren in a white four-door Ford. She looked around suspiciously as she walked into the restaurant. She and Derek came to the table at the same time.

It was 11:03. We were still missing Michael. Maybe I was wrong. Maybe Michael wouldn't show up. I went ahead and made introductions.

"Thank you all for coming," I said.

"Why did you call all of us here?" Derek asked.

"I wanted to discuss the murder of Ralph Meeker. Like I said on the phone, I believe I know who killed him—and it wasn't Senator Puckett."

CHAPTER 20

"You know who did it? This is exciting," Barbara Warren enthused. "I feel like I'm in an episode of 'Murder She Wrote'."

"I've already bought everyone a Grand Slam breakfast, unless you'd rather have something else," I offered.

Everyone accepted, except for Dr. Chander.

"I am a vegetarian," he explained. "And I do not have time for a luncheon."

He folded his arms across his chest and stared out the window. I looked, too. Into the parking lot came Michael Harris in his red Jeep. He flew around the corner without signaling. The car behind him blew its horn. Michael flipped them off. He whipped into a parking spot and bumped into the cement curb. His Jeep had a bicycle hooked on the back; its one wheel was spinning and spinning.

"That is a good way to get shot," Dr. Chander commented.

Everyone else murmured about my forthcoming revelation and hadn't noticed, but I nodded in agreement. I figured Michael must always drive like a maniac. Meanwhile, our food had arrived. We spent a few minutes getting our plates and glasses passed around and arranged.

"Whose plate is that?" Jolene asked about the extra plate. "Dr. Chander didn't want any."

"I guess it's mine," Michael Harris said as he approached the table.

Jolene dropped her fork upon seeing him.

"Hello, Michael." Her tone was steady and warning.

"Jolene." His acknowledgment was the same.

"What are you doing here?" she asked.

"He asked me to come," he answered, pointing at me.

"You didn't say anything about him being here," she accused.

"I'm sorry," I apologized. "I didn't even think about that. I just invited all the interested parties."

Barbara's attention flitted from one to the other, her mouth busily working on her eggs.

"I am not interested," Dr. Chander corrected.

"I'm interested in you," I explained. "Not necessarily the other way around."

Michael took one of the remaining two seats, farthest from Jolene, and began to eat.

"Well, then let's get started," I said.

"Yes, let us," Dr. Chander agreed, drumming his fingers impatiently.

I took a deep breath. Everyone's eyes were on me expectantly. I'd swear none of them were breathing they were so still. Everyone had stopped chewing. I know their hearts must have been thumping like mine.

"As you may have heard, Ralph Meeker was murdered and Senator Allan Puckett committed suicide," I began. "However, this is not the true story. The same person that killed Ralph Meeker also killed Allan Puckett and made it look like a suicide. I've been conducting an investigation of the crime to prove it. I have questioned all of you as suspects."

They exchanged suspicious glances, but I could see they all seemed to agree with me, more or less.

"What actually occurred was a double murder, and I have reasons to believe that each and every one of you had the motive and opportunity to kill Ralph Meeker and Allan Puckett—"

"I had no reason," Jolene interrupted.

"Me either," Derek complained.

"Let him finish, or we will be here all day," Dr. Chander commanded.

"Each of you had the motive and opportunity, but only one of you could have done it," I continued.

"I couldn't have done it," Jolene said. "I—"

"Let me rephrase that," I interrupted. "I was unable to confirm your alibi, if you even gave me one. Samir, Derek, and Barbara didn't give me any alibi. Jolene and Michael did, but I couldn't confirm them. I thought I'd give you all the opportunity to explain."

"I thought you said you already knew who did it," Derek said.

"I believe I do know, however, now is the time to speak up. I'm hoping this meeting will confirm my suspicions, and we can all expose the killer," I said, melodramatically; however, the facial expressions at the table indicated I probably overdid it.

"I told you who I was with," Jolene piped up. "Didn't he tell you we were together?"

"Jolene, you probably have someone lying for you. You always were a liar," Michael accused. "And a whore."

"You bastard!" She kicked at him under the table. "You're the one with the police rap sheet. You're such a hot head, you probably killed him!"

"Please watch the language—" I urged on deaf ears as the couple next to us got up and left the table, ushering their two young children away.

"I was on a plane," Michael defended, turning pleading eyes upon me.

"I couldn't get anyone to confirm anything for either one of you, beyond a doubt," I explained.

"Why didn't you tell me? I can get whatever information you need," Michael said.

"What about them?" Jolene pointed at the other three. "They don't have any alibi at all."

"I didn't have a motive." Derek chewed his food thoughtfully. "So I don't need an alibi."

"I thought we had everything straightened out, Paul." Barbara placed her hand on mine.

I laughed. "Hardly. You came to me and confessed to the crime."

That was a showstopper. Everyone else at the table stopped eating and bickering. I wondered what the other restaurant guests and the waitress thought of this conversation. Two women that looked like they had spent a lot of time with soap operas were staring on happily.

"She confessed?" Dr. Chander asked.

"Yes, but according to the police her facts of the murder were all wrong. Therefore, she is either entirely crazy or covering herself by pretending to be crazy," I said.

"For your information, I'm not either one, and I do have an alibi," Barbara snapped.

"What is it?" I asked.

"We've already discussed this and I don't believe I have any obligation to tell you anything beyond that," she huffed.

"Why don't you cut the crap and tell us who did it, if you know so much?" Michael said.

"All right, Michael. I believe it was you," I said. "You were being blackmailed. You planned to kill Ralph Meeker, so you hastily bought a plane ticket the night of the murder, but you were never on the plane. You were at Ralph's shop pulling the trigger," I surmised.

"I can get you the plane records. I bought that ticket weeks ago, and I had to use my identification to board the plane. No one else could use my ticket," Michael pleaded. "I didn't do it."

"Doctored, all doctored records, no doubt." Jolene rolled her eyes. "He has so many connections, he could frame the president for treason if he wanted to."

"Shut up, Jolene," he warned.

"You can't make me. You lost that privilege when you divorced me, you arrogant ass."

I heard gasps and "oohs" from the few remaining guests around us. "Please watch the swearing," I reminded.

"If he has proof of his whereabouts, then who could it be?" Dr. Chander addressed me, obviously ready to dispose of the notion that Michael had anything to do with the murders in order to get on with it.

"It must have been Jolene," I said. "She feels Ralph cheated her out of some money. She may have killed Ralph intending to frame Michael for it. In order to create her alibi, she had to get people to lie for her. A waiter from the party may be covering for her during the time she was at the shop killing Ralph, so her alibi is suspicious, questionable at best."

"That is absolutely ridiculous," she challenged. "If I wanted to do something to Michael, I'd kill him, or rip his foul tongue out, but not by murdering some moron art collector—"

"Rip my tongue out, huh? That's a little drastic," Michael interrupted.

Jolene rolled her eyes and continued, "If anything murdering that art guy would have helped Michael, and that's the last thing I'd ever do. You know I was with Johnny, and it can be proven if you'd do a little more research. Idiot," she muttered under her breath.

"You couldn't even give me the guy's last name," I said.

"But you found him, didn't you?" she asked.

"Yes, but he wouldn't tell me you were with him until he knew your story first. That made me suspicious."

"Assume she's telling the truth; where does that leave us?" Michael asked.

"Then it would have to be Derek," I concluded.

"This is stupid. You don't have squat on anyone," Derek defended himself. "You have no idea what you're talking about. You're just going around the table throwing out random accusations."

"You were being blackmailed," I said. "Although you deny it, I know it's true. You have no alibi. You seem to be doing very well financially even without Ralph. Maybe his death actually helped your finances?"

"You better check your facts or evidence or whatever you want to call it," Derek said with his mouth full of bacon. "I was *not* being blackmailed, I have money because of my family; therefore, I don't need an alibi. However, if you must know, I would have been at home asleep in the bed, alone."

Barbara Warren jumped in. "That's not too convincing."

"You should worry about your own story," he retorted. "You confessed. Why would you do that?"

"My guess is she wanted revenge," I said. "She wanted to get even with Ralph for blackmailing her and her daughter. After she murdered him, she placed herself above suspicion by framing Senator Puckett for the murder. She killed the Senator in a fake suicide so he couldn't deny the charges. When she confesses to the wrong crimes, everyone thinks she's crazy, but I'd say she's brilliant."

"Yeah, that is a good plot," Michael agreed.

"I didn't do it!" she objected. "I was trying to protect my daughter. I thought she did it."

"Why would you think that?" Jolene asked.

"I thought she killed him for me. She hated that I was involved with him, and she really is crazy. She would do something like that. She needs help." Barbara buried her face in her hands.

"You should be an actress." Derek clapped his hands together slowly in a display of feigned admiration.

"So why isn't her daughter here? Couldn't she be a suspect?" Jolene asked.

"No. She and her husband were out of the country at the time. I've checked it out," I said.

"Barbara, why don't you tell us where you were? What is your alibi?" Dr. Chander urged.

"I was at home," she cried.

"I thought you were at the grocery story?"

"I was. I was at the store then I went home."

"Were you alone?" Derek prodded.

"Yes," she sniffed.

"Oh, boo-hoo. Yeah, that's much more convincing than my story. What the hell is wrong with you people? You're all crazy." Derek threw his arms up in the air.

"If you're so smart, who do you think it was?" Jolene asked.

"Obviously, Dr. Chander; he's the only one left," Derek concluded.

"That is very possible," I agreed. "Dr. Chander, I believe you were being blackmailed as well, and you have no alibi either. You could have killed Ralph in his shop to put an end to the blackmail. You also have a bad temper, which I've seen for myself."

"What?" He stood up from the table. "Have you totally lost your mind? I hope you have a good lawyer, because I will sue you for libel. I have strict religious beliefs that would not allow me to do such a thing. It would bring bad karma."

"Obviously your religious beliefs don't affect your nasty temper," I said.

"What are you so surprised about, Doctor? You knew he was going to get around to you, didn't you? Let's face it, he's not going to get anywhere with this. He has no proof of anything he's said about any one of us." Michael stood up to leave, but eyed his plate full of food.

"You've got a police record; I'd say that makes you a prime suspect in my book," Derek said.

"You have a police record, too," I added.

"Who asked you?" Derek barked, his eyes flashing.

"And look at that temper!" Michael said.

"Watch it, asshole," Derek responded.

"Nobody calls me that unless they want to find out what I have a police record for," Michael warned.

"Arrogant asshole," Derek smirked.

More "ooohs" erupted from nearby eaters. The argument continued as I surveyed the room. We were attracting the attention of most of the restaurant now. Guests were caught between the urge of flight and an overwhelming desire to see how this would turn out. A waitress was going to approach, but changed her mind. At that precise moment Michael had heard enough. He lunged across the table at Derek, fork in hand. Plates and glasses scattered everywhere. An orange juice dumped into my lap. Everyone jumped up. Eggs and pancakes landed in the chairs and on the floor. It was a good thing the dishes were plastic or there would have been broken glass, too.

Dr. Chander intercepted the fork. The table tipped and collapsed under the weight of the three men in the struggle. Dr. Chander and I then wrestled Michael into submission on the floor.

Everyone in the restaurant was frozen in horror at the scene. Customers sat staring wide-eyed with forks halfway to their mouths. Some stopped mid-chew like some movie's special effect where the only people moving were the ones at my table. The room looked like a photograph, stuck in time. I was the first one to move. I approached the waitress. I apologized and told her we would all leave immediately and that I would pay for all the damages. I think she was scared of me, and she probably would have called the police if I hadn't been standing over her. I insisted on her taking my charge card number for the bill and any other costs. I apologized again as I left. I wanted everyone to get out of there before we all ended up with police records. Jolene, Derek, and Barbara had all left by the time I took care of the bill and got outside.

"Michael, you better go, quickly," I suggested.

"I will. I'll get the plane information for you," he assured me, brushing squished egg from his shirt. "I know I'm a hothead, but I never killed anyone."

I nodded. He sure did put on an excellent display of using a fork as a deadly weapon. He left in the same maniacal manner in which he had arrived. Dr. Chander was leaning against his car waiting for me.

"Mr. Grey," he said. "I understand your suspicions of me, and I have no alibi. However, I have too much respect for human life to take one. That is why I became a doctor in the first place. Life is a miracle that should never be wasted."

I nodded in agreement. Demoralized, he got into his car and drove away.

"That didn't go too well," I sighed as I drove home soaked with orange juice and sticky syrup. We gave new meaning to the Denny's Grand Slam breakfast. What on earth had I been thinking? Had I really thought that would work?

All was not lost. I had learned some valuable information from my conversation with Margie and my foray at Denny's. I added this information to each suspect's respective card. I learned that Michael and Derek both had police records. Michael and Jolene were adamant about my checking their alibis further. This convinced me they were innocent or putting on the biggest bluff hoping I wouldn't call it. If I dug further and they were lying, they'd be found out. If they were telling the truth, my efforts would only confirm it. At this point I felt I should focus on those suspects that didn't give me any new information—namely Barbara Warren, Samir Chander, and Derek Leeds. At this point no new information was just as important as getting information. It meant I still had suspects and hadn't followed every lead to its end.

At home I made notes of what type car each person drove. Derek and Barbara each drove a light-colored four-door similar to Allan's car. This could be good information no matter what else happened. I made a note that Barbara had made a false confession. It was significant because it meant she had lied to me.

Then I set to work on the coded papers from Meeker. I knew they contained the clues I needed if I could just figure them out. I knew it had everything to do with the blackmail. Sitting on the edge of the sofa in the living room and leaning over the coffee table, I went to work on them. All previous attempts to solve the code had failed, so I brainstormed and tried new methods.

I tried using the letters to unscramble them into words. Using all the letters to make words, I came up with gibberish. It didn't make any sense when I was finished.

Each letter could be the first letter of a word, a sort of mnemonic device. Using the first seven letters I came up with Students Usually Remember Never Walk On Elephants, but it could just as easily be Sleeping Under Rutabagas Normally Warms One's Ears. If that was the type of code it was, I'd never get it in a million years time. And how could Meeker ever have remembered it all?

Lindsey was in and out of the living room, doing chores. Then she worked in the office for a while and popped out every so often to check my progress.

"Any luck?" she would ask.

"No," was my depressed response.

She would give me a sympathetic look and return to her work.

I tried sounding each letter out phonetically, but soon gave up on that idea, too. Spelling the words backwards by reading from right to left and up and down the columns of letters and even diagonal revealed nothing. I tried finding words hidden in the page like a word find, but the words I found didn't have any significance. I found a whole list of three- and four-letter words that added up to nothing. That couldn't be it. I tried using every other, every third, and even every fourth letter. Still nothing.

I'd been working on it for two or three hours by then. The pages were spread all over the table. I had to keep changing my sitting positions to keep my legs from going to sleep. I was sitting on the floor, and I decided to try my original idea again—that it was a cryptogram. I tried that method again by substituting letters, but it still didn't work. Nothing worked. It was driving me nuts!

In exasperation and tiredness, I laid back on the carpet. I turned my head and looked at the floor. It was dirty and needed vacuuming already. The ceiling at least was cobweb free. I let out a sigh as I lay there discouraged. *What a waste of an afternoon,* had just entered my thoughts when miraculously, the solution came to me and the secret was revealed.

The columns of letters on each page all began in the same location on the paper. But lay one on top of another so they were slightly off center and the columns of the two pages would appear like one solid page of letters when held to the light. The first pairing didn't say anything but BTRAATAEASRMN, but I knew what to do.

I held onto the one page and swapped the second. I held each one of the other pages up to it in succession until—voila! The top line read: BARBARAWARREN. Or BARBARA WARREN once a space was added. I proceeded to match up the remaining pages until they were all stapled in complete sets and could be easily read. Then I held them up to the light and read them. It took a few minutes to get used to it because there were no spaces in the text; I had to do that mentally.

I realized Ralph Meeker had done his homework. He had compiled lists, or as I might call them, financial biographies of each of his intended victims. There were names I didn't recognize. I focused on the ones I knew. Each person's dossier detailed their annual income, dividends, saving and checking accounts, stocks, and net worth. All the numbers were spelled out in long form. An *8* would be *eight,* so it was more difficult to read and figure out. At the bottom was Meeker's calculation of how much money he could safely extract. He knew exactly how much each person could afford. Unfortunately for him, he had miscalculated what each person would stand for, because one of them had killed him.

There were pages for Mark Benton, Michael Harris, Allan Puckett, Samir Chander, Barbara Warren, and Stuart Newsome. There were no pages for Jolene Harris or Derek Leeds. I knew Mark Benton, Stuart Newsome, and probably Michael Harris were clear, so that left Samir Chander and

Barbara Warren as possible suspects. Now that was progress! Now I could really focus my search.

I was ecstatic, and I showed Lindsey. We both jumped around the living room in excitement.

"I think I'll call the police and tell them what I've found. Maybe they can keep an eye on those two," I suggested.

The police politely informed me they had already broken the code, two days after they had received it. It was confidential evidence containing several names, and they would need to confiscate my papers. I quickly took notes and copied as much as I could.

About an hour later Detective Jeffries arrived at our home. I invited him in.

"I heard you stirred up some trouble at Denny's today," he said, laughing.

"How did you know that? The hostess said she wouldn't call the police if we left," I said, astonished.

"She didn't. We've been tailing you to make sure you don't get into any trouble. There was an officer at the restaurant with you. That's one reason why you seemingly got away clean. He spoke to the manager."

"Tailing me? What are you doing tailing me? Don't you have criminals to catch? I can't believe you're following me around—" I wasn't just astonished; I was also angry.

"Yeah, why aren't you trying to find the person that killed my father?" Lindsey demanded.

"Listen, Mr. Grey, we got a report that you illegally searched a person's place of business, and so we've started an investigation. You, sir, don't have a license to go parading around town asking people questions and causing disturbances. We're just trying to prevent trouble. We know you're not a criminal which is why I'm not going to arrest you," he continued with a smile. "Although I'm sure if I questioned the guard at Mr. Newsome's range he'd turn you over in a flash. I don't intend to press charges. Mr. Newsome won't either. Just turn over the papers you have without a fuss," he said.

"No problem. I've already read them, so I don't need them anymore," I retorted.

"And keep out of trouble. You've done enough already. Let us check up on the two names you gave us. We'll let you know how it goes, OK?"

Lindsey nudged me. I could see in her eyes she was ready for me to give up my pet project.

"OK." I gave in.

"If you'll excuse me, I've got to get back," he said and headed out. On the front walk he turned to me and said, "Remember, Big Brother is watching!"

"I will." I shut the door and then turned out the lights.

Lindsey and I retired for the night, but not before she berated me about my careless, law-breaking sleuthing spree. I planned to get up early and go jogging. I didn't do that very often, except when I needed to think and clear my head. I needed to figure out what I was going to do, if anything. I had all but promised to give up on the case. Even if I wanted to pursue it, I hadn't a clue what to do next.

I didn't get up early though, because I was plagued by bad dreams all night. They weren't the someone-is-chasing-you-and-you-can't-run type, they were more the repetitive stupid kind where you've forgotten to wear clothes to work, or you forgot you were still in school and today is exam day. Because of this, I woke up later than I had planned. It was about 10:30 when I got up to shower and dress.

"I can't believe you're going to shower and then go to the park to run and sweat." Lindsey shook her head in disbelief. "And I probably shouldn't tell you this, but my friend Charlotte called this morning."

"Which friend? The one at the FBI?" I asked, trying not to show my eagerness.

"Yes. She said that painting you asked about is stolen property. It was stolen five years ago from a private collection. It's been missing ever since."

"Really? That long ago? That's interesting," I pondered.

"Why is that interesting?" she asked, her curiosity aroused now.

"I'm not really sure what it means, yet," I said. "I'm going to go run. It'll help me think. I'll talk to you when I get back."

"How long do you think you'll be?" she asked.

"About two hours," I said and gave her a kiss.

"Two hours? You better take some water or something; it's already hot outside," she warned.

"I'll stop at the gas station and get something," I promised.

She followed me to the front door.

"You haven't been running in a while; don't over do it," she called from the doorway. She always worried too much.

"I won't." I started the car and turned on the air.

I reached into the backseat for the few fast food bags.

"I'll take that inside," Lindsey offered as I walked up the sidewalk, trash in my hand. As I approached her, I heard the familiar clicking noise of the engine cooling fan coming on—just one CLICK, not too loud. And in the next two seconds my world was torn apart.

CHAPTER 21

There wasn't time to scream, or blink, or duck, or run. I was propelled forward by a hot blast, stumbling on my feet, until I tripped and fell into a somersault. I felt things ripping at my legs and back. I landed somehow sitting upright, legs apart, on the other side of the shrubbery. I had a burning sensation on my arms and legs. My first instinct was to check that all my parts were still there. I could see everything, but I was bleeding, a lot. It was enough blood that I wondered if I was alive or not.

My second instinct was to make sure Lindsey was okay. I tried to get up, but I couldn't. I tried to turn, but I couldn't. Panic set in. I was sure I had snapped my neck or back. I had no feeling in my legs. I concentrated on my feet. I couldn't make either one of them wiggle. My legs were bleeding. My blood was mixing with the dirt and grass. Scraps of paper littered the yard. I sat there not moving. I tried to speak, but the sounds that came out were not words; they were unearthly sounding. My heart was racing—that I could feel. *I need to stay calm.* Help would be coming. An explosion like that would be noticed in our quiet neighborhood.

Some feeling was returning to my legs. They were tingly and painful, like when they've been asleep for a long time and the circulation is returning. I could move my head a little. I turned to look at my car—what was left of my car.

It was burning. The metal frame was contorted like the strange metal sculptures at Derek Leeds' studio. The glass had shattered out of all the windows and lay glittering on the driveway like dark crystals. The glass in the front window was fractured and hanging together tenuously. The seats were still intact, but they were burning along with the flooring and paint. A billow of black smoke drifted from the car like a huge thundercloud, raining down bits of cinder and floating ash. I'm sure the flames were snapping and crackling, but I couldn't hear anything except a ringing in my ears.

Enough feeling returned in my legs and arms that I turned onto my stomach. I couldn't stand, but I could crawl, slowly, the dirt and grass rubbing into my legs with each painful movement. I crawled through the shrubs to the front stairs. I couldn't make myself go up. I could see Lindsey's foot and ankle in the doorway. She wasn't moving.

"Lindsey," I tried to call to her, but the sounds came out all wrong.

"Paul?" she called. I could hear sounds faintly now.

"Are you OK?" I asked, but the only word that came out was "OK."

"I'm afraid to move," she said. She could talk better than I could, that had to be a good sign. "I hear sirens. Just lay still."

"Uh-huh." I reached up to try to touch her ankle, but I couldn't reach. I was as close as I could get. My arms could go no further. I lay shaking and bleeding, waiting for someone to come.

I remember the flashing lights when help did arrive. I could look up from where I was sprawled and see the reflections on the windows of the house. Two windows were shattered, one was intact. I could hear mumbled voices from all around as they lifted me onto a stretcher and immobilized me. I didn't like the feeling of being strapped down. I tried to turn my head to look for Lindsey, but I couldn't. As they lifted me in the ambulance, I heard an EMT reassure me they had Lindsey taken care of.

Immediately inside, they slammed the doors; the siren rang out and they stuck me with a needle. I don't know what it was, but it was effective. My eyes shut.

I remember operating room lights. I opened my eyes to see four or five faces hovering over me. The lights were very bright and I tried to lift my arm to shield my eyes, but I was still immobilized.

"Patient is coming around," a nurse warned.

I heard a doctor command an additional dose of medication. His voice was low and long and distorted. Then I faded out again.

Next thing I knew I woke up in a hospital room, alone. I had no idea what time it was or what day it was. It was dark outside, but so bright inside I wondered for a minute if I was in Heaven, except my pain told me otherwise. I was sore all over my body, aching with each throbbing heartbeat.

I struggled to sit up in the bed. I wanted to get out of the bed, but I was connected to wires and machines that prohibited much movement. I itemized the equipment—oxygen, blood pressure and pulse, and an IV. Nothing which appeared to be life sustaining. I was no longer in my running clothes. I was in a loose-fitting, blue hospital gown. Again, my first instinct was to be sure that all my parts were still in place. Everything was intact—a relief. However, I realized right away I had lots of stitches and bandages on the backs of my arms and legs. Areas on my chest had been shaved to accommodate sensors. Some hair had been shaved off the back of my head. At my age, I hoped it would grow back.

I looked around the room. I'd never in my life been in a hospital room.

I know that is unusual, but I never had the need or opportunity before. It had a potent, disinfectant smell, like alcohol. Everything in the room, including the walls, fixtures, and chairs, were a tan, putty color, except for the sheets, which were a bright, sterile white. A television hung from the ceiling near the wall across from the bed. There were two open doors, one to the bathroom and one to the hallway. I could hear voices carrying down the hall, but I couldn't see anyone. There was one window, but I couldn't see out because of the glare. Next to the bed were the light switch, the television remote, and an intercom with a call button.

Then I realized there was a second bed—empty. Where was Lindsey? Was she OK? I pushed the call button. No response, so I pressed again and again. *Why won't they answer the damn buzzer?* There had to be a nurse around somewhere. I could hear them a moment ago in the hall. I pressed the call button and held it. *A doctor is coming. Is he coming for me? Yes? What will he say? Is she dead? No, he walks past my doorway. Where is the nurse? I could be dying here. Please, answer the buzzer.* Finally, in desperation I yanked my own heart monitor. A series of panicky alarms sounded. Nurses appeared out of nowhere. Now I would know.

"Where is my wife?" my words garbled. I hadn't realized I couldn't speak.

They understood. "She's down the hall, sir," came the reply as they readjusted my wires.

"I want to see her," I said and gestured.

"I'll get her for you. She's been treated and released. She's been talking with the police."

I lay back in the bed to wait. A few moments later, Lindsey appeared. She hurried over to me and wrapped her arms around me tight. It hurt, but I didn't complain. I'd have rather had every moment of that painful embrace than to never have her again.

"I'm sorry I wasn't here when you woke up," she cried. "You're going to be all right."

I nodded and ran my hand through her hair. *I'm not worried about me, I'm worried about you* was the look in my eyes and she read my mind.

She smiled through her tears. "I'm fine. I have a little burn on my face, like a sunburn, and I had the breath knocked out of me. The police said I was lucky I was in the doorway. I was mostly protected from the blast. It just knocked me over."

Her cheeks were rosy pink.

"Hurt?" I asked as I touched her cheek softly.

"No." She shook her head. "Do you hurt?"

I nodded.

"I'll get the nurse to give you something," she said.

"Got to get out of here." I found if I whispered I could get more words to come out.

"We can't. They want to keep you for a full twenty-four hours, maybe even forty-eight, for observation, just to be sure," she explained.

I sat up in agitation and shook my head. "No. Can't stay here."

"They just want to make sure you're OK," she repeated.

"Fine." I struggled to really say the words. "I'm fine. We need to get out."

"You need to rest. You can't even talk." She pushed me gently back onto the bed. Then, again reading my mind, she continued, "The police are investigating. They'll find out who did it. You're safe here and so am I. You need to rest."

I wasn't in the mood to argue with her. I just wanted to leave. I began pulling off the heart monitors again as the nurse was reapplying them. She tried to restrain me.

"Oh, Christ!" the nurse exclaimed as she tried to sit me back down. "You're going to mess up the IV. Stop it."

"Not staying here." I resisted her attempts although the IV did hurt my hand with each movement. "Someone tried kill me."

"Sir, sit down before you hurt yourself," she commanded.

Lindsey had backed up out of the way. Another nurse had come in to assist in calming me, the unruly patient that I was.

"Lindsey," I pleaded as the room began to spiral.

I turned suspiciously to the nurse. In her hand she had an empty syringe, which she had just emptied into my IV line. About three seconds later, I had to lie down. I had no choice; all my muscles were giving out on me.

"You're not going anywhere," the nurse said, laying me back.

I looked at Lindsey. The room was fading in and out, still slightly spinning.

"I'm staying here with you," she came back to the bedside and took my hand. "The police will want to talk to you tomorrow."

Whatever it was the nurse sent coursing through my veins didn't take long to have an effect. It was like being possessed. I had no choice but to drift off to sleep, no matter how much I wanted to go, I physically couldn't. Thoughts I had no control over moved in and out of my consciousness. How could there be a bomb in my car? There is a bug on the ceiling. What about Derek? His Manet was stolen five years ago, so long ago. It couldn't be related to Ralph Meeker. I really could use something to eat, a sandwich. I need the police to check something for me.

"Lindsey," I called. My voice didn't sound like my voice. In fact I wasn't really sure I'd actually said anything.

"What?" she asked.

"Check Allan's painting."

"What do you mean?" she asked. She was leaning close to my lips. I must have been whispering, but inside my head it sounded like I was shouting.

"When it was stolen—anything strange."

"Why?" she asked.

"Just do it," I said.

"What do you mean strange?" she asked.

I couldn't talk anymore. *I wonder what that blue spot is on the ceiling. Sleep.* Once I got over the strange thoughts and got to sleep, it was the most restful night I'd had in weeks. I slept until almost noon. Lindsey woke me. She'd gone home to get some fresh clothes for me to change into. They had torn my running clothes off in order to stitch me up.

"You went home?" I asked, not angry, but scared for her safety.

"Detective Jeffries took me," she said. "He's waiting downstairs to take us to the station."

"Don't go anywhere alone," I said.

"OK, I won't." She patted me on the shoulder.

"What time do I get out of here?" I asked impatiently as I dressed.

Sometime during the night, my IV had been removed and the machines unhooked and removed. I was still sore, mostly my arms. The stitches in my legs pulled tight as I lifted each leg to put on my pants.

"Two," she said. "But if we get ready now, they'll probably let you go early."

"Let's go then," I said.

"I'll go get the nurse. You'll need a wheelchair." Anticipating my response, she added, "It's a rule."

She returned with a nurse and chair.

"I tell you what," I said, addressing the nurse, "that's some powerful painkiller or sedative you gave me last night. Best night's sleep in years. Can I get some of that to go?"

She gave me a disapproving look—no sense of humor. "No. The doctor has prescribed something for you."

I sat obediently in the wheelchair as they took me out. Detective Jeffries was waiting. He took us directly to the station to fill out yet another report.

We sat in the same room that was used before, only it was Lindsey and I, Detective Jeffries, and now an agent of the FBI present.

"I need you to tell me the names of every person you may have made angry in the last two weeks, whether you think it's relevant or not," Detective Jeffries insisted.

"That's a lot," I said. "I guess it would include everyone at the Denny's incident."

"And?"

"And Mark Benton, um, Megan Rawlins, and Stuart Newsome."

"Stuart Newsome?" Detective Jeffries asked.

"Yes."

"Who was at Denny's with you?" he asked.

"Barbara Warren, Jolene and Michael Harris, Derek Leeds, and Dr. Samir Chander." I watched as both the police detective and the FBI agent jotted down the list.

"Do you think you made any of them mad enough to want to hurt or scare you?" Detective Jeffries asked.

"Probably. One of them killed Ralph Meeker and Allan Puckett," I said factually.

"Do you know which one?" he asked.

"If I knew that I'd have told you a long time ago!" I threw my arms up.

"Would you?" he paused, pen in hand, one eyebrow raised. "You wouldn't be saving the information for the opportunity for a little fame or fortune?"

"What are you implying?"

"You wouldn't try to blackmail the killer? Or try to reveal him or her in front of the media or sell the rights to the story, something like that? Something spectacular to clinch your wife's election?"

"No." I shook my head. "I just want to help Margie and clear Allan's good name so my wife can win her election fair and square."

"OK. I thought so, but you understand I have to ask."

"Yes."

"Tell me what you remember about the explosion of the bomb."

"Well, I'd started the car to let the inside cool off, then I cleaned out the trash and was walking over to Lindsey when it blew up."

"What happened right before and right after it blew up?" he asked.

"I don't know."

"Did you see anyone or hear anything?"

"No. I didn't see anyone, but the cooling fan came on."

"Why did you let the car cool off? Why didn't you get in right away?" he asked.

"I always cool it off. I hate being hot. I stick to the seats."

"What are you doing while it cools?"

"Usually I just stand nearby or something."

"I'm going to tell you what we've discovered about the bomb so far," Detective Jeffries said. "It was hooked to your exhaust pipes near the gas tank. It wasn't very big. Only large enough to detonate into your gas tank and then cause a larger explosion. Luckily there wasn't but a gallon or two of gas in your tank. We believe it was held on by Velcro straps, but tests on that aren't done yet. It was a temperature-sensitive detonator."

"What does that mean?"

"It means that it wouldn't go off until the car exhaust pipes reached a certain temperature. When they got hot enough, they caused the detonation."

"Why would someone do that? Why wouldn't they just hook it up to go off when I started it?" I asked.

"Two possibilities. One: they couldn't get into the ignition and wiring to be able to hook it up that way, so this was easier and quicker, and if the tank was full it would still either severely hurt you or kill you. Or two: because they knew you were almost on empty or wouldn't be in the car when it went off, they just wanted to scare you. I have the feeling the culprit fits the first description better."

"I agree. Someone wants me dead or at the least incapacitated."

"This person doesn't know your habits. He or she hasn't been stalking you. It's probably the same person that tried to get into your house but didn't know you had an alarm system. If he'd been watching you, he would have known that."

"Do you think it's the person who called us with the threat?" I asked.

"It could be." Detective Jeffries shrugged. "I'm sure the whole chain of events from phone call to the bomb were directly related to your prying and questioning."

"I can't remember whom I had talked to by the time I got the phone threat." I rubbed my forehead.

"It doesn't matter. If someone knew you were sleuthing around, they might have felt threatened before you ever even met them."

"Like Stuart Newsome," I suggested.

Detective Jeffries checked his list of names and nodded. "I really should have put a stop to your activities a long time ago."

"I wouldn't have listened," I insisted.

"I warned you this type of questioning behavior would be risky." He pointed a finger at me.

"I know, but I never listen to anyone. It's one of my faults," I confessed. *I have to learn on my own. I thought I was going to figure the whole thing out like some television sleuth. I never thought it would come to this.*

"Well, it's too late now. No reason to dwell on 'I told you so'," Detective Jeffries said. "This is what we're going to do. We're going to post a car outside your house *all night*. We're going to find out what the components of the bomb were and check to see if any of those angry people you mentioned have bought any of it in the last two weeks. Then we'll go from there. You are not to pursue the topic on your own. Is that clear?"

"So this proves the case is a double murder. Someone killed both Ralph Meeker and Allan Puckett." I avoided an answer to the directive.

"What do you mean?"

"The real killer has tried to kill me. It couldn't have been Allan; he's dead," I said.

"It may not be the 'killer' as you put it. It may be someone you angered. And I wouldn't be doing my job if I didn't check up on you."

"What do you mean?" I was shocked.

The FBI man, a silent witness until then, stepped forward to reply. "You may have set the bomb yourself as a desperate attempt to clear the Senator's name and help his wife claim the insurance check, not to mention how it helps your wife's political game. That sort of thing is not uncommon, never quite this extreme, but not uncommon."

"I can't believe it. You're going to investigate me?"

"We have to. It doesn't mean we want to," Detective Jeffries assured me. "I have instincts, too, Mr. Grey. We talked about that before. Just remember that my instincts are tempered by my duty."

"I understand," I said, although I really didn't. "Did you check on Allan's painting? Anything strange about it?"

"It's a replica of a painting that was stolen several years ago," he replied.

"What do you mean a replica?" I asked.

"We didn't know at first. We thought it was an original, but when we tested it, we found out it was a fake. We gave it to an art expert just to be sure. He said it was definitely a fake, but it was very good."

"How could he tell?" I asked.

"They used x-rays to determine the chemical compounds in the paint. Barium sulfide and titanium dioxide were both present, and they weren't around when that painter painted," the nameless agent replied.

"Also carbon dating proves the canvas had been artificially aged." Detective Jeffries handed me a report.

"How do you age a canvas?" I looked at the FBI agent.

"Heat it for an extended time at a low temperature," the agent replied.

"How strange, a fake. What a waste, blackmail and murder over a fake." After a few seconds I added, "Doesn't that help? If it was fake, why would Allan Puckett have paid anyone blackmail?"

"He would pay it if he thought it was an original. It probably never occurred to him that it might not be real," Detective Jeffries replied.

"Oh. Well I guess you have things covered then." I shrugged.

"Yes," he responded.

"May we go?" I felt a little testy, a little angry.

"Yes, you're free to go anytime."

Lindsey and I left. I didn't say anything about Derek Leeds' Manet or Mark Benton's Metcalf or any of the other paintings I suspected were out there that should have been tested, too. I don't know why I held back the information—stupidity maybe?

CHAPTER 22

It was about quarter till three when the police dropped us off at home. They inspected the house and Lindsey's car, which had also been parked in the driveway. "We'll be right outside, if you need us," the one officer said.

His voice was deep and gravelly. He was a big, muscular man with charcoal skin and a big bald head. He carried a large sidearm. I was glad he was protecting us. I had no fear while he was on watch.

I finally had time to think and think clearly. All the pieces in the puzzle now seemed to be creating a picture of Derek Leeds. Lindsey, although not happy with my persistence, had to agree.

"So Derek had a stolen Manet, yet he wasn't being blackmailed. Why?" she asked.

"Probably because he was 'Rembrandt', the fence that Barbara Warren told me about. If Derek was stealing or selling the pictures, then Ralph would never know what Derek kept for himself. Ralph would only know about the ones that Derek gave him to sell to others." I paced the floor.

"Derek has the right cover and background, too. He would have a legitimate reason to go to museums and art shows where he could decide what to nab." Lindsey flopped onto the sofa, pulled her knees up to her chest, and wrapped her arms around them to hold them there.

"That part all makes sense, but what about Allan's painting turning out to be a fake? Is it possible they were all fakes?"

"Maybe. If Ralph found out all the paintings were fake, would that be enough reason for Derek to kill him?" Lindsey cradled her chin in the groove between her knees.

"Would he care?" I shrugged. "I mean, as long as people paid the blackmail, would Ralph care whether the paintings were fake or not?"

"Probably not. Maybe the police should test the other paintings—"

"Not yet. I want to think on this some more." I sat beside her and rubbed my forehead. "I want to get a clearer idea of what was going on first."

"But—"

"Lin," I said and patted her hand, "just let me think about it through dinner."

Lindsey didn't reply. She threw her legs out from under her and sped into the kitchen. I followed, my legs stiff and sore; I wasn't able to keep up too well.

"Don't be mad, please." I approached as she poured herself a glass of water.

"I'm not mad." She thumped the cup down, spilling some. "I'm just worried about you. On one hand I think you need to pursue it—for yourself, for me, for Margie. We seem to be in danger and there isn't much the police can do except keep us prisoners in our own home." She lifted the kitchen curtain and peered at the officer's car parked on the curbside. "On the other hand—" she dropped the curtain, letting it fall back into place, "it may be safer to quit now, cut our losses. It's almost become an obsession with you, where you don't seem to care about the danger, but I do."

"It is not an obsession. I do care about the danger—"

"Paul, I can't lose you." She sank into a chair. "If something were to happen— "

"Quitting now isn't the answer." I stood beside her and ran my fingers through her hair. "The threat of danger, that won't go away until the person is caught."

She nodded but wouldn't raise her eyes to look at me. "OK, think on it through dinner, and if you don't have a clue by the end, promise me you'll stop."

"I promise." I lifted her chin and tenderly kissed her cheek.

She reached her arms around me and held me. I could have used her input, but it was better if I worked on my own now. I returned to the living room to hash out the case. It was possible that Allan's painting being a fake was a fluke and neither Ralph nor Derek knew it. Maybe Derek stole it, thinking it was real when in actuality it was a decoy. That still didn't tell me why Derek would have killed Ralph and even less why Derek would have stolen these paintings up to five years ago.

I needed a fresh perspective. When you try to think of something, sometimes it just won't come up into your memory. The harder you try to remember, the farther into the dark recess of your mind the answer falls. I felt certain the answers would come to me, if I could just relax. I took out two pieces of paper and wrote on one, "Things I Know." On the other I wrote, "Things I Don't Know." Then I began to fill them out.

THINGS I DON'T KNOW

Who is Rembrandt? Is Derek the thief that supplied Ralph with paintings? How did Derek get his Manet? Did Derek kill Ralph and why?

THINGS I KNOW

Derek was not being watched the night the bomb was planted. Derek was one of the five suspects at Denny's because he had no alibi. He is a painter that has a stolen Manet. Allan's painting was from Ralph, but it was a fake. The real Degas was stolen a couple of years ago.

There was enough information that I was sure Ralph and Derek worked together, but it was all guesswork or could be explained as circumstantial. I needed something solid.

I set the lists aside while we ate supper. I didn't talk much; I was too busy thinking. I had a deadline. I ate slowly.

"Are you OK?" Lindsey asked.

"Yeah, I'm fine." I fiddled with my mashed potatoes.

"Did you figure anything out yet? I know you've been working on some idea."

"No, nothing."

"You're just full of talk tonight. I'm getting the impression you're mad at me because you haven't said diddly since we started dinner." She plunked her fork down.

I stopped mixing my potatoes. "What did you say?"

"I said I've got the feeling you don't want to talk to me." She folded her arms across her chest. "I'm just looking out for your safety, for us!"

"No, that's not what you said." I shook my head.

"Yes, it is."

"No, it's not." I waggled a finger at her. "You said you were getting the *impression* I was mad at you."

"Yeah, so?"

"That's it!" I jumped up, bumping the table and spilling my drink. "I don't know why I didn't realize it before!"

"What? What is it?" Lindsey had hopped up from the table as well and was mopping up my mess.

"Impressionism. It links them all together," I explained.

She shook her head. "I don't follow."

"Allan's painting was by an Impressionist painter. So is the Manet at Derek's place. All of the other paintings I've seen—like the one at Mark Benton's house and at Stuart Newsome's office—they were *all* Impressionist style. Derek paints in the Impressionist style." I took her waist and swung her around, then released her, hurting myself in the process. I was too excited to care. "I did it! I'm a real detective!"

She was still frowning, her hands on her hips.

"Don't you see? Derek painted them *all*. That's why Allan's painting turned out to be a fake. They're all fakes."

"I understand." She followed me into the living room.

"Derek creates forgeries of real impressionist paintings. Then he ages them in his double-sized oven. He sells them to Ralph—"

"—who then sells them as originals," Lindsey finished my thought and continued. "Wouldn't the purchaser discover he had bought a fake eventually? It's kind of risky."

"The buyer would believe they were the real thing because the real ones are missing. Unless the original is found, this would only add to the illusion. Ralph is free to blackmail his buyers."

"The buyer might try to have the painting authenticated." Lindsey picked up my two lists from the table.

"The buyers all thought the paintings were stolen, so they wouldn't take one to get it tested unless they wanted to lose it." I flopped onto the sofa. "Ralph and Derek had the whole scheme planned."

"So Derek made the Manet for himself," Lindsey handed me my papers, "but you still didn't answer the last question on your list. Did Derek kill Ralph and why?"

"I'm not sure he did. Ralph Meeker was valuable to him. He needed him to sell his forgeries to."

"Maybe Derek got greedy and wanted to run the whole scheme himself. Maybe Ralph didn't pay him," Lindsey suggested.

"Both of those are possible, but Derek has lots of money. I'd be surprised if greed had anything to do with it."

"Let's call Detective Jeffries and tell him what you've come up with." She reached for the phone.

"No!" I grabbed for the receiver. "I need some real proof."

"I don't like the sound of that. I think those painkillers have gone to your head, because you agreed to stop right after dinner."

"No. I agreed to stop if I hadn't gotten any new clues, and besides we haven't finished dinner yet." I still had my hand over the phone.

That was the deal and Lindsey knew I was right, but she kept her hand on the phone as well. My eyes pinned to hers in a staring contest. Her brows knitted, her lips curled, she looked like a wild animal ready to bite. This was her "lawyer" stare, the way she always looked in a challenge. I knew the look. It didn't bother me, because I knew it wasn't anger; it was a contest. I would have to do some fancy talking to convince her.

"I know there has to be some record or evidence to connect Derek Leeds to Ralph," I began.

"Like what?"

"I don't know. Papers or records of payments, or another painting. There has to be something that could link them together."

"I doubt it. I'm sure Ralph covered his tracks very well." Lindsey was always ready with a counterattack. "I think we should let the police handle it."

"The police are already doing what they can. There's no proof of any of this, so they can't do anything more. It's up to us."

"Us? I don't think so." Lindsey released her grip on the phone. "The police told you to quit."

"I'll go alone." I let go of the receiver as well.

"Alone? Go where?" she asked in surprise.

"To Ralph's shop to look around."

"Oh, no you won't. You've already been there once and found all you could."

"Actually, there is one other thing I found, but I never told you about it. Now the police are investigating me, and it could make me look bad."

"What? What are you mumbling about?"

"I found an ID badge from your dinner party. It was Allan's." I paused to let this sink in.

"Allan's?" She realized the significance of this, too. "That's further evidence to prove he did—he did it."

"No, it's not, because it's not there anymore."

"Where is it? Where did you put it?" She clutched my hands.

"I burnt it and put it in the ashtray of my car," I replied, lowering my eyes.

"And now the FBI has your car, and they will find it. You tampered with evidence? It makes it look like you've been covering up for Allan. It'll make them think you set the bomb yourself."

"Then they'll drop the investigation for the real killer and maybe even come after me. They are going to want to know why I have Allan's badge. They might even think I did it, all of it." I paced to the window.

"If you try to go to Ralph's shop, you'll be followed by the police." Lindsey came up behind me and placed her hand on my shoulder.

"Only if they see me leave." I turned to face her.

"I'm going to be angry at you for a long time for this." She folded her arms, but it was the signal she gave in. "What's the plan?"

Around 11:00 P.M. we turned out all the lights and went into the bedroom.

"Now watch television for about thirty minutes, then turn it off and go to sleep," I instructed.

"I'll never be able to sleep." She grabbed me and gave me a clingy hug.

I peeled her off me. "Well, then just turn it off and lie there pretending to be asleep."

"What are you going to do?" She reattached.

"I'm going to sneak out the back." I pulled her away and reassured her. "I'll be fine."

"Promise?" she asked as she turned on the television.

"I promise." I turned out the bedroom light.

Then I crept down the darkened hallway. The television noise faded. At the back door, I looked around before stepping out. I had changed into dark clothing, and I had brought some quarters, cash, and a flashlight. I stepped into the backyard. I didn't see anyone. There was a bright, full moon. My eyes were already well adjusted, so I sped across the lawn to the back fence. I scaled the chain link and dropped onto the other side. I felt a few stitches pull. I felt the back of my leg—a little blood oozed through my pants. I crept quickly and quietly through the neighbor's yard, trying to remember if these neighbors had a dog or not. I prayed not. I emerged from behind their house and out onto the road. I went left toward the main street of the subdivision.

A few houses had dogs that barked at me, but mostly it was quiet. Just the sound of my footsteps and the crickets. There were some cars parked on the road, but I didn't see anyone in them. A few houses still had lights or televisions on inside. I could tell by the bluish glow through the curtains; but no one peered out. At one point a car turned down the road, and I jumped into some nearby bushes. Not a smart thing to do. The people in the car saw me and drove by very slowly, staring at the bushes and the house to make sure nothing was amiss. Then they pulled on by. I was sure they would call the police as soon as they got home to report the suspicious character in their neighbor's yard. Also, I'd suggest checking the species of bush before leaping with wild abandon. This particular bush was a prickly, messy holly, which bit me through my clothes, adding insult to injury.

I hurried now. I wanted to get out of the subdivision before anyone else saw me. At the subdivision entrance, I went to the right. It was still a long way to the closest gas station, which is where I was headed.

Once I arrived at the gas station, I used one of my quarters to call a taxi. It was almost midnight. I wondered if they would pick up a man dressed in black with a flashlight at that time of night. In about thirty minutes the cab arrived. An older Asian man was driving. He had a big toothy smile.

"Where are we a'going tonight?" he asked.

I gave him the address.

"Do you have a'money?" he asked.

"Yes."

"Let me see it," he said, all the while grinning ear to ear.

I held open my wallet.

"OK, get in." He apologized. "I have to be a'careful nowadays. I've been ripped off one too many a'times."

"That's OK," I said.

He spent the drive telling me stories about some of the fares he'd picked up in the past. Being only slightly distracted I just uttered uh-huh at appropriate intervals. I had him drop me off about a block away. I would walk the rest.

"You need me to a'wait for you?" he asked.

"No. Thanks." I paid him his fare through the passenger's window. Then he pulled away.

I could see Ralph's shop from where I stood. It looked deserted. There were no cars or lights. I approached slowly. I wasn't exactly sure how I was going to get in. I hadn't thought about that, and I hadn't brought any tools. There was still a fair amount of traffic on the road. I had to try the doors and windows during breaks so as not to arouse suspicion. They were all shut and locked.

I surveyed the surrounding area. About a quarter of a mile down the road was a gas station. Maybe they would have some tools. I walked down.

"Excuse me," I said to the clerk. "I hope you can help me. My car broke down and I was wondering—"

He cut me off. "Gas cans are five dollars."

"Oh, no, it's not the gas. I was wondering if you had any tools?" I asked.

"Tools?"

"Yeah, like a wrench or screwdriver or something," I suggested.

"Um, I think there are some things in the back." He stepped out from behind the bulletproof glass.

He went through a door in the back by the drink case. He emerged a few seconds later with a screwdriver and a hammer.

"That's great," I said, reaching for them.

"Five dollars," he insisted, and then added, "Each."

"Just the screwdriver, thanks."

I got out my wallet. *What an entrepreneur.* All said and done, I took my five-dollar screwdriver and used it on one of the windows. The locks were old and surprisingly easy to pry loose. I crawled inside pulling my stitches again.

Immediately I donned a pair of latex gloves from the box by the gun case. The darkened gallery gave me the creeps. Chill bumps covered my arms. I fumbled for the loaded revolver in the gun case and then tucked the weapon into the back of my jeans. Sensing that uncanny feeling of being watched, I spun around to face the empty gallery. I wanted to remain there, frozen like a rabbit, to avoid being spotted by prey, yet I also had a task that needed to be done. Once I began moving around the gallery I felt a little more secure, so I searched it in detail. I looked under the rugs on the walls. I went through the cupboard in the corner. I looked under the chairs. I even looked under the lining in the jewelry case. I checked inside every vase and cup and under every plate and saucer. On the shelves were books and boxes. I flipped through each and every book, and I opened every box.

One carved box caught my attention because it appeared some of the wood pieces were loose. I recalled something Jolene Harris had said about a secret box. I fiddled with it for a few minutes and discovered a large secret compartment. Thank you, Jolene! In the hidden area I found stamps Ralph had used to mark the fakes—each one created for a different museum's or collection's name. I didn't remove or touch any of them in case they might have fingerprints. Another box on the same table had some papers inside, but they were old and falling apart. I read them, but there were no secrets. Nothing to connect Ralph Meeker and Derek Leeds. Then there were the racks of paintings. I looked at each one, stopping only to pull out anything that looked Impressionistic, but again, like on my first visit, there wasn't a single old master. I thoroughly searched the bedroom and bathroom—every nook and cranny, underneath the mattress, and inside the medicine bottles. Still nothing.

I headed then for the office. I figured a more thorough search of Ralph's papers might reveal something. The floor was still stained with blood. The windows had been shut and locked for a few days, and the summer heat had made the smell stronger. Everything was exactly the same, except for an additional layer of dust. Well, not exactly the same, I thought of the glasses I'd found which I no longer had. I couldn't remember where I'd had them or put them. Shrugging to myself I resigned myself to the tedious and tiring work of pulling out every file from the file drawer and flipping through them one leaf of paper at a time. By 2:00 A.M. my eyes were strained. My flashlight was weakening.

Then I heard a noise.

CHAPTER 23

I flipped off the flashlight. Then I heard another noise, a scraping sound. I quietly got up from the desk. I walked to the doorway of the office, hugged the wall to one side, and peered around the corner. The moonlight danced in creepy shadows on the floor of the gallery. Someone was there. A person was climbing in through the same window I had opened. I held my breath and didn't move.

The figure had a blocky, masculine shape and was wearing jeans and boots. He pulled himself upright, but his face was shrouded by shadows. He crossed the room to the opposite corner and with his back to me, began flipping through the rack of pictures, holding several into the moonlight for a closer look. As I watched, I realized the intruder had a purpose and a method. Those pictures that he pulled out were examined front and back.

Then I did something really stupid. I took the gun out of my pants and flipped on the lights. I wanted to see who it was. I wanted the element of surprise.

It was Derek Leeds. I surprised him all right.

"What are you doing here?" I asked him, gun not aimed, but clearly visible in the now brightly lit room.

"What are *you* doing here?" he asked me as he replaced the painting he held in his hand.

"Looking for evidence," I said. "But I asked you first. What are you doing?"

"Same thing," he replied.

"What do you mean?" I asked suspiciously.

"I'm looking for evidence, too. Only I'm sure we have entirely different purposes." He turned his back to me and began flipping through the pictures again.

His voice and posture were confident, considering the firepower I held focused on him. I doubted I could answer questions so swiftly, so cocky, if positions were reversed.

"What specifically are you looking for?" I asked.

Derek didn't look at me, didn't move toward me. He didn't seem to care what I did or that I was even in the room. He didn't acknowledge my question. At that time it never occurred to me that Derek might also have a weapon and therefore wasn't concerned about me. He bent down beside the picture rack with a canvas and frame and pulled the two apart, removing a large manila envelope from between them.

"What are you doing?" I took a few small paces, instinctively raising my gun toward him.

Sensing my approach, he pulled a weapon from his boot, stood up and spun to face me. Thinking I was about to see my life flash before my eyes and without thinking about the weapon in my hands, it went off. I don't remember squeezing the trigger. My eyes were closed. The bullet went whizzing off somewhere in Derek's general direction, but strayed widely from the mark—a complete miss. He was still standing. I was still standing. I had only heard one shot, and even if Derek had fired at the same time, I doubted he was as bad a marksman as I was. That meant only one thing—Derek didn't fire.

"Why didn't you shoot me?" I asked, curiosity outweighing the risk of putting an idea into his head.

"I don't want to hurt you. I never meant to hurt Ralph. This whole thing is a big misunderstanding."

"Two men—dead! You call that misunderstanding?" I gasped, the adrenaline rush creating problems with my speech. "I call it murder."

"You think, you think that I killed two people? You think I murdered them?"

I nodded.

Derek shook his head in dismay. "I didn't."

"I believe you'll try to kill me, too, when you can find a way to make it look like an accident."

"The only reason I pulled my gun was because you had your gun out first and were coming at me. I thought I needed to protect myself."

"The only reason I pulled the gun on you first was because you sneaked in on me!"

"And because you think I'm a murderer. Enough excuses." Derek waved his gun around. "I realize you fired your gun because you were scared. By the way you have terrible aim; I'm really not so worried about you now."

My arm was beginning to tire from holding the gun at arms' length. The added insults about my shooting skills didn't help. They flustered me. I grew hot around collar in embarrassment.

"It's obvious I don't want to kill you, or I would have already done it," Derek dropped his stance and lowered his weapon.

He lay the pistol down on the shelf beside him and took a step back. The muscles in my arms were burning with strain.

"Move into the office," I ordered. "And bring that envelope with you."

I wanted to get to a phone. Derek complied, slowly. I rather think he relished the idea that I had to struggle to keep my aim steady. He smiled as he passed by me at a safe distance and through the doorway.

"Go sit in that corner." I motioned with the point of the gun.

He obeyed. I kept my eye on him as I reached across the desk to dial 911.

"Wait!" he shouted. The gun almost went off again. My adrenaline was pumping and my heart couldn't take much more of this.

"What?" I demanded.

"Please, please don't call the police. I promise, I didn't murder anyone. Just let me explain first," Derek pleaded uncharacteristically.

"If you didn't do it, you have nothing to fear from the police." I picked up the receiver.

"They'll think it was me. I'd kill myself before going to jail for something I didn't do. Let me explain. I'm not any danger over here in the corner and you've got the gun— "

Derek's self-assured, cocky attitude had dissipated. His hands were shaking. He held them together to stop their movement. He sat folded up into a fetal-like position in the corner. I replaced the phone and sat down at the desk across from him, ready to listen. The gun never left my hands. My finger never left the trigger. If given a second opportunity to shoot at Derek, I wouldn't miss.

"Explain until your heart's content. There's nothing you can tell me that I don't already know," I said, confidently.

"Ralph and I were working together. I provided paintings for him to sell. Ralph then blackmailed his buyers, telling them the paintings were stolen—"

"—But they weren't; they were fakes." I finished his sentence to prove I knew this much.

"Yes. That was how it happened, but please don't call them fake. They were as good as the originals. Call them forgeries or duplicates, but not fakes." Derek demonstrated a little of his artistic temperament as he rocked back and forth in frustration.

"Did Ralph know they were forgeries?"

"Yes." Derek examined his fingernails and chose one nail to bite.

"How did you create them?"

"If a client expressed an interest Ralph and I would find a matching art piece that had already been stolen. It wasn't hard. On average there's a major piece of artwork missing for every zip code in the country. Pieces are stolen from museums and private collections and it's difficult to keep up with and track. I'd use photographs of the paintings, often provided by the owner after the theft in hopes of getting the piece back, and I'd look at other examples of the style and painting technique of the artist. From these I'd create a duplicate. To most people, they looked very authentic; although they'd never stand up next to the real thing. We even aged the paintings."

"Most people have never seen the real one since it's already missing. And they didn't question the authenticity for fear of being revealed. A well put together scheme," I surmised. "How much money did you make? I mean, that's why you killed Ralph, right? For the money?"

"No!" Derek spit out the piece of nail he'd severed. "I never took any of the money. I gave all my share to Ralph because I'm already wealthy."

"So, what did you get out of it then?"

"Respect. Respect for my artistic talent that I couldn't get with my own art." He ran his fidgety fingers through his hair.

I noticed that he looked even more unkempt than usual. His hair looked like he had slept on it. He still wore the old T-shirt and jeans that he had worn to Denny's.

"Ralph sold your paintings. It was through him that you earned your 'respect'. Why would you kill him? Did you want to take over the blackmailing?" I asked.

"No!" Derek went back to picking his fingernails. "Blackmail wasn't even part of the original plan. At first I was just to paint for Ralph and he'd sell them and that would be it. But soon he got the hair-brained idea of blackmailing the buyers, too. I knew it would be trouble in the end. A few of the buyers were beginning to revolt."

"What do you mean?"

"They called Ralph's bluff. They said they'd rather turn the painting in than pay any more."

"Who said that? Specifically?"

"Well, the Senator and Stuart Newsome." Derek shrugged. "I don't know who else."

"That's why you killed them? To end the blackmail and to keep from being discovered?"

"No." Derek sighed. "I don't even know how it all happened."

"Bull-shit. I don't believe you. Everything you've said gives you motives to have killed them both. All the evidence I've gathered points to you." I picked up the phone. *What a scam. I kicked myself for getting hooked into his rambling story.*

"You don't think I know that?" Derek shouted and threw his arms up in the air. "That's why I was here looking around. Ralph shouldn't have, but he kept all the notes and records on the people he blackmailed and on our dealings."

"What do you mean, dealings?" I put the phone back down again.

"You said you didn't take any money."

"Sometimes Ralph would trade an antique or something for one of my paintings. Like I said, I wouldn't ever take money, so he would feel bad and give me something. The real cause of all my problems isn't the deal, it's the notes, photos, and documentation of our preparation and creation of the painting. Some of those papers have my handwriting and fingerprints on them." Derek dropped his head into his hands and let out a sigh. "In fact all my sketches and notes were kept here because at the time I felt it was safer. If I kept them at my house I would be automatically implicated, but if I kept them here I knew Ralph wouldn't roll over on me if he was caught. He wouldn't give me up in life, but in death, that's a different story."

I waited in silence for him to elaborate. Laboriously, he took in a deep breath and looked up at me. His eyes glistened. Either he was about to tell me something that truthfully hurt him or he was the best actor I'd ever seen.

"We always did our deals late at night. That night, the night Ralph died we'd just finished a deal and Ralph hid all the papers," Derek indicated the envelope he still clutched.

"May I see—"

"Ralph— Ralph got shot, by accident." Derek choked on the words in his throat.

"Go on," I encouraged.

"He offered me a gun, in exchange for a Manet I had painted. He didn't tell me it was loaded." Derek shook his head and wiped his face with the sleeve of his shirt. "The fool kept all his guns loaded."

"Let me get this straight," I said. "The gun went off accidentally?"

"Well, no, I definitely squeezed the trigger. I was testing it, you know, seeing how it worked. I had it pointed, pointed in Ralph's direction, not really aimed, just kind of toward him."

"From over there? In the doorway?" I motioned.

He nodded, "I shot it, expecting it to just click. I'm so stupid. I know about guns. I knew better— "

"So what happened?" I asked, trying not to feel sorry for Derek.

"I—I thought he was faking. I mean, I heard the gun, but there was blood. Lots of blood spilled, all of a sudden."

"Did you try to help him?"

"Of course! He was my friend. I tried. I tried to take his pulse, but I couldn't find it. He didn't answer me. He wasn't breathing. I couldn't see him breathing. I couldn't help." Tears were in Derek's eyes again. "I don't know CPR, or first aid. I didn't know what to do or if I should even touch him, or how to get the blood to stop."

"You just let him die?" I asked, aghast.

"He was—he was already dying—already dead. Don't you see? I couldn't do anything for him, and if I stayed there I'd go to jail for art fraud.

I called for help, but I didn't stay."

"Then you had to kill the Senator to cover up what you did," I concluded.

"No! I have no idea what happened to Mr. Puckett. He was a friend of my dad's. I wouldn't have any reason to—"

"Except as a cover. He was seen publicly arguing with Ralph, so you chose him."

"No, no, no. After Ralph—after, I tried to make my cover up there, at the shop. I wiped the gun clean and then put it next to Ralph's hand, like maybe he had it and shot himself. I grabbed my painting, checked the desk for any leftover papers, and locked up as I left the house, so it would look like he was alone."

"Ralph was shot twice, the second time in the head. Did you do that to finish him off?"

"No. I only shot him that one time, by accident, and then I hurried out in case there was some chance the ambulance could save him. I wanted to get the records of our dealings, but I didn't want to take the time then. I figured we had hidden those papers well and I could come back for them later."

"But Ralph was shot twice," I insisted.

"I don't know how. I only pulled the trigger once." Derek shrugged. "Maybe the person that took the gun to Senator Puckett's house shot him the second time."

"That would explain time span between the two sounds the old lady heard," I mumbled.

"What?"

"If someone else arrived right after you left and found the grisly scene, he or she might have panicked thinking the blame would fall on them. You said you checked the desk for papers? Did you see a pair of glasses?"

"I looked at the desk, but there were no glasses. I told you before, Ralph doesn't—didn't—use glasses."

"So you were looking for papers tonight?"

"Yes. He kept the records in this envelope tucked into the back of one of the canvases," Derek shifted positions, stretching his legs out from under him.

"Why did you wait so long to get the papers? Why not come back right away?" I asked.

"Well, I tried to come back early the next day, but the house was a crime scene and I couldn't," Derek replied, eyes downcast. "Then as it turned out I figured I wouldn't need the papers because Mr. Puckett was blamed for Ralph's death."

"Sounds too convenient to me." I frowned, not sure whether to believe any or all of this wild tale.

"I know. I thought so, too. The saying if it's too good to be true, well, anyway, I read about Mr. Puckett being found after committing suicide. The report said it was the same gun. I thought it was a real stroke of luck for me, although I really don't know how he got that gun."

"Why did you decide to come back for the papers now?" I furrowed my brows.

"Because you started getting nosy. I decided it'd be better to have the papers and destroy them before I leave town."

"Leave town? Where were you planning on going?"

"I've had all my money transferred to a new name, an offshore account. I'm getting out of the country because the police will be after me."

"What do you mean?"

"Well, you're so nosy, you're meddling has made the police aware of Ralph's blackmail. With these papers, Derek waved the enevelope, the police would eventually figure out who made the paintings and be after me. I don't want any evidence left around. I made the mistake of thinking you were a threat. I called you to scare you and set off your alarm at your house—"

"You blew up my car!" I thumped my fist on the desk.

My fears of losing my life, of losing Lindsey, flooded back over me. I was prepared to go over the desk and kill him with my bare hands.

"No! No, I really am sorry that happened but I didn't do it. I do feel guilty though, all that's happened to your family is because of me. I know Margie hasn't been able to collect any insurance money and the retirement fund is empty. I put a money order in your mailbox to cover the costs, because I really am sorry," he said.

"You what? You sent her money?" I sat back down, shocked.

"Yes, to cover the costs of my mistakes"

"I still don't understand why you came back for the papers if you're leaving. Why not just tell the police what happened?"

"They won't believe my story. Frankly, I wouldn't believe it either. Getting rid of the papers is just one less piece of evidence against me. I don't want to be extradited or something. Besides, one day when this all blows over I might like to return. And if I ever do get caught I don't want enough stuff on me for a conviction. I want the jury to have doubts."

"You seem to have it all thought out. What about your gallery?"

Derek shrugged. "I left it to Mimi, an artist friend."

"Why run?" I asked. "Why not confess and explain everything to the police and trust they'll believe you and treat you fairly?"

"I don't know. Maybe the same reason you didn't trust them to solve this case?"

He had me there. In so many ways I found myself wanting to believe him. I almost wanted to let him go. Derek sat huddled in the corner, feeling sorry for himself, as I picked up the phone to dial the police. The lines were all busy. I had to wait for an operator.

"I'm telling you, Im not going to jail," he called across the room.

He slowly stood up. I stood up as well and raised my gun.

"I'm not going to hurt you," he quietly explained. "I'm taking my papers. I'm going to walk along this wall to that doorway," he pointed, "and I'm going to go through the door, pick up my gun and go out the side window. You won't ever see or hear from me again. My flight out of the country is waiting."

"No," I warned, waving the gun. "Stay put. I may have missed you the first time around, but it won't happen again."

"Shoot me if you have to." He edged along the wall, eyes on me. "I won't shoot back. I'm not going to the police."

"Stop. No," I repeated.

He didn't stop. He picked up his gun and continued toward the window. He bent down and had one leg out. At that same moment, I heard tires in the driveway. Red flashing lights pierced the shadows of the gallery and lit the mirrors on the walls. Derek looked up at me, his movements still calm as he continued to move out the window, but his eyes were wild.

"Shit," was my response to this new development.

Derek was in the yard now. I didn't know where to go. I felt it would be in my best interest to get out of the house, out of the line of fire, but the opportunity didn't present itself.

"Put your hands up. Drop your weapon," were the commands issued to Derek.

Through the window I could see Derek did not comply. Derek was sweating, droplets gleaming in the flashes of light. A spotlight, meant to disorient and blind him, lit him up like daylight. The commands to disarm were repeated more aggressively. Derek waved the gun around wildly, not taking aim.

"You want to shoot me? You want to kill an innocent man? Go ahead!" he barked. "Kill me!"

"Drop your weapon and put your hands up," multiple voices screamed over and over.

The exchange repeated. Sensing the police were not going to do the job, Derek placed the gun in his mouth and squeezed the trigger. Multiple shots rang out. Officers had tried to maim him at the last moment to prevent him from taking his life. They were not successful.

CHAPTER 24

At the police station, filing reports again, was the last place I wanted to be. I sat in a small office with a trash can between my knees, fighting off waves of nausea. I'd just seen a man die before my very eyes. I'd seen the life slip away. It was the most terrifying thing I'd ever seen and the realization that Derek might not have been guilty of anything but poor judgement made it worse. It made me realize how temporary, how lucky we are that we're allowed to remain walking this planet. The sermon-like words of Dr. Chander, about life being too precious to waste, came to haunt me.

Through the open doorway I watched the officers scurry about like so many people hurry through their lives. The buzz of multiple conversations, the endless ringing of phones, the shuffle of papers all exploded in my ears. I had a headache like a vise-grip.

"It's a full moon." Detective Shope approached, explaining the furor. "We're always like this on a full moon. All the weirdoes come out or something."

I nodded. I had heard something similar about hospitals and babies.

"I know this has been a tough time for you, but we need to get a statement while the events are fresh." Detective Jeffries stood sideways in the doorway, leaned back to it, bent one knee, and braced himself with his foot against the frame.

I was ready to cooperate, to get the whole thing out in the open, to get away from there as fast as possible. I recounted everything Derek had said.

"What a wild story." Detective Shope shook her head.

"Of course, it's all untrue," piped Detective Jeffries. "Derek Leeds did them both in. He just fed you that line to try to get away from you."

"He could have killed me," I said, "but he didn't."

"He was better off to let you go. Sending you off believing he was innocent puts you in his corner and is much better than another dead man, which only complicates things for him," Detective Shope explained.

"I think congratulations are in order." Detective Jeffries changed his balancing foot, like a flamingo. "You got your man."

"Yeah," was my sullen reply.

"Aren't you happy? You found the murderer of Ralph Meeker and Senator Puckett. You're practically a celebrity. Isn't that what you wanted?" Detective Jeffries asked.

I shrugged.

"Don't tell me you believed Mr. Leeds?" Detective Shope warned.

I didn't answer.

"How did you know where to find me?" I asked at length.

"We called you to give you an update on the bomb. The bomb investigators claim now they know the culprit definitely wanted to kill you. The location and components all indicate this. Some of the material is being traced to see if anyone you mentioned bought any. The FBI checked into your story first. I thought you'd want to know you were in the clear. Anyway, your wife told us where you were, she was so worried," Detective Shope replied.

I sat silently thinking about Lindsey and how sorry I was to keep her worrying all the time.

"Do you have anything else you need to tell us about Derek?" Detective Jeffries asked.

"Why would Derek call the police for help if he wanted Ralph dead?" I asked, hoping they would have a really good answer for this.

"He didn't. An anonymous caller made the 911 call from a pay phone about a block from the shop," Detective Jeffries replied.

"The anonymous caller could have been Derek," I insisted. "And the neighbor reported a gap of about fifteen minutes between the first and second shots. Isn't it possible Derek shot Ralph by accident and then a second person finished Ralph off?"

"Derek's motive can be established by papers we found on him. Derek had to get rid of both Ralph and Allan Puckett. It's the only logical solution," Detective Jeffries replied.

I was so tired of hearing them talk about logical solutions. Nothing about murder is logical—ever.

"His bull-shit story to you was a cover. He wanted you dead, but he didn't have the opportunity or the advantage. If he was leaving the country he didn't need to go get any papers. He just wanted to tie up you—his only loose end," Detective Shope said.

"If he was leaving, why would he need to do me in?" I countered.

"If he got rid of you maybe he wouldn't have to leave."

"Did you check with the airport? Did he have a ticket? He had all his money transferred." I said, then added, "And if Derek set things up to make it look like the Senator killed Ralph Meeker, how did he get the ID badge back to the shop?" I asked.

"What ID badge?" both officers replied in unison, bewildered.

"Allan's ID badge, from the party. I found it at the shop the day I went and looked around."

"We didn't find it in our search. Derek must have brought it back and planted it later on," Detective Jeffries replied.

"I wish you had mentioned this earlier." Detective Shope was writing notes. "Evidence doesn't just appear. It would have clued us in there was something wrong."

"That's not the only thing that appeared. According to Derek there were no eyeglasses on the desk, yet there was a pair when I was there."

"Where are they now?

"I don't know," I shrugged. "It's too late now anyway. Why do you think Derek would kill himself?"

"Fear of prison." Detective Jeffries moved to a chair.

"That's the same reason you gave me for why Allan might have committed suicide. Does that really happen all that often?"

"Mr. Grey, why are you so worried about details?" Detective Jeffries jumped to the defensive. "You were right on with your suspicions of Derek Leeds. Don't let anything he said affect your judgement now. It's over."

"OK, I'll drop it if you can tell me just one more thing, what about the dead bartender? I almost forgot about him. How does he fit in all this?"

"Oh, him, he doesn't. We found evidence to indicate his girlfriend did it. She's in custody."

"If that does it, we'll take you home," Detective Shope offered.

I nodded. At least I could agree to that.

Lindsey greeted me at the front door with a smile, hugs, and tears. We were both in need of some rest, so we cuddled and slept for a while before getting up for a late breakfast.

"I'm so proud of you," Lindsey exclaimed as she stirred scrambled eggs in the frying pan. "You really did it. Not that I had any doubts."

"Yeah, right." I winked at her humor.

"At least now Margie will be able to make her claim, and things should improve for my campaign."

"That's great," I replied as I sorted through a stack of papers.

"What are you looking for?" She took the eggs off the heat while she got two plates.

I had already found what I was searching for—the stack of unopened mail. In the pile was a plain white envelope with only my name on it, no return address, no postage. I turned it over and used the side of my finger to open it. It was a cashier's check make out to Margie for two million dollars.

"Oh, my God." I had to sit down. I suddenly felt very sick.

"What? What is it?" Lindsey practically dropped the eggs rushing over to help me to a chair.

"It wasn't Derek." I blinked. "I've really messed up. It was someone else. Someone else killed Allan."

"What? Are you OK?" Lindsey got me a glass of water. "I think you need to rest—"

"No, that's not it. Derek Leeds was telling the truth."

"The truth about what?"

"He said he didn't want to hurt me. He sent me money to cover the hospital bill," I said.

"What?" Lindsey grabbed the check from my hands.

She got weak in the knees seeing all those zeroes. She also sank into a chair.

"He felt guilty, even though he never tried to hurt us. He said he shot Ralph by accident, and he left the gun there at the shop and locked up. The only person that could get into the locked shop to get the gun would be Barbara Warren. The glasses I found were hers, I'm sure of it now."

"But, why would she want the gun? Why shoot Ralph if he was already dying?" Lindsey put the check down on the counter.

"I don't know, but I'm going to find out. Let's invite Detective Jeffries to lunch," I said.

Lindsey shrugged. "Why?"

"I'll need you both there to witness Barbara Warren's confession. Tell him to bring a pair of handcuffs and a tape recorder."

"Handcuffs? Recorder? Confession to what?" Lindsey asked.

"You'll see."

A little before noon, Lindsey, Detective Jeffries, and I were all in position. We sat in the restaurant in two back-to-back booths—Lindsey and the detective in one, and I, alone, in the other. Lindsey faced away from my booth so as not to be recognized.

"Barbara Warren should be here any moment," I whispered. "Go ahead and order your food."

No sooner did I get those words out of my mouth when Barbara appeared in the entrance to the restaurant, frizzy hair flying in all directions. The waitress pointed out my table and she hurried over.

"Glad you could make it." I stood up as she took her seat.

"What choice did I have? Miss out on free food? I don't think so." She laughed.

"I ordered your drink. Sweet tea, right?" I handed her a menu.

"That's fine. This place has great desserts. Will we be ordering dessert?"

"Sure," I smiled. "You can order anything you like."

"How generous," She smiled and placed her order with the waitress.

"Well, I just fell into some money," I confessed.

"Really? How nice." She sipped her tea, half interested.

"The money came from Derek Leeds. You met him at Denny's. He was Ralph's artist friend."

"Really?" Still she showed little interest, gazing out the window.

"Yes. Derek told me a very interesting story."

"I like stories." She glanced back at me.

"Derek told me how Ralph died."

"Eeeooo, how morbid." She shuddered. "Was he the guilty party?"

"Sort of. It seems Ralph's death was a mishap. Derek shot him by accident and left him there."

"Is that why you wanted to see me? To tell me what really happened to Ralph? Because I already told you, I wasn't too sad to see him go. I don't care that much for specifics." She fanned herself with a wine menu.

It didn't seem that hot in the restaurant to me.

"Actually, you can help me out," I said. "You see, as Derek left the shop, he dropped the gun and locked the door. I was hoping you could tell me how someone could get in to remove the gun, unless they had a key, such as yourself."

Barbara thought for a moment to formulate a response. "They could break in through a window or the door."

"Yes. I already thought of that, but I was there last night and all the locks were intact."

"Really? Well, then I guess someone would have to have a key." She shrugged.

"Like you?" I asked.

"Not me, but someone like me, yes."

"I don't know anyone else that had a key, besides you." I took a drink, playing it cool. I didn't want to scare her off. I wanted a confession.

"Who knows how many ex-girlfriends Ralph gave keys to?" She rolled her eyes.

Our lunch salads arrived at the table.

"He could have given out lots of keys, that's true. How many of those ex's would have shown up at his place the night he was killed? I would think only the current lover would do that."

"What are you saying?" Barbara folded her arms.

"I'm saying you were at Ralph's right after he was killed, after Derek left and right before the police arrived. You found Ralph, not quite dead yet, so you took the gun and finished him off. You've made it crystal clear you were glad to see him dead."

"I did not." She shook her head. "I was at the grocery store, remember?"

"May I see that receipt? You never could produce it before."

Hesitantly she opened her bottomless pit of a bag and searched for the elusive slip of paper. When she found it, she handed it over.

"You said you have lots of cats?" I asked.

"Huh? Yes." She frowned.

"Well, if you have so many cats, why did you buy a litter box that night?" I pointed out the purchase on the receipt. "I don't think you have any cats, except Charlie Brown. You arrived at Ralph's, finished him off, took the gun, and his cat. Then you had to go buy supplies to take care of it. You wouldn't do that unless you knew for a fact that Ralph Meeker was dead."

"I don't know what you're talking about." She placed her napkin on the table like she was getting ready to leave.

"Look at the time of check out. You were at the store well after the time Ralph was shot."

"I was shopping, that takes some time."

"You didn't buy that much. You had time to kill Ralph and then do all this."

"No it didn't."

"I think the police will see it the way I do. You also have the pair of glasses I found. It wasn't until today that I remembered where they went. Two pieces of evidence showed up at the scene after Ralph was shot by Derek. One piece was a nametag that points to Allan and the second piece is the glasses which implicate you. I assume the glasses were yours, that's why you took them the other day in the restaurant, even though you already had a replacement pair. And I think you planted the name tag which when checked will probably contain your fingerprints."

She didn't know the name tag had been destroyed, yet she didn't attempt to respond, so I continued, "I'm trying to figure out why you shot Ralph when he would have died if you had left him there. I can understand why you didn't care if he died—he didn't seem like a very nice guy, but why take the gun to Allan's house? Why kill him?"

At length, Barbara answered softly. "I panicked."

She fiddled with the straw in her drink and continued in a whisper, "I knew the police would think I did it, or worse, my daughter. I mean, blackmail is a motive. There I was with a key to his place, a dead body, and a history with the man—

"Stupidly, the first thing I did when I arrived was set my purse and glasses down on the desk so I could check him. I picked up and moved the gun. It would have my prints on it. Ralph would never have left me or my family alone if he had lived. I was so angry with him for making me, you know. I was standing there with the gun in my hand so I shot him again, in the head. I kind of figured if I was going to be blamed for something I might as well have done it. Then I grabbed the cat and took off. I had the gun with me.

"After I left, I wondered if maybe I should have tried to get rid of the body somehow. I realized I'd left my glasses, and I really freaked. I had to cover my tracks or they'd be after me for sure."

"You thought you had to shift the suspicion off yourself and onto someone else?" I asked.

"Yes, and at the same time I didn't know who had shot Ralph the first time. I suspected everyone, even my own daughter. I had to protect her. I wracked my brain all night long trying to come up with a plan. I couldn't just ditch the gun and expect the whole problem to go away. The police would question me. They would suspect me, especially if they knew anything about the blackmail. Then I remembered I'd seen Senator Puckett arguing with Ralph only a few hours before. I knew they were arguing about the blackmail money, and it was a perfect opportunity."

"You thought you could pin it on the Senator?" I interjected.

"It was the only way out as far as I could see. I decided to sneak into his house that next morning to hide the gun there, so it could be found with him. I popped the lock on the door, it's not hard with a credit card as long as it's not bolted. But I didn't know the Senator was still home. He came out of the bathroom where he had been shaving and caught me putting the gun in his dresser. I had to act. I had to think fast. I threatened to shoot him. He was so terrified he was willing to cooperate, only I didn't know what to do next. There were pantyhose in the dresser drawer—"

"You tied him up? He wasn't restrained when the police arrived on the scene, what did you do?"

"I restrained him, hand and foot, and gagged him. He kept talking and I couldn't think. I spent a long time pacing and thinking when all of a sudden the idea came to me so quickly, such a devilish plan, I scared even myself. I could make it look like the Senator had killed himself—murder-suicide. I made him get in the tub. I took out the gag and untied his hands and told him to sit down. I think he believed I was letting him go. I don't think he would have gotten in if he'd known—"

She stopped there.

"You shot him," I finished for her.

"Yes." She answered so quietly I could barely hear her. "I did it very quickly. He didn't have the chance to try to stop me. I didn't want to kill him."

"Just send him to prison for the rest of his life by planting evidence," I said.

"It was him or me," she justified. "Before I left I took the panty hose off his feet and put the gun in his hand. I tried to be sure to wipe my prints off everything. I saw his ID badge on top of the dresser and took it. I hid it at Ralph's shop later to make it look like the Senator had been there."

"Why the phony confession earlier on? That was little risky, don't you think?" I asked.

"I guess. At the time I thought it would throw you and the police off my trail, really confuse you. It fit right in with my past. The police never questioned me any further after that. However, you didn't quit, so then I had to slow you down."

"Did you set the bomb in my car? To kill me?"

"Yes, I did. Nothing personal," she shrugged. "I needed you out of the way."

"Didn't you think that would be suspicious and might eventually lead the police to you?"

"No. I thought it would lead them to Derek."

"You know you're going to jail for this—not as long as if you had planned it, but for murder just the same."

"But Mr. Grey," she sort of smiled, "there's no proof of any of this, only what I've told you."

"There's enough evidence to make a case. The FBI will find somehow that you purchased materials or had the bomb made. I'm sure we can find a latent print or two at the Senator's and bloodstains on clothing and shoes at your house, maybe the panty hose if we're lucky," Detective Jeffries said and stood up with Lindsey. "Certainly we'll be checking the autopsy records and crime scene photos for indicators that restraints were used and then removed—smudges in the blood patterns. We'll also check around at local eyeglass suppliers. I'm sure you bought that replacement pair after your first pair got left at the scene of the crime."

Barbara Warren's face turned as red as hot coals, and her eyes grew wide with shock.

"You tricked me into a confession. You can't do that— " she stuttered.

"Oh, yes, I can." Detective Jeffries had his cuffs out and was clasping them on Barbara's wrists.

"She'll use the insanity plea, just wait and see," Lindsey whispered to me and then added aloud, "We'll send Mayson to see you."

The waitress approached with Barbara's apple cobbler. "What about your dessert, sir?"

"I'll take it to go," Barbara replied.

EPILOGUE

Finding out what truly befell Allan was both a blessing and a curse. It was relief to both Lindsey and Margie to have the truth, but a lengthy trial for Barbara Warren lay ahead. The days of trial reopened the pain of losing Allan over and over, and many of those days were grief filled. In the end, Barbara Warren was sentenced to twenty years for the murder of Allan Puckett, but she was found not guilty of the murder of Ralph Meeker. The prosecution couldn't prove whether Mr. Meeker had still been alive when she shot him the second time—you can't murder a dead man. Barbara Warren suffered a stroke in prison and years later when she got out, she moved to Wisconsin to live with her divorced daughter. Last I heard she ran a dog grooming service. She sent us a Christmas card every year. I never quite understood that, but that was Barbara.

People like Mark Benton, who had dished over lots of cash to Ralph Meeker, were given some compensation out of his estate. All Ralph's belongings from his shop were sold at auction (Jolene Harris was there bidding, trying to create a new life for herself) and then the building was razed to make room for a gas station.

Once the truth about Allan was in the media, things improved for Lindsey's campaign. She won her election by a wide enough margin. I was extremely proud of her. We celebrated with the best steak dinner fifty bucks could buy and ceremoniously ended our lease at the strip mall in favor of her new office at the capital. Not too shabby, they had free coffee.

I was spared a police record, only because Detective Jeffries liked me. I was charged with obstruction of justice and breaking and entering, but only for show. Eventually, those charges were dropped and I was left with a five-hundred-dollar fine for conducting an investigation without a license. I realized I had only solved this case by luck. It had been totally accidental that I caught Barbara Warren in the end—a case of beginner's luck.

Luck or no, I was bitten by the private eye bug, and I began training to become a licensed private investigator. It took several months to finish the course work, but then I gave up my job at DataCOM, which I hated anyway, and joined an investigation firm in Atlanta where I began a two-year stint searching out insurance fraud. Once my great-aunt returned from Europe, I bought a used Toyota Camry, something that would blend in, which I parked safely locked away in the garage. And last, but not least, I bought a gun. Yes, a gun. In my future line of work, I was going to need it.

ACKNOWLEDGEMENTS

I would like to thank my family for their support of my writing and desire to publish, especially my husband for all his technical expertise when it comes to computers. I need to thank Mary Chamier and Erin Woods for all the hours we spent in our writer's critique group. I couldn't have done it without your suggestions and friendly criticisms. I have a better book because of you both. I would like to thank Leslie Santamaria for her suggestions and editing work. Hopefully the majority of her proofreading changes have survived my last minute revisions! Thanks to Witherells.com for the cover photograph. And last I need to thank the educators, evaluators, and agents of the Harriett Austin Writer's Conference in Athens, Georgia for the wealth of information on mystery writing and crime, and the guidance they have given me over the last few years.

COMING SOON!

Other books in the Paul Grey Series:

Runner's High

Open House

Going Postal